LET'S PLAY A GAME

NANCY SAVAGE

BLOODHOUND
BOOKS

First published in 2026 by Bloodhound Books.

www.bloodhoundbooks.com

Print ISBN: 978-1917705790

To my six Rs

PROLOGUE

The morning air feels thick, as though suspended in the weight of the previous night. The tortured echoes that rebounded among the dense thicket of trees have since been swallowed and muted, the group's presence having all but vanished. Though one trace remains.

The ground this far from the worn-down trails of the deep Santa Barbara woodlands rarely sees the tread of human feet; the only disturbance, ordinarily, coming from the light footfall of foxes and coyotes. Scavengers waiting for their next meal.

The vultures and condors that circle above, intently scanning the ground, don't discriminate when it comes to what feeds them. Whether it's a deer carcass, a disease-infested rodent or, on this occasion, an eighteen-year-old girl lying lifeless on the damp, fertile ground, they'll pick away at it all the same.

And today, it's a multitude of animals and insects who will feast on this generous offering, left discarded as though just for them. Her arms and hands are tucked below her narrow chest, defenseless from their advances.

Her long blond hair, once carefully brushed and folded into

a neat braid, has come undone, frizzy strands now stirring gently around her neck in the soft breeze. Her legs are extended, as though poised to run away from this unsettling scene.

A shallow stream of water that lightly licks at her face will provide the hydration the animals need in the harsh heat of this Californian summer. A heat that will greatly speed up the decomposition process; breaking down skin and muscle until all that's left for the stragglers and latecomers are bones to pick apart, scattering the fragments so far and wide that the only remnants of what transpired that night are the memories imprinted on the minds of those who left her lying there. Memories that pull and twist at the very fibers of their hearts, slowly eating away at them until it begins to feel as though *they* are the ones who are now decomposing—rotting and putrefying—from deep inside, where nobody will ever see it.

CHAPTER ONE

NOW

I once read that couples who are truly in love are like trees. They have roots that grow deep down, below the soil. And while those roots are forming, they are overtaken with passion; a beautiful explosion of lust, affection and excitement. They bloom with first kisses, stolen glances and the thrill of discovering each other. A time where every moment feels electric and even one touch, skin to skin, can send a sharp current through your whole body. But as the seasons change, the flowers of that initial excitement fall from their branches and in their place lingers a gentle comfort. And in all that has settled, the couple will find that what remains is something even more beautiful than before. Because underground, below the surface, their roots have now entwined together. And they have become one tree, instead of two.

That's Seth and me.

We're not just husband and wife, we're two halves of a whole. We fit together as perfectly as a jigsaw and are so tuned in to each other that even the briefest of looks between us can convey a message ten pages long. Where I stumble in life, he soars. Where he falters, I flourish. And we move through each day like it's a dance we've practiced a thousand times.

Every morning, I wake up to his arm draped over my side, the scattered hair on his chest tickling my back. He nuzzles my neck and lightly kisses my shoulders until I roll around and kiss him back. We shower together and wash each other's bodies in turn. Sometimes there's a little lingering if we're both in the mood, sometimes not. We brush our teeth side by side, alternating spitting and rinsing so as not to get in the other's way. He flosses, I don't. He tells me I really should, and I promise I will that night, knowing I won't remember to. We get dressed together, and his eyes always stray suggestively to my bare skin as I slip on my clothes. There's something ruthlessly appealing about the way Seth looks at me, hungry, like I'm the only woman in the world. He then makes coffee as I prepare eggs and toast. While the smell of fresh brewing coffee fills the air, he gets Penny out of bed and dresses her while I pack her lunch for preschool before we all sit down to eat breakfast as a family.

In the evenings, we sit around the dinner table and talk while we eat. There's never an awkward silence and Penny always has a new story from preschool to tell us. After dinner, I'll bathe Penny in her nightly bubble bath before getting her into the pajamas that Seth leaves out on her bed. After that, Seth tucks her in and quietly reads her to sleep. We'll then watch a show together, usually a crime thriller or sometimes a documentary, go to bed, make love, then read our books side by side and fall asleep before starting the routine all over again the next day. It's like a well-practiced dance that we know off by heart and follow along to the letter. And most importantly, we enjoy it.

Nobody ever believes me when I tell them this, but Seth and I have never once in our fifteen years together had a fight.

You can roll your eyes all you want but it's true. We were dealt a winning hand in the marriage department, I guess.

That's not to say we haven't had our disagreements and gotten annoyed at one another, like any other married couple. We're only human. But it's never anything big enough to divide us.

There was the time Seth bought a Groupon voucher for a white water rafting experience for two. I flat out refused to go, and he got annoyed as he tried to persuade me it would be fun. I think that particular disagreement stemmed from the fact that he's always wanted to go white water rafting, while I have never wanted to go white water rafting. But we always solve our issues without raising our voices in anger or letting conflict drive a wedge between us. And most importantly, we're always there for each other when we need to be.

Take today, for example. I was supposed to be collecting Penny after work and taking her to a friend's birthday party. There's some kid's party most weeks since Penny began preschool, so I've gotten used to scouring toy stores for generic gifts that a child I've never met might enjoy. And today I meant to go to the store on my lunch hour to buy something I could stick in a gift bag for this one's birthday. But there were only three of us at the bakery this morning, and I was flat out getting finished on an order for a three-tiered anniversary cake as well as four dozen cupcakes for a Little League celebration and I never got the chance to slip away. I messaged Seth to ask if he could help organize a gift, and not an hour later he showed up at the bakery with a perfectly wrapped set of toy ponies with accessories, tied up in a big pink bow. He'd even bought a card, which he'd written inside of, wishing Penny's friend a happy birthday from her. He left them sitting safely on the countertop, walked up to me while I was elbows deep in chocolate frosting, pecked me on the cheek then winked and left. It wasn't some sweeping, extravagant gesture but it meant the world to me. He didn't even stop for recognition or praise. He knew I was busy, and he just wanted to make my load a little lighter. That's the kind of guy he is. He's always ready to drop what he's doing to help me out, and he'll even go the extra mile to make sure I'm happy. And of course, I'd do the same for him. I'd do anything for Seth.

I once gave away tickets to see my favorite band (Creed, don't judge) so that I could stay home with Seth and tend to him while he had bronchitis.

"Go, Jade, you've been waiting for months to go see them. I'll be fine here alone, I promise."

He tried to persuade me to go out and enjoy myself, but how could I possibly have had any fun while he was stuck on the couch under a blanket, coughing and struggling through every breath? There was no way I was going to leave him there to fend for himself and I told him as much. I stayed right by his side that night, watching his favorite movies with him, making sure he was okay and even cooking him chicken noodle soup for dinner.

In sickness and in health. I took that vow seriously. We both did.

We were high school sweethearts, each other's first loves. We tied the knot after six years together then had Penny five years later. We've had ups and downs but our relationship is built on solid ground and I truly believe there's nothing better in life than to have a foundation that's completely unshakable.

I have girlfriends who have had relationships come and go, and there's always something that has whittled away at that all-important core, knocking it down bit by bit until all that remains is rubble. It's heartbreaking to watch: arguments about finances, a dead bedroom, differing desires for their future, a lack of trust, a hidden addiction.

There was a guy I used to work with at the bakery who found out his girlfriend had been hooking up with her ex behind his back for over two years. He discovered this the day we were all sent home early after a small fire broke out in the kitchen and he arrived home to find them going at it on the back porch. I just wonder why someone would do that—why not just leave him and spare him the pain of betrayal?

There always seems to be some kind of hidden drama lurking below the surface of people's otherwise enviable relationships. I have one friend who divorced her husband of two years because he became lazy and unmotivated, choosing online gaming and weekends on the couch over the romantic outings and affectionate displays he'd hooked her in with.

I'm so thankful that I don't have any of those issues with my husband. With Seth, I never have to second guess myself or feel alone, he's always there for me, both in a practical way and emotionally. I know this all probably sounds super cheesy and too good to be true—our relationship couldn't possibly be this dreamy—but it is. Our life together really is perfect.

I mean, as perfect as it ever could be after we dumped that girl's body in the woods.

CHAPTER TWO

"Ah ah, girlfriend. You know the rule," I scold Penny, who looks up at me with her pleading doe eyes. She thought she could sneak away from the dinner table without finishing her food.

"But I don't like broccoli!" she whines, pronouncing it 'bwoccowi.'

It takes everything I have not to melt in defeat at her little voice. But I stand my ground, placing my hand on my hip. "That may be, young lady, but how are you ever going to grow big and strong if you don't eat your vegetables?"

Seth, who has just finished filling the dishwasher, scuttles over and scoops Penny up into his arms. "Well, that's where Mommy is wrong. You're already the strongest person I know."

Penny giggles and squirms in her father's arms.

"Just look at this," Seth gloats, placing Penny on the table and prompting her to raise her fists. "Go on, Penny, hit me as hard as you can."

With a steely look of determination, Penny makes little knuckles and pulls back both arms before driving them squarely into Seth's belly. He flies back dramatically, landing against the wall and slumping down to the floor, his eyes closed, tongue lolling out to the side. Penny erupts into a fit of giggles and shouts, "Again, Daddy! Again!"

But rather than indulge her, Seth gets up and places her gently back in her seat. "We'll do it again once you've eaten all your broccoli, okay?"

Penny grumbles in complaint but proceeds to shove a large piece of broccoli into her mouth.

I have to give it to Seth, he knows how to make even the hardest parts of parenting just that bit easier. And he's not wrong. Our little girl is the strongest person I know, too.

Not long after Penny was born we started to notice something wasn't quite right. Sometimes when I was trying to get her dressed or holding her in my arms her body would become rigid for minutes at a time. As new parents we thought maybe this was normal, but soon enough these instances grew more frequent. When her eyes started darting around wildly, we knew there was something wrong. She was just one month old when we rushed her to the hospital late one night, scared out of our minds. It didn't take long to receive the epilepsy diagnosis and by the time she was two, she began having full-on seizures. There's no way to describe what goes through your mind when you see your child having a seizure. It hurts more than anything to hold back and watch it happen, unable to intervene for fear of making it worse.

We joined a support group, learned everything we could about the disorder, put her on special diets and tried all sorts of methods to stop the seizures, but it just kept getting worse. Ultimately, she was put on a strict regimen of anti-seizure medicine twice daily and will likely be taking it for many more years to come. I hate that my little girl needs medicine just to function normally each day, but the upside is that it has given us our life back. Even a trip to the store used to be nerve-racking, but now we can leave the apartment for hours at a time, take a trip to the zoo, or even pack up and leave the city for a weekend without having to worry. Last year, we took off down the coast, Penny built sandcastles and dipped in and out of the ocean water for the first time in her life, splashing about and enjoying it just like any other child. There was a time when I worried that would never happen.

"Finished!" Penny declares through a mouthful of broccoli before running over to Seth and knocking him down to the floor and jumping on him like a trampoline.

I leave the two of them to roughhouse it out (another important part of our evening routine) before taking Penny to prepare her bath. She takes the bottle of bath foam and shakily pours a capful, spilling a little down the sides before emptying it below the flowing faucet and I stir the water to get the bubbles forming. Once she's in and resembles a little cherub on a fluffy white cloud, I sink down onto the floor beside the tub and squeeze my aching feet in my hands. Eight hours standing at the bakery, followed by another two at Chloe Lindman's unicorn-themed birthday party, chatting with the other parents while a gaggle of hyperactive four- and five-year-olds ran around screaming, has me beat. I'm hoping to sweet-talk my way into a foot rub from Seth once Penny's in bed. I need it badly.

It used to be the other way around. Until recently, I only worked mornings so I could spend the afternoons with Penny at home after preschool while Seth was at work. But since the company he was working for went under and he's been temporarily out of a job, I've taken on extra shifts at the bakery, now becoming the primary breadwinner—no pun intended. This arrangement is okay for now, we have enough savings in the bank to get us through at least a month or so but we're beginning to run behind on our credit card payments, with one bill arriving today with a sticker saying FINAL NOTICE in bold red letters. Still, I trust that Seth will find work soon.

Though I can sense that all this job hunting is starting to wear on him.

Big bubbles converge around Penny and I watch on, smiling, as she scoops them upwards, water hitting the walls. A flash flood rushes over the sides of the tub right into my lap, and I lean across to splash her back. "Oh, you think you're funny, huh?" I tease. "I am *so* getting you back!"

"Mommy, no!" she squeals happily as I splash her.

Even after four years I can't stop marveling at how this small human can bring us so much joy. And chaos, to be fair. I run my fingers through her flattened wet curls and breathe a happy sigh for moments like these that help to remind me why all the stress is worth it.

The last six months have not been easy on our family. Putting Penny into preschool felt like tossing her into the ocean without a life jacket. My heart still tugs at every drop off time. With her medical issues, every step of independence feels like a giant leap away from the protective bubble we've built around her. On her first day there, I had to hold back big fat tears that threatened to fall as I watched her walk into the classroom, her backpack much too large for her little back. I wanted to run after her, scoop her up, and take her back home where it was safe and I could keep my eye on her. And while it's gotten a little easier day by day, I still have to fight the urge to call the preschool and check if she's okay on a daily basis.

"Alright, girlie, let's get you out," I say, lifting her out of the tub, water dripping off of her. I wrap her in a fluffy towel and carry her into her bedroom, her wet legs flapping back and forth as we go. I expect to find her pajamas laid out on the bed where Seth leaves them for her each night, but they're not there. It's a small thing, but it strikes me as odd. He never forgets to put out her pajamas while I'm bathing her.

As I'm searching inside her drawer for a fresh pair, I hear

voices coming from down the hall. Somebody must have come over. That explains why Seth was too distracted to put out Penny's pajamas. But I can't think who would show up at our apartment this late in the evening.

I dry Penny off with the towel and get her pajamas on her before picking her up and walking down the hall toward the kitchen. But halfway there I hear a voice I recognize and it stops me in my tracks, a familiar dread crawling up my spine.

Not her. Anyone but her. She's the only person in the world who could take everything Seth and I have worked so hard to build over the last fifteen years and smash it into tiny pieces.

I peer quietly around the kitchen doorway and my heart drops when I see her sitting across the table from my husband. She turns her head and raises an eyebrow before waggling her fingers at me in greeting.

Sacha.

CHAPTER THREE

THEN

The trailhead parking lot is deserted. It's just us and a rusted old pickup that looks as though it was probably abandoned years ago.

The hood of Seth's Nissan almost glows, illuminated by the full moon hanging high above. I watch an oak tree's shadow quivering on the dry ground and fireflies flickering as they weave through the nearby treeline. It's too damned hot in here. I grab the closest thing to hand that remotely resembles a fan—a battered-up car owner's manual—and begin to flap it back and forth in front of my face, trying desperately to cool myself off.

"Can you at least try the cold air again?" I plead with Seth.

"There's no point," he repeats the same words he said ten minutes ago. "It's broken. It hasn't worked since my dad bought me this piece of junk."

I roll my eyes but keep quiet.

Seth has no idea of the privilege he comes from. He thinks because his dad bought him a twelve-year-old car for his eighteenth birthday, and his family only went on vacation once every couple of years growing up that he had it hard. Meanwhile, I can't even bring myself to tell my boyfriend of six months that my mom routinely had to wash our clothes in a bathtub of cold water to save on our electric bill and has a wallet stuffed full of coupons just to keep food in the fridge. And I'm pretty sure she'd switch that off to save money, too, if it were an option.

It's not like I want to keep secrets from Seth but these aren't things he needs to know about me. I'm sure he wouldn't think any less of me but next to a guy like Seth, with his stellar grades all through high school and now the big news of his scholarship, I sometimes feel inferior. Like, a lot inferior. I didn't come out of high school so well and I still have no idea what I'm going to do next while most of my friends are moving on to college.

"Come on, let's get out of the car, it'll be cooler outside," Seth suggests.

I step out of the car, my sandals slipping slightly on the twig-scattered ground. He's right, it's not as hot out here as it was inside his car, but I'm still sweating in my T-shirt, and I can only hope I don't have damp circles forming under my armpits.

"Where is everyone?" I ask. "We said nine thirty, right?"

"Relax." Seth slides his hands around my waist, kissing me softly. "They'll be here soon."

"Well, if they aren't, can we just go back to your place? There's DVDs and air conditioning there," I say, knowing I sound like a whiny child but not caring.

"Come on, Jade, this is going to be a great night," Seth promises, his voice echoing in the stillness.

I force a smile, trying to match his enthusiasm and failing miserably. In the distance, headlights pierce the darkness and I squint to see who's coming. Before long a car brakes to a halt, tires kicking up dirt. It's Brady behind the wheel, his laugh loud enough to reach us before he even pulls up.

"Ladies and gentlemen! Brady DuPont has arrived!" he shouts like a fool, swinging the car door open and stepping out.

Roman exits out the passenger side, scooping back his shoulder-length hair and taking in the empty parking lot. His linen shirt, like all his others, is crinkled and scattered with blim holes which, according to him, each tell their own story of a time he was somewhere cool, doing something cool, while stoned.

Seth strolls over and clasps the guys' hands in turn, knocking shoulders together. "What happened to meeting at nine thirty?"

"Yeah, sorry. We had to make a quick stop on the way," Brady says, glancing back at his car.

I stand awkwardly, trying to ignore the unsettled feeling that lingers in my chest. It's not that I don't like Seth's friends, I do, but Brady tightropes on the borderline of obnoxious when it comes to his confidence level. He's tall, dark, built like the insanely talented athlete that he is, and don't worry, he knows it. Roman, on the other hand, with his curly hair and stoner eyes, possesses a kind of laid-back aura that makes it hard to get on the same level as him.

"Hey, Jade," Brady's voice booms as he strides over to me. "You ready to party?"

"Sure," I reply tepidly.

"Not sure 'sure' is going to cut it." He grins, his eyes challenging me. "We've got to bring the energy because we're turning this place upside down tonight!"

Before I can respond to these meaningless hype words, the back door of his car swings open and out steps Sacha. She's stunning, as usual. Wild auburn hair, intense brown eyes and an unbridled confidence that draws the attention of every guy around her, and she knows it.

Lucky for me, I'm the only girl around who isn't in competition with her, since it's her twin brother I'm dating and not some other guy (literally, any other guy) who could easily be stolen away, should she wish to take him. And just like her brother, Sacha is the kind of person that makes it easy to feel inadequate when next to her. At only eighteen, she's got the confidence of a woman twice her age. When I'm around her, I always feel like a wannabe.

I shake my head, trying not to focus on my insecurities.

"Who's got the music?" Sacha raises her arms and shakes her hips like she's ready to get dancing.

"I think DJ Brady's got it covered." Roman smirks as he watches Brady struggle to get his oversized portable sound system out of the trunk.

I notice a lingering shadow inside of Brady's car. There's someone still in there, hidden in the darkness of the back seat. It's supposed to be just the five of us here tonight, celebrating our last days of summer before Brady begins his internship and Seth and Roman start college—so who is that?

Brady finally fishes the sound system from his trunk and awkwardly props it up on his shoulder. He's wearing our old high school sweatshirt for the occasion. "Are you people ready for the private event of the summer? It's going to be unforgettable!"

I can't help but roll my eyes as I lean against the hood of the car, wondering how many more party-boy platitudes he can cram in before the end of the night.

While the guys begin unloading the supplies, Sacha sidles up close and looks me up and down. "Hot out here tonight, huh?"

I quickly cross my arms when I see her smirking at the sweat stains that are beginning to bloom under the pits of my T-shirt.

"Who's back there?" I ask, nodding at the darkened rear seat of Brady's car.

"Oh, yeah," Sacha lowers her voice. "That was the *stop* Brady was talking about. Roman's cousin, Squeak. His aunt and mom asked him to hang out with her more often. Get her to socialize. They obviously don't know how we like to party..."

"Great," I mutter under my breath. Just what we need, to babysit for the night.

Although it's not really babysitting because Squeak is actually the same age as the rest of us. It just doesn't seem like it. She's small and painfully thin, and she always wears her hair in a long braid down her back. She also dresses like she's a middle-aged woman, if middle-aged women wore knee-length floral skirts with chunky leather boots and woolen cardigans. Her name isn't really Squeak, of course, it's Linda Bernotti. But she's quiet as a mouse and must have always been because even her family don't call her by her real name anymore.

"Looks like the party's about to get wilder," Sacha scoffs sarcastically as the car door finally opens and the tiny figure emerges.

Squeak steps out of the car, her posture lamppost straight. Her eyes survey the area cautiously, as though she's searching for something or someone to save her. Even in the low light I can see her cheeks glowing, maybe from the heat of the car, but it looks more like the telltale flush of nervous anticipation.

Sacha hollers wildly into the air above, the noise ringing through the night as she twirls over to Squeak's side, her exuberance seeming strained, if not completely artificial. Squeak flinches, a mouse cornered by a cat, as Sacha approaches her.

"What's wrong with you, Squeak? Liven up." Sacha gives her a chuck on the chin like she's a small child. "You're not afraid of the deep dark woods, are you?"

"No, I'm not," Squeak answers, her voice trailing off as she turns away, eyeing the trees that surround us.

"Atta girl. But you know... you'd better be careful." Sacha

lowers her voice to a purr as she leans in close to Squeak's ear. "A girl like you could get swallowed up whole in these woods."

CHAPTER FOUR

NOW

"Auntie Sacha!" Penny squirms her way out of my arms and beelines straight toward my sister-in-law.

I'm a little shocked that Penny even remembers her name considering she last saw her a year ago at her grandfather's funeral. But I guess Sacha must have left an impression on Penny, as with everyone else who's ever met her.

I step into the kitchen and survey Seth's face as he sits across from his sister, his brow furrowed as though trying to parse something complicated.

Sacha leans forward in her chair as she wraps her arms tightly around my daughter. Her hair is darker than the last time I saw her, it's now a deep burgundy that hangs loosely around her shoulders. She's wearing a dark gray T-shirt and faded jeans and her eye makeup, though not smudged, looks about two days old.

"Mommy! Look! It's Auntie Sacha!" Penny squeals from her perch on Sacha's lap.

"Hey there, sweet pea!" Sacha coos. "I've missed you so much!"

Seth shifts uncomfortably in his seat, his gaze darting

between me and Sacha. I catch his eye and send a sharp glance his way containing a question that I know he will receive: *Why is she here?* But it seems Seth is as perplexed as I am, because all he does is shrug and look away.

I can't imagine he's any happier to see his sister than I am. For as long as I've known them, Seth and Sacha have hated one another. As twins and each other's only siblings, there has always been a rivalry between them that surpasses the norm. There was never a time when they weren't butting heads. As teenagers their relationship was a mess of competition and resentment, and their parents did nothing to help the situation. Even as an outsider, it was plain to see that their mom and dad had a soft spot for Seth. In their eyes, he was the golden child, the one who could do no wrong. While Sacha was the wild child, impulsive and reckless. When Seth and Sasha turned eighteen, Seth got a car. Sacha didn't. And when he received his scholarship, his parents were so proud that they would speak in verse to anyone who would listen about their son's achievement. They'd never mention Sacha and would quickly change the subject if anyone were to ask about her or her plans after school. Nobody ever expected Sacha to go far, least of all her parents.

If this all sounds unfair, it's probably worth mentioning that Sacha never did herself any favors. All throughout high school she struggled with her grades and spent her time partying and making a reputation for herself with the boys. Some of the male teachers, too, if the rumors were to be believed.

Like me, Sacha went straight from high school to studying culinary arts at a local community college. Unlike me, she ended up dropping out when she met a hot French guy and returned to France with him to pursue a higher vision: living off a hot French guy's money in Paris. His name was Antoine, and he barely spoke a word of English but even that didn't stand in the way of him soon figuring out that Sacha was trouble. He sent her packing after a year. She mooched around the capital for a while before eventually making her way back home, by which time Seth had finished college and been awarded a position at a local tech startup. So when Sacha arrived back at her parents' house with her tail between her legs and nothing to show for herself since graduating high school, this only confirmed the feelings that had been simmering under the surface in their family for years: Seth was the successful one and Sacha was the screw-up. Since then, Seth and Sacha's relationship has become practically non-existent.

Which is why I'm now lost for words as I watch this woman bounce my daughter up and down on her knees while water droplets fall from the ends of Penny's wet hair onto the kitchen floor.

"Sacha, w-what are you doing here?" I stammer.

"What, an aunt can't come and visit her only niece once in a while?" she says defensively, the rasp in her voice telling me she still hasn't kicked her packet-a-day habit.

"It's not that, it's just," I glance at the kitchen clock, "it's nearly 8pm and we weren't expecting you."

And the reason we weren't expecting her is because we've never given her our home address or invited her over before. And yet, here she is. The only way she could have known where we live is either from her mom or Seth, and I know he would have told me if he'd invited her here. Also, he'd never invite her here.

"Yeah, well, I was in the area and I thought I'd come and see my family."

Family.

The word hangs ironically in the air.

If we are her family, then why did she never call when Penny was sick in the hospital as a baby? Or send birthday wishes for any of her four birthdays? Probably the same reason she's never taken an interest in anything that doesn't immediately serve her—she's selfish and doesn't care about other people's feelings.

"Hey, guess what?" Sacha squishes her nose against Penny's, staring straight into her eyes.

Penny giggles. "What?"

"I bought you a gift!" Sacha reaches into her bag and pulls out a packet of sugar-coated gummy worms before promptly ripping it open and handing the whole thing to Penny.

"Woah, woah, woah!" I snatch the packet away before she can reach her hand inside. "We don't do gummies, sorry."

Penny's mouth falls agape and her bottom lip begins to wobble, threatening a full-blown tantrum.

"Are you serious?" Sacha narrows her eyes at me. "It's just candy, Jade. Not drugs."

"It's Penny's bedtime and sugar would keep her awake all night," Seth finally speaks up and I throw him a thankful glance.

I'm not being unreasonable here, Sacha is. Who shows up at night-time with candy for small children? Witches. That's who. And Sacha has always struck me as a bit of a witch.

Penny's eyes are now glistening as Sacha consoles her quietly and I stand there trying to figure out how I'm suddenly the bad guy.

"Look, sweetie," I say to Penny. "How about you have a couple of gummy worms tomorrow, okay?"

"Okay." Penny sniffs and I give a silent thanks for having such a great kid. She knows our rules on candy and she could have made that a lot harder for me.

"Now, let's thank Auntie Sacha for the gift and then she can get going while I take you to bed," I say, reaching out my arms to Penny before directing my next words at her aunt. "In the future, maybe you could call before showing up and we can arrange something for a better time."

I keep my arms held out, but Sacha pulls her hands tighter around Penny's waist. "Actually, I was just talking to Seth and he said I could stay here for a while."

I have to stop myself from laughing because I know that's not something Seth would ever say without consulting me first. But when I look his way, his expression is stony and unreadable.

"See, I moved out of Ryan's place a week ago," Sacha continues. "And I've been staying with a friend since then, but her parents are coming to visit her and she needs the extra space. So I thought I'd use this as an excuse to come and get to know my precious little niecey-weesey!"

She pinches Penny's nose and Penny grins up at her like she's the best thing in the world.

I'll assume Ryan is another cog in the giant wheel that makes up Sacha's list of ex-boyfriends, but surely she has other friends she can lean on post-breakup rather than insert herself back into our lives, unannounced.

"I…" I glance at Seth, hoping he'll speak up but he remains quiet. "I don't know, Sacha. I mean, we only have two bedrooms and they're both taken."

Sacha shrugs. "That's okay, I'll sleep on the couch."

I don't know what to say to this. I know when family show up at your door asking for help, the right thing to do is open it wide and let them in. But Sacha is different. Every single fiber in my body is screaming at me to turn her away, to show her the door. But from the expectant look on my daughter's face, I can see that I have no choice but to let Sacha stay.

CHAPTER FIVE

A gentle crackling noise accompanies the amber glow of the cigarette sticking out from Sacha's mouth. She takes a long drag before shooting out a thick plume of smoke into the still night air of the balcony.

I've known Sacha since she was fifteen years old and even back then she smoked. Seth did, too, although he gave up cigarettes when we began dating because he knew I hated his charred breath when we kissed. I know how hard it was for him to give them up and it meant so much that he would do that for me. Sacha, on the other hand, didn't even give up when her own father died of lung cancer last year. You'd think that might have been enough to scare her out of her addiction, but apparently even staring the deadly consequences of her longtime habit right in the face didn't convince her to quit.

I study her features in the dim light and wonder how this lifestyle of cigarettes, alcohol and a revolving door of bad relationships hasn't left more of an imprint on her face. But there isn't so much as a hint of a wrinkle on her smooth skin. Whereas I—at the same age as Sacha and having never smoked or consistently drank in my life—am left pondering why even my expensive retinol regimen hasn't halted the slow creep of fine lines that have taken a comfortable residence around my eyes. It's hardly fair. Damn genetics.

Seth is reading Penny night-time stories in her bedroom and I suspect it will take much longer than the fifteen minutes it usually takes for her to fall asleep after the excitement of her aunt showing up.

"So why did things end between you and Ryan?" I ask, already having a fair idea how this conversation will go.

It's always the same. Sacha falls quickly in love with some tall, dark and preferably well-off enough to keep her fed and housed kind of guy, he's hooked on her for roughly six months or so until she gets too comfortable and begins to let her true self slip out, at which point he (understandably) bails before it's too late and she can weasel a ring out of him. Though only one of her relationships ever got to that point. His name was Diego and they were two months away from tying the knot before Sacha cheated on him with one of his groomsmen. Poor Diego was torn up about it, but he'll never know how lucky he was, finding those racy texts between her and his best man. It saved him a lifetime of misery, marrying a woman who would have either stayed with him, sucking his bank account dry over the years, or take him for everything he had the second she caught a glimpse of something better. Either way the result would've been the same. And I guess it showed Diego who his true friends were, too.

"Why did things end with Ryan?" Sacha repeats my words back, smoke flowing out with them. "Well, I guess it ended because I stupidly brought up the B-word."

I rack my brain. Bank? Barbados? Boob job?

"I'm lost," I say, giving up.

Having smoked her cigarette down to the filter, Sacha throws it to the floor of the balcony and twists it under her sandal before kicking the mangled butt over the edge, onto the street below.

"*Baby*." She coughs before leaning both arms down on the metal ledge. "I'm thirty-three, Jade, and sometimes these thoughts come creeping into my mind. God forbid I say them out loud, though. Ryan couldn't get me out of his apartment fast enough after I brought up the subject. Why is every guy in the world a commitment-phobic asshole?"

I almost want to commiserate with Sacha on this crude observation of hers, but as a sane person standing on the outside of this issue, it's clear to me that she's missing one crucial element as to why every one of her relationships has failed miserably. The common denominator is *her*. It's like she wants so desperately to be the victim in her own tragic love story that she can't see the real villains aren't the men who've left her, but the shadows of her own stupid choices that will forever lurk just behind her.

"A baby?" I ask. "You really think you're ready to have a child?"

"Why not?" She shrugs. "Idiots all around the world pop out kids every day, it's not like it's hard. And I'm great with kids."

I stifle a scoff. "You just tried to give Penny candy at bedtime!"

"Yeah." She brings her hands up and out, as though I'm only proving her point for her. "And did you see how happy I made her? That kid worshipped me."

I'm just about to clarify that it was most likely the candy that Penny worshipped and not Sacha herself when she turns to me suddenly with a sour expression. "I know what this is! You think you *own* motherhood. Like you've done it for a couple of years and now you're what, like, an expert? And because I'm not exactly like you, I couldn't possibly do it right."

I cross my arms, knowing I should drop this right here and now but for some reason I buy into this woman's never-ending rage bait. "Sacha, raising a child isn't as easy as just throwing sugar their way and hoping for the best. Babies need constant attention, they need a stable home and, God forbid, your child had any medical issues, like we've had with Penny. Kids are expensive. Then there's school and tantrums and imaginary friends and scraped knees and a million and one other things every day you have to deal with when you dedicate your life to being a mother."

"My kids wouldn't have any medical issues," she says brilliantly. "And what was that? Imaginary friends? Normal kids don't actually have those, do they?"

Normal kids? I don't even want to know what Sacha means by this, so I don't bother to ask. "Yes, actually. Even Penny has one. Izzy-Bella."

"Dear God." Sacha grimaces. "Aren't you afraid that it's not actually an imaginary friend at all, but some kind of demon that's going to convince her to stab you and Seth in your sleep?"

I roll my eyes. I can't say I'm surprised by this reaction from Sacha. Even I thought imaginary friends were a weird concept until I came home from work one day last week and Penny rushed up to me, gushing about how Izzy-Bella had visited her that afternoon, describing her long blond hair and pink dress and how she wanted to have a tea party with her someday soon. At first I was confused, but when Seth explained that Penny had just invented this little girl, I found it quite cute. And after searching online, I discovered that many kids go through the imaginary friend phase before eventually growing out of it. I'm not sure Seth loves the idea, though. I overheard him one night asking Penny not to talk about Izzy-Bella anymore. I don't see why he'd have a problem with it but I guess his feelings are more aligned with those of his sister.

"No," I say. "I'm not afraid that it's a demon. I'm happy that Penny has a great imagination and when she tells me about what she and Izzy-Bella get up to while I've been at work, I listen and play along because I'm her mother and being supportive is all part of the job."

"Hmm." Sacha looks unconvinced. "Well, please keep this Izzy-Bella well away from me, I don't feel like waking up tomorrow in a pool of my own blood."

CHAPTER SIX

THEN

The heavy-duty flashlight Seth brought with him from his dad's garage shoots a bright beam down the dirt path as we venture deeper into the woods.

The air is warm with the resinous scent of pine, and the sound of night critters chattering floats all around. I stick close to Seth, his hand wrapped around mine as I focus on trying not to trip over fallen branches and raised tree roots. Sacha's voice echoes through the trees in front of us. She's been talking nonstop since we set off ten minutes ago.

"Come on, Brady, can we just stop here?" she shouts. "We've been walking for ages and this spot is fine. Nobody will be able to hear us from the road."

Brady, who was the one to suggest we come out here tonight, shoots a grin her way. "You know, if you keep on yelling the bears are going to come for you."

"Maybe that would liven things up," Sacha flings back, her tone playful. "Plus... a bear would only go after the runt of the group." She punctuates this statement with a pointed look at Squeak and a sarcastic kiss blown her way.

Squeak ignores Sacha and continues walking quietly. I

don't think she's said a word since we set off. I really don't know why Roman brought his cousin, she doesn't seem like much of a party person. He said it was a favor to his mom and aunt, to try to get Squeak out of her shell and among people her own age, but she looks as though she'd rather be anywhere else, her eyes cast down as her long braid swings back and forth behind her. She keeps her arms crossed as she steps over fallen logs.

"Don't worry, Squeak, she's joking." Brady drapes his arm around Squeak's shoulder. "Besides, I was messing around. We don't need to worry about bears in this area."

"You sure about that?" I ask, rethinking the idea of coming out here tonight.

"Trust me." Brady grins. "I was a Boy Scout for six years. I know what I'm talking about."

Squeak does nothing to remove Brady's lingering arm from her shoulder, but I see her stiffen at the unwanted physical contact.

Even in the darkness, Sacha's eyes visibly flash when she spots Brady sidled up next to Squeak. She's had her sights set on Brady for a long time, but up until two weeks ago he was in a nearly three-year-long relationship with Celine Hutchins. With that over, I'm pretty sure there's no end to the lengths Sacha would go to in order to get her catch.

"Well, if there are any bears," Sacha says, stopping short and facing us all. "I'll just startle them like *this* while you guys run."

As if to prove my point, she pulls the bottom of her shirt up to her neck, flashing her bright pink bra to the entire group and winking at Brady. He and Roman both laugh and I see Seth's jaw tighten beside me as he tries to ignore his sister's grab for attention.

"Something tells me you won't be running away, Brady," Sacha says suggestively before grabbing the edge of his T-shirt and pulling him away from Squeak, who looks relieved to finally have his arm off her shoulder.

"Are you okay?" I ask Seth quietly as we keep walking.

He squeezes my hand a little tighter, his eyes narrowing at his sister. "I just wish she'd stop making an idiot of herself."

"She's just trying to have fun," I say, unsure why I'm defending her.

"Yeah, my sister is a whole *heap* of fun," he murmurs under his breath, but Sacha hears this and turns around, glaring his way.

"What's your problem, Seth? If you're not having any fun, then maybe you and your girlfriend should just go back home."

I don't know why Sacha is dragging me into this weird sibling squabble, but I want nothing to do with it. I keep my mouth firmly closed.

"Shut up, Sacha. Who even invited you?" he flings back so casually that I wonder if this is how they've spoken to each other since they were small children.

It's always like this when Seth and Sacha are around each other, but tonight it's like watching a slow-motion freight train hurtling toward us, threatening to ruin our night. And, as usual, I'm stuck in the middle wanting to scream at them both to just grow up.

I can feel the heat of Seth's frustration from beside me. It's not just Sacha's antics that are getting to him tonight, it's something deeper. Something I've sensed brewing under the surface of their relationship for a while now. Sacha ignores her brother's dig and strides on ahead, though it looks like her bravado is fading.

Once we're a safe distance behind the group and out of earshot, I turn to Seth as we walk. "Hey, I've got an idea," I say, trying to pivot his attention. "Once we've set up camp, how about you and I slip away and go make some fun of our own?"

Seth's mouth twitches up at the edges, a smile cracking through. "Really?"

I waggle my eyebrows at him and he laughs, his shoulders relaxing a little.

Despite the strained energy between my boyfriend and his sister, I'm starting to feel a little prickle of excitement for tonight. When Brady first suggested coming out to the woods for our last big party together before he starts his internship and Seth and Roman go off to college, I wasn't exactly into the idea. Getting drunk in the woods and sleeping inside a pop-up tent didn't sound like my idea of a great time. But now that the six of us are out here, getting closer to our stop for the night, I have this sudden resolve to make the most of it. With everyone's lives shooting off in different directions, it could be a long time until we're all together as a group again.

We follow as Brady leads us deeper into the woods. I hope he knows where he's going because without any signposts or landmarks, everything here looks the same to me. I know the real reason he wants to get far away from the trailhead, and the portable sound system he's carrying with its large speakers has a lot to do with it.

Brady is the kind of guy who never says no to anything. He's loud, he's confident, and if there's a good time to be had, he's always right there in the middle of the action. He has a lot more in common with Sacha than her own twin brother does, and it's clearly gotten her attention because she's pulling out all the stops flirting with him tonight. Though I have to admit, it's more than a little amusing to witness the hard work she's putting in to grab Brady's attention, before being left pouting miserably as he attempts to strike up a conversation with Squeak instead. Good luck with that, buddy. I don't really know Squeak, but when Sacha and I once enquired about Roman's verbally challenged cousin, he told us she'd spent a few weeks in the hospital as a child for a heart condition and when she came out, she barely spoke anymore. Hence the name.

I'm getting tired of walking. Even stoic Roman—who's been quietly trudging along with two pack-away tents while the other guys carry the drinks in a large cooler—seems to be showing signs of fatigue as we press on. Everyone is more than a little relieved when Brady runs ahead suddenly, his voice cutting through the woods. "Guys, over here! I found the clearing!"

Sacha bounces ahead, her auburn hair reflecting the moonlight as she catches up with Brady.

"Let's make some noise!" Brady calls out into the night, before the thumping sound of his speakers starts up from where he crouches on the ground.

Roman drops the tent bags and Seth doesn't waste any time opening the cooler and passing around cold beers, which we all happily accept after hiking for twenty minutes in the warm night air. Even Squeak accepts a beer, which surprises me. She looks like the type who'd squeal on you for underage drinking, but I guess I've never really seen her outside of school before, so what do I know? She's always been so quiet, I don't know how to get a read on her. But I get the feeling that behind that mousy face and prairie-rebel style, there's a lot more to Squeak than meets the eye.

CHAPTER SEVEN

NOW

By the time I've already gotten out of bed, showered, dressed and have breakfast cooking on the stove, Sacha emerges from her slumber on the couch and joins Penny at the table.

Seth is still showering. We usually shower together, but our beloved routine has been interrupted by Sacha's presence and I'm both surprised and a little annoyed that he didn't put up more of a fight when she asked to stay.

He wasn't jumping for joy over her sudden arrival, that much was clear from the grim expression on his face last night. But, I guess, despite the tension that's simmered under the surface their whole lives, they're still brother and sister.

Twin brother and sister. That's got to count for something.

I don't have any siblings, so I don't really know how these things work, but witnessing Seth's relationship with his sister over the years has been enough to convince me that I don't ever want to have another child. I want Penny to always be number one, to never have someone else undermining her bond with us. I want her to know that she's the center of our world and to never feel like there's a competition to win our love. Having been an only child, I never had to share the affection of my parents growing up. And I turned out fine. Mostly.

When Seth and I talked last night in bed, he told me Sacha had assured him she'd only be staying for a week or so, while she gets herself back on her feet. But without a job, I don't see how she could afford to get a place of her own and it's most likely that she'll be couch surfing until she finds another man (read: sucker) to fall for her charms and support her passive existence. I just hope she has a few friends scattered around the city with places to crash at though, because she's only been here twelve hours and I already want her gone. I had to carefully avoid knocking over the collection of toiletries she'd left scattered around our bathroom vanity while trying to access our hand soap this morning, and then on my way to the kitchen I nearly tripped over the giant quilted duffle bag she'd left lying open on the floor.

I don't mind playing host, but most people try not to impose too much when they're a guest in someone else's home. Sacha, on the other hand, seems to have no problem unloading her stuff anywhere she spots a space for it.

"Good morning," I greet her, my tone neutral.

Sacha responds with a nod and smooths her ruffled hair back before pouring herself a cup of coffee from the pot on the table. I load plates with scrambled eggs and buttered toast and serve them to Penny and our houseguest, pleasantly surprised when Sacha mumbles a thank you, then sit down to eat my own.

"What are your plans for today?" I ask Sacha, uncomfortable with the idea of leaving her alone in our apartment.

"Not sure." She inspects a single lump of egg sitting on her fork before placing it into her mouth and slowly chewing. "I thought I might spend some time with my little princess here."

Penny grins as Sacha reaches out and tickles underneath her chin.

"She'll be at preschool until two this afternoon and Seth will be out at a job interview until then," I point out, hoping that last remark might spark some inspiration for her.

Sacha hasn't had a steady job since I've known her. She's dabbled in everything from bar work to retail to peddling 'wellness' shakes online for what I'm pretty sure was one of those sleazy multi-level marketing companies, but it seems like every time she meets a guy, she gives it up in favor of a more sedentary existence, living off him until he gets sick of her crap and kicks her to the curb. If she could just stick with something long enough to earn some money and get a place of her own, she might be one small step closer to her newfound aspirations of starting a family. As awful an idea as that sounds to me.

"Seth has a job interview? What happened to his old job?" Sacha asks, draining the last of her coffee and pouring more into her mug.

"The company he worked for went under a few months back, so he's been trying to find something else since then," I say, trying to sound casual. "His skills are kind of specific though, so it's just taking a while."

This is downplaying the situation somewhat. It's not like Seth can just walk into any job, his is a highly specialized field. Cybersecurity and network defense are the kinds of things that require a deep understanding of intricate systems and protocols. And since the company Seth worked for eventually went under, it complicates things even more. For one, the hiring process for these positions involves a lot of vetting. Employers need to trust that candidates can handle sensitive information and the background checks that are undertaken are no joke. Seth's previous employer's closure adds a big layer of scrutiny. It's not as straightforward as just listing his skills on a résumé, this is a whole different ball game than most professions.

He even enlisted the help of a career coaching service, something I'd never heard of until he brought it up. They're called the Vanguard Career Group and apparently they specialize in placing professionals in high-stakes roles like his. "These guys have a solid network and they know exactly how to navigate the job market for people like me. It's a competitive landscape, Jade, and hiring Vanguard will be an investment that will pay off, I promise," he'd said.

It took a lot for Seth to convince me the cost was worth it, but they've been working to help him find a position for a couple of weeks now. There may not have been any bites yet, but I have faith he'll land something soon. He'll have to. We're beginning to struggle on only one income.

"Finished!" Penny sings, shoving the last bite of egg into her mouth. "Can I have the candy now?"

I should have known Penny wouldn't forget about that so easily. It's like my daughter is Odysseus and candy is a siren's call she just can't resist. Though tying her up to stop her from succumbing to its allure won't help in this case. And I did promise her just a couple of pieces this morning, so I decide to use this to my advantage. Anything to get her medicine down easier before preschool.

"You sure can," I say. "As soon as you take your medicine."

Penny pouts, her small brows furrowing as she weighs up the proposal.

"Medicine? What medicine?" Sacha's eyes narrow.

"It's an anti-seizure medication she has to take each day," I explain. "It helps control the electrical activity in her brain."

Sacha stares at me blankly, clearly confused.

I take a breath, searching for the right way to explain it so she'll understand. "It's kind of like... a safety net for her brain. It stops the seizures from happening by stabilizing the nerve activity. It's not going to cure her, but it helps keep her safe so long as she takes it each day."

"What happens if she doesn't?" Sacha asks.

Penny's face scrunches up at this, the memory still fresh.

"The bad thing," she whispers to her aunt.

Sacha's eyes widen, and I feel the familiar twist in my stomach, the guilt still eating at my insides.

It happened three months ago, not long after she started preschool. I went to give Penny her medicine one morning but got distracted by a call. By the time I got off the phone we were running late, and I quickly bundled her up in her coat before we ran out the door, forgetting the medicine still sitting on the kitchen counter. That afternoon I got a call I'll never forget. Penny had suffered a seizure during playtime in the yard and hit her head on the edge of a stone path. By the time I got to the preschool she was in the care of EMTs and was screaming for me, a dressing covering the gash on her face. She was terrified by the whole ordeal. She had to spend the night in the hospital for observation, and as much as the doctors told me not to blame myself, I'll never stop feeling guilty about it.

Since then, we've never forgotten a dose, and hopefully never will again. We were lucky that day. It's terrifying to think of how much worse it could be if something like that ever happened again.

CHAPTER EIGHT

It's late afternoon by the time I arrive back at our apartment building, the mouthwatering scent of spices from the Indian restaurant next door setting off a small but angry growl from my stomach. I hit the button for the elevator before the doors open and I get inside, leaning against the wall and letting the coolness of the metal panels sink into my back.

It's no wonder I'm hungry, I didn't even get a chance to eat lunch. Today was a mess. Darina stuck me with an order for a four-tier wedding cake on top of everything else, and of course one of the kitchen hands chose today not to show up. No call, no warning. It felt like I was playing a game of Whac-a-Mole, one minute piping roses the next sweeping up spilled flour and trying to keep the kitchen in order.

On the fourth floor, I step out and begin counting down the seconds until I can collapse on the couch. I'll happily sit and brush knots from a doll's synthetic hair with Penny for a whole hour if it means getting to take the weight off my feet.

Inside the apartment, I find Penny seated at the kitchen table, coloring with crayons while her little legs swing about underneath the chair. "Hi, Mommy!"

I lean down and plant a soft kiss on her cheek. "Hey, pumpkin. What are you working on?" I ask, glancing at her masterpiece: an abstract swirl of colors that only a mother could appreciate.

"It's a rainbow unicorn." Her eyes sparkle with pride.

"It's beautiful. Is that you standing next to it?" I point to the squiggle with long hair and hands that are two times bigger than its face.

"That's Izzy-Bella."

"Oh. Did she come to play today?" I ask, because for some reason, Izzy-Bella never shows up when I'm at home. I think she must be Penny's way of dealing with separation anxiety.

"No." She sounds disappointed. "But I played with Auntie Sacha."

This is something I'm glad to hear. I'd kind of expected Sacha to just sit around all day doing nothing, so the fact that she took time to bond with Penny after preschool is a pleasant surprise.

"Where are Daddy and Sacha?" I ask, looking around.

"Outside. Auntie Sacha has her stinky stick." Penny pulls a grossed-out face, her nose scrunching up.

I chuckle softly. "Got it."

I slip off my shoes and step into the living room, the wooden floor cool on my feet, but when I spot the balcony door ajar and hear raised voices from outside, I freeze in place. I stay back, hugged against the wall, listening.

"...that's bullshit and you know it, Sacha! What do you really want from me? Money? Because I'll give you money if you just get away from my family and leave us alone. Forever." Seth's voice is an all-too familiar echo of the way he used to speak to his sister when they were teenagers. But it almost feels like I'm listening to a stranger now. I never hear him talk like this anymore. So emotional and angry.

"Don't be so dramatic." Sacha's voice comes out a little muffled, a cigarette hovering in her mouth, lighter clicking away before she takes a large drag.

"It's not dramatic, Sacha. You're talking about ruining my marriage! You and I *both* played a part in what happened to Squeak that night, and if you tell Jade–"

My heart begins thudding wildly in my chest as I clutch the wall.

Sacha cuts Seth off mid-sentence. "Oh, relax. I'm not going to tell her anything. I just want to spend some time with my niece. Is that such a terrible thing? But Jade deserves to know about Roman. She'll find out sooner or later anyway."

I'm sure that they must be able to hear the blaring rhythm of my heartbeat from where they stand, but a moment later they move further out on the balcony and I can no longer hear what they're saying. I quietly return to the kitchen, unable to understand what Seth meant by those words. He and Sacha both played a part in Squeak's death? What does that mean?

It's been fifteen years to the month since that night in the woods, and not a day goes by that I don't think about it. We'd all agreed to never say a word, that was the only way. The only way Seth and Roman could continue on to college with their scholarships still intact. The only way Brady could start his internship, without a tarnished reputation. The only way Sacha and I could move on with our lives and not always be blamed for what happened.

I've always believed that despite our actions, despite the sickening choice we made, none of us could be sure of the cause of her death. But after hearing Seth's words out on the balcony just now, everything I thought I knew has been thrown into question.

A moment later, my nerves are still shot as Seth returns to the kitchen, Sacha in tow. "Oh hey, honey. How was work?"

How was work? How can he act so normally after he and Sacha were just fighting?

"Um... yeah, it was fine," I say, putting away the loose crayons scattered around the table.

Sacha casts a pointed look at Seth, and he sighs before turning to Penny. "Hey, Pen? How about you go put on a cartoon for a minute?"

"Really?" Her eyes narrow. She knows she's only allowed cartoons on the weekends, so I don't blame her for being suspicious.

"Just this one time, yes," he replies.

He doesn't need to tell her twice, because she shoots off to the living room faster than Wile E. Coyote on a rocket.

"What's going on?" I ask him once she's gone.

Sacha leans against the countertop, watching us. She hasn't so much as said hello to me. Seth takes my arm and leads me to a chair. He sits across the table from me and leans my way. "It's Roman..." he starts, and I already know from his tone.

I already know because I've heard that tone before.

It's Brady.

"What... what happened?" I ask, tears already in my eyes.

Seth heaves a sigh and chokes up a little as the words come out. "He... he's dead. He decided to leave us."

What a strange way to put it. *He decided.*

Did he really decide? Or was he forced? Forced by the rot in his heart. The rot that has infested all our hearts since that night. The same one that drove Brady to alcohol in the months after Squeak's death, that made him get in his car with enough liquor in his system to kill a small elephant before he crashed into that truck.

I haven't seen Roman in over a decade, but I know he suffered more than any of us in the years after that night. Squeak was his cousin. His mother and aunt trusted him with her life. I saw the pain in his eyes when the search began, when his aunt put out the desperate plea for anyone who had seen her daughter to help them. Roman told her she never showed up, that our party was on the other side of town. They never even searched the woodlands. They never knew we'd been there.

The rest of us only had to deal with *our* guilt. With *our* pain. Roman had to deal with the pain of his family, too. The kind of pain that shadows every moment of every day, and rips families apart.

And now he's gone. He couldn't live with it all anymore.

"So, what are we going to do?" Sacha asks, crossing her arms.

"What do you mean?" I flick between her and Seth.

"I mean," Sacha says, lowering her tone, "if Roman felt so guilty about Squeak's death that he couldn't face another day, don't you think it's possible he might have written a parting note confessing to what we did?"

CHAPTER NINE

THEN

I lean back against the rough bark of a tree as I take a sip from my red paper cup. The taste is a familiar blend of cheap rum and cola that burns my throat and tingles my tongue. It's not the ideal drink for a warm summer's night like this, but it's delicious and smooth and I'm beginning to feel a numbing buzz inside my veins.

Any worries I had about Seth and Sacha's brewing animosity ruining the party atmosphere are long gone, because since we set up camp and the drinks have started flowing, they're suddenly playing nice. They've stopped bickering and are now both immersed in an animated conversation with Roman about his plans to go traveling after college.

Roman has always had an untamed spirit, he's never just gone along with the crowd. I sometimes think that if Seth and Brady hadn't been friends with him since kindergarten, they would have never found each other. And once Roman finishes college and goes hiking up mountains in Tibet or living among goat herders in India while those guys follow the tracks that have been pre-laid for them here at home, it'll likely be difficult for them to all keep in contact.

Sacha tells Roman about her dreams of visiting Paris, her voice far louder than it needs to be over the music, and every time she laughs, I'm sure I hear another owl or bat fluttering off. At this rate she'll have the whole forest cleared in no time and we won't have to worry about not having a campfire to scare off any unwanted natural predators.

These woodlands are prone to wildfires in the summer months, and as tempting as it is to light a fire to sit around, none of us are stupid enough to actually risk it. Luckily, it's still warm enough for me to sit comfortably in just a T-shirt but I know the chill of the night air will begin to spread soon enough.

Brady's speaker is blasting techno-pop down by his feet, although he's turned it down a little since we first arrived and he's now sitting on a log next to Squeak. She almost looks like a child next to his six-foot, broad-shouldered, athletic build. But despite her size, she's on at least her third beer. I'm surprised when I see her talking to Brady. In high school I never saw her say more than a couple of words to anyone, but now I'm wondering if all it takes is a little Dutch courage to get her going. I lean forward, straining to hear what they're talking about but the noise of the music is drowning out their words, and when I try my hand at lipreading, I'm even less successful. Unless Brady really *did* just ask Squeak if she wanted two medium-sized frog bombs, but that seems very unlikely.

It looks like I'm not the only one who's noticed them getting closer, because as Sacha yucks it up with the guys, I see her eyes stray to Brady and Squeak every so often.

Sacha has been waiting for years to sink her claws into Brady DuPont, and now that her chance has come, he seems more interested in the quiet mystery of Squeak's allure than Sacha's blatant in-your-face advances. I bet this is killing her.

No matter what she's doing, Sacha always exudes this totally effortless kind of confidence, as though she owns every inch of the space around her. I'd never admit this out loud, but in high school I used to try to emulate her style and mannerisms. I'd even search through clothing stores for items that looked like hers. If she came to school on Monday with white Adidas sneakers, slouchy jeans and a layered camisole, then you can bet your ass I'd be out at the mall that weekend, scouring the rails to recreate the look as best I could. Somehow, nobody ever called me out on it, but that's probably because they were all doing the same thing, too. At least the girls who hung around Sacha were, anyway. And I was always just on the outside of that friend group. Not pals, not rivals, but the only time we'd ever converse was on school grounds, never outside of them. It wasn't for my lack of trying, either.

I would 'accidentally' bump into them in the movie theater lobby, hoping they'd invite me to come watch a film with them. They never did.

I'd slow down a little as I passed their lunch table each day, praying they'd stop me and ask me to sit with them. They didn't.

I'd even hang out with boring Jill Clarkson in the hopes her older sister Emma would strike up a friendship with me and be my gateway into Sacha's coveted group. But nothing ever worked. I was basically invisible to them.

Of course, this all changed when I began dating Seth. It's not like I was only interested in him because of his sister, that would be creepy and weird. But it just so happens that when there's a beautiful, perfect-in-every-way girl who happens to have a twin brother—a person made up of the same unfairly blessed genetic concoction—he's going to be as hot as the sun. And somehow, I managed to get his attention. I didn't even mean to.

I'd just gotten off the school bus one day when I turned around and walked straight into him. Well, his nose really. But once we'd stemmed the blood flow, we were able to laugh about it, and we've been inseparable ever since. It just so happens that my relationship with Seth came with the huge social advantage of having a close tie to his sister. Suddenly she and I would spend evenings in her bedroom talking endlessly before Seth got home from his job delivering pizzas. She would confide in me about all the ins and outs of her friend group, their stories, their secrets.

And, naturally, that was when I became completely disillusioned.

Because this cool girl I'd followed around, this *everyone wants to be her or be with her* kind of girl, turned out to be a giant whining, self-centered bitch. And a crappy friend to boot. I mean, I would never say that out loud, and frankly, I don't have to because Seth says it enough for both of us—but my days of longing to be just like Sacha are now well and truly over.

That doesn't stop me from wishing I had her confidence though, because as I sit here feeling a little like an imposter, a shadow lurking in the background, I watch her radiating the kind of energy that draws everyone in. And while I stuck with the safe combo of a plain white T-shirt and jeans tonight, she chose to flaunt her skin and her curves with a short button-up shirt that boosts her assets and barely covers her navel. Her long, tanned legs are accentuated with cut-off shorts that hug her hips, and when she laughs, her wild, untamed hair swings about her shoulders. She's the kind of girl who has never had to fight against the mirror's reflection, and that's something I'll forever be envious of. She's also someone to always push boundaries, and apparently tonight is no different.

"Let's play a game!" she shouts, reaching down to turn the music off.

I exchange glances with Seth and Roman, who both look about as skeptical as I feel. Squeak, still sitting quietly on the log, pulls her knees to her chest. It doesn't really look like there are any takers, but if I know Sacha, that isn't going to stop her in the slightest.

"We're not kids, Sacha." Seth sighs. "We're not going to play hide-and-seek in the woods."

"Did I *say* hide-and-seek?" she hisses at her brother. "No, I did not."

I can see the tension building again between them. If they weren't related, someone would tell them to just give it up and kiss already, but since this is the kind of tension built on years of hurt feelings and jostling for the love and affection of their parents, it feels like there will never be a time when it's not just right under the surface, ready to bubble over any second.

"No, this is different," Sacha insists, looking at each of us in turn. "You'll all love this one. It's called Truth, Truth, Lie."

CHAPTER TEN

NOW

Roman is dead. I've been trying to process it for the last twenty-four hours, but I still can't believe it.

It's easy to sound cliché, but Roman was nothing like the other guys at our school. He never cared for normal. He kept his hair long, despite the constant remarks from the teachers and other students. He serenaded whole classrooms with poems he'd written. He once brought a live chicken from his neighbor's farm to walk around the halls with, feathers flying, before kicking off a speech about how eggs don't just magically appear at the grocery store and proclaimed that poultry cages were torture chambers. He even set up a choir in our science lab and had a bunch of us sing in rounds to a row of potted plants to test the theory that it would help them grow faster.

There's no question that there's a huge void in the world now that Roman's gone. He made life a little more vibrant and ridiculous, and even though Seth and I weren't in touch with him for many years, I found it comforting to know he was out there somewhere in the world spreading his unique brand of weirdness.

But now I'm wondering if that guy I knew died long ago.

Long before his heart stopped beating. Because what happened in the woods that night changed us all, and each of us learned to cope in our own different ways.

Brady immediately turned to alcohol, which led to his tragic death in a car accident at just nineteen. Roman eventually went through with his plans to travel the world, though I think his motive changed from wanting to explore to wanting to run away. Sacha seemed to freeze in time, never really growing up or evolving from the wild eighteen-year-old she was back then. And Seth and I turned to each other. We created a bond so strong and unshakable that we always had steady ground to stand on, no matter what.

A toll was taken on all of us that night. And Roman was hit the hardest. While the rest of us went home and kept quiet, he had to face his family. He looked them in the eyes and lied to them, telling them Squeak never showed up. That we'd partied on the other side of town, never mentioning the woods.

Roman had a huge heart for humankind, animals and the earth. And I guess the lies he told to protect the ones he loved must have been a burden he could no longer bear.

His funeral is being held tomorrow in Hawaii, where he's been living for the past ten years, and I know that Seth wishes we could go. We both do. But the thought of facing his family, their grief, their pain... it makes my stomach churn. What would we even say? "*We're sorry for your loss*"? It sounds so hollow in my mind. I can already see the questions in their eyes, questions that we hold the answers to but can never share. I can't bear the thought of their pain. And just like every other day for the past fifteen years, the weight of our silence pins me down like an oppressive force.

I sit beside the bathtub as Penny splashes about and wrap my arms around myself, a half-hearted attempt to shield my body from the guilt that gnaws at me. If I could have one wish in the world it would be to turn back time. But it's too late. And nothing will ever bring Squeak, Brady and Roman back.

Now there's just me, Seth and Sacha left. And the question on all of our minds is: Did Roman leave a note confessing everything? It's a terrifying thought. And one that I try to put to the back of my mind as I hoist Penny from the tub and pat her dry.

I find her pajamas laying out on her bed—Seth remembered them tonight—and I begin putting them on Penny as we talk about her day.

"Bodhi got glitter on my picture," she continues on from the preschool recap she'd started in the bath, "but Miss Carol said it made it even gooder. So I put lots and lots and *lots* more on but then she took away the glitter."

"Oh, I see." I nod. That'll explain why her school bag looked like Rip Taylor had gotten into it.

"And what did you do when you got home? Did you play with Izzy-Bella?" I ask, doing up the last button of her fleece shirt.

"No, I told you before, she doesn't come when Auntie Sacha's here," Penny scolds me, like I'm slow to keep up.

"Oh, yes. I remember you said that yesterday."

"Daddy says I'm not essposed to talk about her." Penny's face drops.

"He said you're not *supposed* to talk about Izzy-Bella?" I correct, remembering the conversation I overheard him having with her before.

Penny nods.

I don't understand what makes Seth so uncomfortable about our daughter having an imaginary friend. It's harmless. But he always avoids talking about it when I bring it up, and I can see that Penny's upset by his dismissive attitude to this little girl she's created to keep her company and play with when she's feeling lonely.

I make a mental note to try to talk with Seth about it again later and encourage him to be a little more accepting of Penny's vivid imagination.

"So, what did you and Auntie Sacha play while I was at work?" I ask as I gently comb through Penny's wet hair.

This is why I have no itch to have a second child. Every evening, I can give my whole undivided attention to Penny, and she feels as though her words are the most interesting thing that I've ever heard. And sometimes they are. I've always been afraid that a little brother or sister would leave her feeling abandoned and resentful. And don't parents always subconsciously choose a favorite child? That's how it always seemed with Seth's parents. His mom and dad always favored him over Sacha, and they didn't even do a good job keeping it a secret. No wonder Sacha has always been so desperate for attention, she had to fight from the moment she was born—sixteen minutes after Seth—just to be seen by her parents.

There's no way I could do that to Penny. She's my number one. My *always* number one. I breathe in the comforting clean scent of her strawberry shampoo as she regales me with stories of the various games she played with Sacha today.

Sacha has always been one for games. My mind quickly goes to a darker place, but I try to shake myself out of it as Penny continues.

"And then Auntie Sacha wanted to play mommies and babies, and I made a–"

"What?" I cut her off, suddenly focused on her words.

Penny turns when I stop brushing her hair.

"What did she make you play?" I ask, trying to keep my voice light.

"Mommies and babies," Penny repeats. "It's fun."

I put the hairbrush down gently. "Okay, time to clean your teeth."

I send her off to the bathroom while I wait in the hall for her to finish. From here I can see through to the living room, where Sacha is lying on the couch, flicking through a magazine. That's where she spends most of her time since arriving two days ago. It's like she doesn't know what to do with herself. I don't know how she ever expects to get anywhere in life if she can't even pick herself up and start looking for a job. It's as though she's totally aimless.

Her words the other night about wanting a child of her own float through my mind. Is that why she was playing mommy to Penny today while I was gone? Is she playing out this new fantasy of hers with my daughter?

I can't quite pinpoint why, but the thought leaves me with a deeply uncomfortable feeling.

CHAPTER ELEVEN

Seth's voice hums low and soothing from Penny's room, the way it always does when he's reading her night-time story.

We've tried other things over time to get Penny to sleep, like playing gentle lullabies, white noise, a lavender scented pillow—you name it, we've tried it. But she just won't fall asleep without one of us there reading to her. I know it's probably a bad habit, but I doubt in fifteen years' time, as we stand there waving goodbye to her as she leaves for college, we'll be regretting that extra twenty minutes we took each night to read her to sleep as a small child.

I take a few minutes to wash the dishes from dinner and wipe down the countertops before sucking in a deep breath, steeling myself as I approach Sacha. She's still sprawled out comfortably on the couch, flipping through channels like she owns the place. I'm worried that she's getting a little too comfortable in our home. When she told us she wanted to stay, she assured us it would only be for a week or so. But since she hasn't said anything about where she's going next and doesn't seem to be job or apartment hunting, I'm beginning to wonder how long exactly the 'or so' part is. It's only been two days, but already I've found her dirty dishes stacked up in the kitchen, power bar wrappers on the living-room floor and I don't even want to think about how much our next energy bill will be if she keeps taking thirty minute showers like the last couple of evenings.

I'm looking forward to her moving on to the next sucker who'll provide her room and board so we can get back to our normal routine here. But that's a conversation I'll leave for Seth to have with his sister. Right now, there's something else on my mind that I want to talk to her about. I gingerly approach her in the living room where she's chuckling at a sitcom re-run.

"Hey, Sacha?" I say, attempting a non-confrontational tone.

She glances up, arching an eyebrow. "Hmm?"

I swallow hard, telling myself not to be intimidated by her. "I just wanted to ask you about something."

Her expression shifts, but not in the way I want. She tosses the remote aside and leans back, a challenge glimmering in her eyes.

"Penny mentioned you two played mommies and babies today while I was at work."

"And?"

"And... she said you suggested it," I prompt, hoping she'll get where I'm going with this.

"Okay?" She draws out the word.

"Well, it's just..." I'm beginning to sweat and I'm wishing I'd have planned out this conversation in my head better before approaching her.

"What?" Sacha looks suspicious. "Did she say I did something to her? Like I hurt her or something?"

"Oh no," I rush. "No, that's not what I'm talking about. It's just..."

What I want to ask is '*Why are you pretending my kid is your baby?*' but I can't seem to get it out.

"Oh..." Sacha nods her head in understanding. "Did she tell you I'm secretly plotting to kidnap her and raise her as my own? Damn it, I made her swear that she wouldn't tell you."

I roll my eyes. "I'm just a little concerned about you setting up a game where she has to pretend she's your baby."

Sacha snorts, flipping her hair over her shoulder. "Seriously? Come on, Jade, don't be that person."

"Why are you acting like it's no big deal? You even told me you wanted a baby of your own." The words spill out before I can stop them, and I feel the heat rising in my cheeks. I hate that I'm confronting her like this, but the thought of her pretending Penny is her daughter gnaws at me.

Sacha narrows her eyes. "Oh, right. Because playing house with a four-year-old is the same as me trying to steal your kid. Look, I'm not trying to replace you. Penny wanted to play, and I played along. It's called being a good aunt."

"A good aunt doesn't pretend she's a kid's mother!" I shoot back, my voice rising.

She sits up, her expression shifting from playful annoyance to something sharper. "You know what, Jade? You've always been like this. Making a big deal out of everything. Have you considered for a second that you might have it wrong?"

I don't know what she means by this, so I cross my arms and wait for her to continue.

"I was eating soup for lunch and Penny asked me if she could try a sip. Then she thought it would be funny to feed it to me, and I said I hadn't been spoon fed since I was a baby. So, she fed me the soup and pretended she was a mommy."

Oh.

"Oh," I say, my mouth no more articulate than my head.

"Yeah, *oh*," Sacha says, mocking me.

"So, she meant she was the mommy and you were the baby."

I wish Penny had just told me that and saved me this

incredibly awkward moment. I've made a mountain out of a molehill, and I'm sure my face is glowing.

"Yes." She throws her hands up in exasperation. "And if you're so worried about it, maybe you should be asking yourself why that is instead of accusing me of having some twisted agenda. Maybe you're worried that she thinks you're boring."

My chest tightens and I don't know what to say to this. I don't know if she's being passive-aggressive or just plain aggressive.

"But you can relax." Her voice softens. "I'm not trying to play mommy. I'm not trying to take anything from you. I just want to bond with my niece. It's not a crime."

I glance away. Something else is pulling at my mind. "About that. I just don't want you to get too attached. Penny is sensitive and if you build a close relationship with her and then just slide right out of her life again, she'll be–"

"I'm not going anywhere, Jade." Sacha's eyes bore into mine and there's something about the way she says these words that makes it sound like a threat.

"But you know..." she continues, the corners of her mouth turning up playfully, "that reminds me of something. What *would* happen to Penny if you and Seth were to... I don't know, die in a plane crash or something?"

I'm sure Sacha is just playing some kind of weird mind game with me, but the question makes me feel like I've been stabbed in the chest with a shard of broken glass. That very question has been a topic that Seth and I have discussed repeatedly since Penny was born and since we have no suitable family, we've never come to an answer.

Seth's mom is out of the running. When she became a widow, she decided to embrace her golden years at a large retirement community in Florida, which is hardly a place to raise a small child. And with my own parents now in their late seventies—and not the sprightly kind—we've found ourselves with no grandparents to fall back on. That just leaves our siblings. And since I don't have any, and Seth has no others, the only family left is Sacha.

I've even considered trying to create a close bond with some of the other mothers at Penny's preschool, but since I have to go to work soon after dropping her off every morning, I never get time to stop and chit-chat like most of the other mothers do. And when I go along with Penny to one of her friends' parties, everyone stands around in a large group and I can't seem to pinpoint anyone who stands out as a suitable mark for becoming my daughter's potential guardian.

We've looked at this from every angle there is and there's no getting around the fact that we have nobody else in our lives who could take on the responsibility of raising our daughter if the worst were ever to happen.

It's a terrifying thought, and probably one we should have had before making the choice to have a baby, but it wasn't until I was already pregnant that the reality struck me: If Seth and I were to suddenly die tomorrow, the only person left to raise our daughter would be Sacha.

CHAPTER TWELVE

THEN

"I've heard of that game before," Brady says, lifting his beer bottle in the air. "You have to say three facts about yourself, and everyone has to guess which one of them is a lie, right?"

"Exactly!" Sacha points at Brady and throws him a wink. "Except we're going to play it with a little twist."

"What do you mean?" I ask, suspicious of the way Sacha's eyes gleam in the darkness.

The trees loom over the clearing, their shadows swaying in the light of the battery powered lanterns set up in a circle around us. I'm nestled against Seth, his arms wrapped around me like a shield. I've only just relaxed into the evening and Sacha's tone is making me worried. If I know her as well as I think I do, then she's got something specific on her mind and this isn't just as simple as playing a game.

"Since some of us know others here so well," she says, "how about we each say three things about somebody *else* in the group? Then the rest have to guess which facts are true and which one is the lie."

"Interesting..." Roman says, but there's a hint of confusion on his face.

Squeak looks uneasy, her fingers twisting in her lap. She's never been one for attention and I can't blame her for not wanting to become a subject in Sacha's game. But we all know Sacha is going to get her own way here, so I don't bother to put up a fight. Seth and Brady say nothing, and Sacha seems to take the resounding silence as a yes.

"It'll be fun!" she trills, her enthusiasm leading. "I'll go first! Three things about... let's say... Seth."

Seth puffs out a breath and looks away, clearly sensing his sister is about to try to embarrass him.

"Okay, let me think for a second..." Sacha taps her chin theatrically.

I catch sight of Roman from the corner of my eye, fiddling with something in his hands, and it takes me a moment to realize he's rolling a joint.

"Okay, I've got it!" Sacha downs her beer and throws the empty bottle to the side. She's the only one standing, the rest of us are sitting on various logs and tree stumps creating a loose circle. "Three facts about Seth. One: he had to repeat the third grade. Two: he still has a collection of action figures in his bedroom from when he was a kid. And three: he once broke two of his fingers when he crushed them in a car door."

The last fact elicits winces from most of us. Even Squeak gasps at the thought. But I'm mostly surprised by how tame Sacha's facts are. Seth is her twin, they grew up together and I'm sure she knows some seriously embarrassing facts about her brother. But it looks like she's really held back. That isn't like her at all.

Seth seems to relax beside me, breathing a sigh of relief. I turn and smile up at him, a look passing between us. I happen to already know which one of these things is a lie. "I'm out, I already know."

"Okay, okay, don't give anything away." Sacha points at me in warning. "Anyone else? Who wants to take a guess?"

Roman is flicking his lighter at his now-rolled joint and lights it up before inhaling heavily. He sits back and blows out a thick plume of smoke over the circle.

Brady raises an arm. "It's obvious, isn't it? The lie is him being held back at school. If anything, Seth should have been put forward a year, the whiz kid."

Everyone concurs and Seth nods in agreement. "I should have been, shouldn't I?" he boasts playfully.

"Brady got it!" Sacha sings, running over and plonking herself down on his lap, uninvited. Brady looks surprised but does nothing to move her as she wraps an arm around his shoulder.

"Okay, okay. But," Seth raises a finger, "let's get it straight, Sacha. I didn't crush my fingers in that car door. *You* did that to me."

"Oooh." Brady squeezes Sacha's sides. "You're a bad girl."

Sacha laughs loudly and looks thrilled at this nugget of attention from Brady.

Squeak is sitting beside them quietly, and I'm wondering if she'll join in our game and share some funny facts about Roman with us. Surely she knows some things we don't, being his cousin?

"Okay, who's next?" Sacha asks, looking around.

"I'll go." Roman rises up and the sweet, pungent smell of weed hits my nose before he passes his joint to Seth and takes a spot in the middle of the circle.

"Okay, three facts about *Brady*," he says confidently, looking like he's already thought of them.

Brady groans. "Go easy on me, Romey, go easy on me!"

We all laugh and Roman raises his brow playfully. "No chance, buddy."

Brady hangs his head in mock-terror and rests it on Sacha's shoulder. She looks completely in her element, finally having pulled Brady's attention away from Squeak and firmly onto her. My guess is that Squeak is relieved at this, too.

I gaze up at Seth, who grins at me and lowers the joint in his hand toward my lips. I take one pull and then nestle myself back up against his side as I exhale.

"Okay." Roman rubs his hands together, apparently ready to play hard. "One: Brady keeps a picture of Dwayne Johnson in his gym bag as inspiration to train harder."

"I believe that one!" Seth shouts from beside me and I giggle.

"It works!" Brady raises an eyebrow, imitating the Rock, and flexes a large bicep.

"You're not supposed to confirm it until after people guess!" Sacha scolds Brady from her perch on his lap.

"Two," Roman continues. "Brady Boy and I started a rock band when we were twelve years old called The Chaos Lords. And three: he failed his driver's test two times before passing it. Once for running a red light."

We all look around the group, hemming and hawing. This is a tricky one. Nobody seems to know which one's the lie. Even Seth, who is good friends with Brady, seems stumped.

"I know." A small voice breaks the silence.

Everyone turns and stares as Squeak raises a petite arm in the air. This is the first thing I've heard her say out loud since we set up camp and I'm kind of shocked at her sudden willingness to join in.

"Which one is it, cuz?" Roman turns to Squeak, his face beaming with pride at his cousin for speaking up.

"Well," she says, her voice slow and controlled. "If Brady already confirmed the picture he keeps in his gym bag then the lie is about the band, because I know that the last one has to be true."

Brady's jaw hits the floor, but his tone is amused. "Wha... But how did you know I failed my driver's test?"

Squeak's eyes flash with something I've not seen in them before as she daintily takes the last sip from her beer bottle and keeps us in suspense. "I was in the car when you drove us here, wasn't I?"

Roman is the first to crack up laughing and Seth follows, leaving the joint dangling from his mouth and loudly clapping his hands her way in praise. I can't help but laugh, too. I can't believe Squeak just spoke up, let alone cracked a decent joke at Brady's expense.

Sacha is forced to stand up from her spot on Brady's lap as he gets to his feet and turns to Squeak.

"You got me." He smiles and extends his arm to high five her. "You got me good."

Squeak raises her hand and hits his gently. It's difficult not to notice the almost comical size difference between their palms.

You could probably knock our group over with a feather right now; Squeak is finally coming out of her shell. I scan the amused faces that surround her but soon get to one that isn't like the others.

Sacha sits on the log where Brady just dumped her from his lap, her arms crossed, features set in a stony glare as she glowers in Squeak's direction.

CHAPTER THIRTEEN

NOW

I hum softly to myself as I scrub the stack of plates from breakfast. The smell of the piece of toast I burned twenty minutes ago still clings to the air, barely covered by the second pot of coffee currently brewing.

Since Sacha's been here, I've had to start making extra coffee in the mornings. Seth doesn't take kindly to arriving at an empty pot before he gets a chance to pour a cup, and I know it's not me who's drinking it all. Like everything else she does in life, when Sacha pours her second cup of coffee in the morning and drains the pot, she fails to think about anyone else and whether or not they got their own coffee yet. It's like her whole personality is just being awkward for the sake of it.

Once I get the last dish cleaned and on the draining rack, I grab Penny's lunchbox and place it in her school bag next to her water.

I used to put so much effort into making adorable bento boxes with cute little rice pandas, veggie flowers, and fruit rainbows. I'd pat myself on the back for nailing the whole *mom* thing. But that phase didn't last long because without fail the box would come back at the end of the day still half full and clearly unappreciated. Eventually, I gave up and switched to the classic sandwich, yogurt, and fruit combo. And, of course, she devours that like a tiny vacuum cleaner. Every single crumb. It made me evaluate how much of this stuff I just do to make myself feel better. Because the only person who ever appreciated all the effort I would put into those elaborate lunchboxes was me. It all worked out though, now I get an extra twenty minutes of sleep in the mornings instead of waking early to slave over tiny pieces of flower shaped watermelon.

"Penny, time to get your shoes on!" I call out, my voice echoing through the apartment.

No answer.

I glance toward the hallway. "Penny?"

I wipe my hands on the dish towel and step out of the kitchen, scanning the living room. There are toys strewn across the floor, but no Penny. I move quickly to her bedroom, but the door is closed. "Penny, are you in there?"

I push the door open but find the room empty. My hackles go up and I dart back toward the living room to see that the sliding door to the balcony is slightly ajar. I pull it open and there she is, bouncing a bright red ball in the warm morning air. My heart plummets.

"Penny!" I rush forward, scooping her up in my arms. "What are you doing out here?"

"The door was open."

"Open?" I glance back at the door, a tightness forming in my chest.

Seth and I never leave the balcony door open. We never even leave it unlocked.

I bring Penny back inside and lock the balcony door behind me, hanging the key safely back up on its hook. I kneel in front of Penny.

"Honey, I know you just wanted to go out there to play, but

it's really important that you only ever go out on the balcony with a grown-up. Okay?"

"Okay." She fidgets with the ball in her hands.

"You'll remember that?"

"Uh-huh."

"Okay, go get your shoes on, please."

An unfazed Penny skips off to find her shoes and a moment later Sacha emerges, her hair still damp from the excessively long shower she just took.

"Sacha, did you leave the balcony door open?" I ask.

"I'm not sure. Maybe," she replies with the enthusiasm of a teenager on a Monday morning.

"Well, I can't think of anyone else who frequently goes outside there to smoke," I say. "So, I think it was you."

"What's the big deal?" She yawns.

"What's the big deal? I told you when you got here to always leave it locked after you've been out there. We live on the fourth floor, it's dangerous. I just found Penny out there throwing around a ball."

"She was just playing? I don't get what the problem is."

I can't contain my frustration anymore. I feel like throwing Sacha right over the balcony and seeing how big a deal she thinks it is then. I can deal with her leaving her mess everywhere and taking up space with her bags and drinking all the coffee, but I won't tolerate her putting my child in danger.

"Just playing?" I erupt. "Sacha, she's four! What if something happened and she fell?"

"Penny isn't stupid, Jade. Do you really have that little faith in your own daughter?"

"She's only four!" I shout. "She doesn't fully grasp the concept of danger yet."

Sacha raises her palms. "It's not going to happen again, okay? Chill out."

Since this is probably the best I'm going to get out of her, I decide to abandon this conversation before it can go further downhill. But the air is still vibrating with tension as Seth walks in a moment later and I can see from the look on his face that he can sense it.

"What's going on?" he asks, his brow furrowing slightly as he surveys the room.

He's dressed sharply in a navy blazer and crisp white shirt, his tie is knotted neatly and he looks much more made-up than usual. I'm hopeful this is a sign of good things.

"Nothing." I force a smile, trying to blow past my anger at Sacha. "Hey, you look nice. Another job interview today?"

Seth looks unconvinced by my shifting the subject. He runs a hand through his dark hair.

"Not exactly an interview," he says. "I have a meeting here at home this afternoon with my career coaches to go over a prospective job opening. It's kind of a big deal."

"Oh?" I say. "That's new."

A meeting at our apartment? That seems strange. He usually meets them in their offices. Seth has had so many meetings and job interviews in the last few months, I can never keep up with the current company he's chasing after. All I know is, a guy as intelligent as he is, with as refined a skill set as he has, it's a crime he hasn't been snapped up yet.

"What time is the meeting?"

"Twelve thirty." He glances at his watch. "I'm not sure if I'll make it to pick up Penny from preschool afterward. Could you take your lunch break late and collect her?"

I hesitate, annoyance pricking at the back of my mind. "Oh. Um..."

"I wouldn't ask you if it wasn't important. I just really need this today."

I'd rather not use my one short break to drive through the

city at lunchtime, but I guess I have no choice. "Sure, I can do that."

Seth nods, grateful, and turns to Sacha who's now perched on the edge of the couch with her arms crossed. "Sacha, I need the apartment free this afternoon. Do you think you can maybe go shopping or something?"

Sacha's eyes narrow. "Shopping?"

"Shopping, drinking bat's blood, slaughtering baby animals, whatever it is you do with your free time, yes, please." He crosses his arms.

"Fine. I need some new shoes anyway," she huffs, clearly annoyed but not willing to push back further.

Their irritation radiates through the air and I sense a fresh storm brewing between the two of them. It's starting to feel like the old days again, and not in a good way.

"Great," he continues, his tone calming. "This is important. I can't have any distractions during this meeting."

As Sacha heads toward the kitchen, she turns back to look at her brother and for a fleeting moment I see a look in her eyes of pure and unmistakable hatred.

Seth busies himself with his phone, ignoring her, but I'm struck by the stench of hostility that still hangs between the two of them. How did brother and sister—twins—get to a point in their lives where they despise each other so much? I've never heard Seth mutter so much as one kind word about Sacha since the day we began dating. And the same with her. It's like they've hated each other since the very beginning of life, while still sharing a womb.

Seth glances up, his expression shifting to one of concern when he sees me. "You okay?"

"Yeah." I force a smile that feels strained. "It's just been a long morning."

CHAPTER FOURTEEN

The air is butter-scented and likely caloric as I hunch over the worktop, carefully folding layers of puff pastry. It's repetitive and fiddly and—helpfully—keeps my mind busy and away from stewing on all things Sacha. I'm deep in concentration when the kitchen door swings open with a soft creak.

"Mercy, it's busy out there!" Darina bounds in, her broad figure hugged by a bright green apron with little daisies embroidered throughout.

"Don't ever trust a thin baker," Darina once told me. "If they're not enjoying their own food, it's not worth eating."

Nobody who has ever set foot inside the Crumb Cottage or has tried the drool-inducing selection of treats, snacks and specialty cakes we offer could ever question Darina's love for her craft. I remember the day I arrived here, having called about a listing I saw for a job opening. I'd barely stepped a foot inside the door and the scent of freshly baked cinnamon rolls transported me back to waking up as a child on a Saturday morning with no worries or responsibilities. Darina had conducted the job interview (it probably couldn't even be called that) while in the midst of neatly swirling frosting onto fifty or so cupcakes.

"Can you bake?" she asked.

"Yes." I nodded without hesitation. "I have a–"

"Well that's a great start." She pointed to the aprons on the back of the door. "Stick one of those on and make me something."

I was totally taken aback. I hadn't imagined she would put me on the spot like that but after looking around and thinking on my feet, I spent the next hour and a half preparing a lemon lavender tart topped with mint leaves and just a dusting of powdered sugar. Darina took me under her wing that day, and the rest is history.

Her cheeks dimple now as she smiles, and I can't help but smile back. "What's got you so giddy, Darina?"

"Oh, Jade! You won't believe the news!" Her voice bounces. "Aria Arts Center is hosting this year's Canvas Gala next Saturday. Art installations, live performances, all the who's who of the art scene are invited. And guess who's catering it?" Her eyes sparkle.

I pause, my fingers freezing mid-fold, and study her eyes to see if she's messing with me, but her gaze holds steady. The Canvas Gala is a big deal for arty types and an event that draws the city's finest snobs and big shots. How the heck Darina scored a job catering for it, I have no idea.

"Darina, that's incredible!" I laugh, wiping my hands on my apron before hugging her. "But... next Saturday?"

"I know, I know. It's totally short notice. But a little birdie let slip that the people they had lined up pulled out... and I know someone who knows someone who knows a guy," she adds with a wink. "We can pull it off, though! We have a week to prepare. I just need you to stay late the night before to help get everything ready, and, if you would, play waitstaff at the gala, too. I promise you'll earn a nice cut of the money, and believe me, it'll be worth it!"

I think of Seth and our ever-growing list of bills. I can't deny the extra cash would really help us. Since Seth has been out of work, our savings have been quickly depleting and unless he finds something soon, we won't get to do that trip down the coast we have planned later this year. We've already cut back on everything: dinners out, new clothes, even groceries. The thought of a spontaneous family outing feels like a distant dream. I want to help ease the pressure he's put himself under to find the perfect new job and this catering gig could be the lifeline we desperately need. The extra cash might cover one of our overdue credit card payments, at least.

"Okay, I'll do it," I say.

Darina's face lights up. Her joy is infectious.

"You're the best, Jade! This is going to be amazing!"

As she rushes off to share the news with the rest of the team, I finish up work on the pastry as fast as I can before clocking out for my break.

I step outside and take a deep breath, glad to be out of the kitchen. It may be mid-summer, but no heat can compare to a two-hundred square foot room with three ovens running continuously.

The smell of butter still lives on me as I make my way to the back lot where my car waits. I slide into the driver's seat and glance at the clock. One forty-five. I'm cutting it close to pick up Penny from preschool.

I decide to take a shortcut through the side streets, a decision I quickly regret as I find myself in a line of honking cars and glaring brake lights.

"Come on!" I mutter under my breath, tapping my fingers on the steering wheel.

The clock ticks on, indifferent to my plight. One fifty. One fifty-five. Traffic crawls and with every slow inch forward, my frustration grows. I imagine Penny's face as she watches her friends leave with their parents, one by one, until it's only her left there with Miss Carol, thinking she's been forgotten.

"Let's go! Move!" I yell at a man in a black SUV poking at a large screen on his dashboard, oblivious to the fact that the light in front of him has turned green.

Who exactly decided that it was illegal to hold a cell phone while driving, yet giant screens installed right in front of you with every single app you could ever want are just peachy? I'm unable to suppress a wave of road rage and beep incessantly at the moron until he sticks his middle finger out the window and starts moving.

I weave through lanes, my heart dropping as I glance at the clock again, it's already after two. I'm officially late. I speed toward the preschool, praying that Penny's too busy to have noticed. I pull into the parking lot and leap from the car, my shoes thudding on the pavement as I rush toward the building. Inside, Penny's classroom is almost empty, there are just a few children packing up their things while their parents wait for them by the door. My shoulders sag in relief that she isn't the only kid left here.

The classroom is a copy and paste of what I remember from my own preschool days: an assault of primary colors with finger-painted pictures hanging on the walls, and small tables scattered about covered in crayons, pipe cleaners, glue sticks and glitter. All the things I'm happy Penny gets to make a beautiful mess with outside of our own home. The play area in the corner is filled with soft toys and building blocks and a soft rug lies in the center, the fibers worn down from countless tiny feet. But as filled with color and art and toys as the room is, my heart drops when I scan every corner and see something is missing.

Miss Carol places a warm hand on my shoulder. "Hi, Jade. It's a surprise to see you here!"

I try not to take this the wrong way, since she's likely referencing the fact that Seth is usually the one who comes to pick Penny up. But my own insecurities make it feel like she's judging me for being a working mom who never has the time to collect my own child from preschool.

"Hi, Miss Carol. Where's Penny?"

Her smile drops, replaced by an odd expression. "Well... she already left. A woman came to collect her about fifteen minutes ago."

Every fine hair on my body stands on end.

"What woman?" I demand.

Miss Carol's mouth hangs open. "P -Penny said she was her aunt."

CHAPTER FIFTEEN

THEN

Sacha has officially lost control of the game.

She keeps trying to rein everyone back in, but she's having about as much success as she would herding cats. Brady is now in the middle of some wildly exaggerated story, gesturing erratically while Roman leans back between tokes, laughing to the point of coughing.

I get up from my spot snuggled next to Seth and grab my sweater. The temperature is dropping now and I'm starting to wish we were able to light a campfire. As I pull my sweater over my head, I notice that Squeak is now laughing quietly beside her cousin as they listen to Brady's animated tales. I think Brady must have noticed too, because he's taken a step backward to accommodate his widening audience.

"I'll be back in a moment, babe." Seth squeezes my arm then gets up and starts toward the trees for a bathroom break.

"Can't you wait?" Sacha turns to him, annoyed. "We're in the middle of a game."

"I'm pretty sure the game is over, Sacha," Seth says, looking around as if to emphasize that nobody is interested in playing anymore.

"It's not over until I say it's over, *brother*." Sacha twists her finger in a circle toward Seth's face.

Seth swats it away and pushes past her, colliding shoulders. "Whatever."

Despite these two constantly bickering, everyone seems to be having a good time. It might be that we're all roughly four drinks in, or that the evening heat has faded, but even Squeak is now mingling and I'm happy to just observe as I take a sip from my can, feeling the warmth of the alcohol settle into my chest.

Brady seems to suddenly notice Seth has left. "Wait, is he going to the little boy's room? Hold on, buddy! I'm coming, too!" He rushes for the trees, arms flailing, and I laugh at our resident joker.

"Farewell, my friends," Roman shouts after them, lifting his beer bottle in a mock-drunken salute. "Until we meet again."

Squeak reaches into her bag and pulls out a pack of potato chips. She opens it up and holds it out to Roman, letting him take a handful for himself as they begin talking. It's such a casual, familial gesture that it makes me wish I had a sibling or a cousin of my own. But with my mother and father having waited until their forties to have me, and both of them also being only children (it's almost like my family are hell-bent on going extinct), I have no idea what that must feel like.

Sacha suddenly plops down beside me, pulling me from my thoughts.

"Look at her over there," she mutters quietly, tilting her head toward Squeak. "What do you think her deal is?"

"Who? Squeak?" I ask.

"The braid. The boots," Sacha sneers. "What's she going for? *Little House on the Prairie* or military-girl? Like... pick a style."

Squeak, who is perched on a log opposite us, looks up for a moment and sees us staring at her. Sacha waves sarcastically, so as to leave no doubt in Squeak's mind that we're talking about her.

"I don't know what they see in her," Sacha huffs, looking down and rearranging her shirt until she's successfully displaying fifty percent more cleavage.

I briefly glance down at my own chest and feel that familiar creep of jealousy as a grudging member of the proverbial 'committee.'

"What do you mean?" I ask, crossing my arms self-consciously.

Sacha lights up a cigarette and looks at me like I've grown a second head. "Jade, come on."

"What?"

"Come *on*," she says, blowing out a cloud of smoke.

"What?" I ask again.

"You can't see it?"

"See *what*?" She's really starting to piss me off.

"Guys love Squeak, Jade." She shakes her head, sighing. "It's gotta be the brooding quietness or the fact she's so small and helpless they want to protect her, or something, because it's not like she's got an irresistible personality, is it? Even your idiot boyfriend has been staring at her all night."

I usually try to ignore Sacha's infernal braying, but this strikes a chord in me. Seth has been staring at Squeak? I haven't noticed that at all. But then I guess I've been cuddled up to his side most of the night, and it's not like I've been watching his face. Though it's much more likely that Sacha is just trying to mess with my head. She'd say or do anything to get at her brother.

Like the time a few months ago when she 'accidentally' let slip that she saw Seth talking to his ex at the mall. It was such a casual throwaway comment, like she was just mentioning the weather, but it drove me straight into a spiral of paranoia. Seth had assured me he was done with his ex for good, but how could I know if he was telling the truth or not? I spent that whole night lying awake in bed, imagining Seth dumping me and running back into Kylee's arms. But it turned out to be a whole lot of stress over nothing because when I finally built up the courage to confront Seth about it, he was dumbfounded and said he hadn't seen Kylee since the day they broke up. It turned out Sacha had lied. She'd planted a seed of doubt in my mind on purpose, trying to make me second guess my relationship with Seth. Now I know not to trust her with anything.

I shouldn't let her get to me but sometimes I wonder what life might be like in the future, if Seth and I really do go the distance. Will Sacha still be there trying to pick away at our relationship even when we're married and have kids?

I'm not sure her intention is to break us up, but let's just say I don't think she'd care if it happened. It's all just part of the elaborate mind games she enjoys playing.

"And have you seen how Brady has been falling over himself for her?" Sacha continues. "It's disgusting, really. If Roman hadn't brought his stupid little cousin, Brady and I would have hooked up hours ago, trust me."

God, this girl cannot stand other females being around. The only reason she puts up with me is because I'm dating her brother and therefore not a direct competitor for the attention of guys she chooses to mark down as her own personal property.

"I don't know what you're talking about." I attempt to blow past it.

"What I'm talking about, Jade," Sacha says, like she's speaking to a moron, "is that for some reason or other, guys find Squeak hot."

I narrow my eyes, finding it hard to believe that this could be true. I mean, I kind of believe the whole 'wanting to protect her because she's small' thing Sacha theorized, but... *hot*? Squeak isn't hot.

Only... now that I look over and see her smiling at something Roman is saying, it's like my eyes have been opened. She obviously feels comfortable with her cousin, and now that she's relaxed a little and isn't so stiff, I'm seeing her in a completely different light. The way her cardigan slips off one shoulder, the delicate curve of her cheekbones illuminated in the moonlight. Her eyes, they have a kind of sparkle that I haven't noticed before. Is this why Seth was staring at her?

I suddenly feel a strange twist in my stomach as it hits me: Squeak is actually kind of beautiful, in her own way. How the hell have I never noticed this before?

No wonder Sacha seems to hate her. Not only is Squeak pretty, but she's got the advantage of not scaring the guys away with her loudmouth antics like Sacha does. Although Sacha clearly doesn't see this as a fault in herself because when the dry leaves and twigs nearby begin to crackle and snap, and Brady and Seth emerge back from the darkness of the woods, she puts out her cigarette and rushes to Brady's side, grabbing his hand and dragging him to sit back down next to her.

"Thought we lost you there, sailor," she says in a low voice. "I was about to come find you, see if you needed any help."

There's no way Brady is dumb enough to not hear what she's implying, but where most other guys in his situation would take the bait and run with it, he just laughs it off.

"Nah, I'm good. I was just talking to Seth," he says, then gets up and goes over to ask for one of Squeak's potato chips. "Thanks." He smiles at Squeak when she lets him take one, then sits down beside her, abandoning his spot next to Sacha.

I watch as Squeak laughs at something Brady whispers in her ear. Her laughter is light and airy and when I see that Seth is now looking her way and smiling, something clicks in my mind. Guys really do gravitate toward Squeak. Sacha was right. It's as if she's a magnet, pulling them in.

I glance back at Sacha, who catches my eye and nods knowingly, seeing that I'm starting to get it. I shake my head like it's no big deal, but Sacha doesn't take her eyes from mine. It's like she's trying to send me a message that I can't quite understand. Then, for a split second, something flashes in her gaze. Something dark. And despite the warmth from my sweater, I feel a cold chill run through my body.

CHAPTER SIXTEEN

NOW

The city passes by in a kaleidoscopic blur as I weave through traffic, my hands gripping the steering wheel hard enough to leave indentations. I pick my phone up from the passenger seat and tap Sacha's number for what feels like the hundredth time. The irony does not escape me. Just twenty minutes ago, I was seething about that guy in the black SUV, his eyes fixed to the screen on his dashboard. Now here I am, glued to my phone, desperate for answers while I navigate the streets with only one hand on the wheel.

"Pick up, pick up, pick up!" I mutter through gritted teeth.

The traffic is a mess. I can't afford to be stuck here. Not when I have no idea where Sacha has taken my daughter. The thought makes my cheeks flame. What the hell does she think she's doing, picking Penny up from preschool without our permission? This isn't just another of her reckless decisions, this is a complete violation of my and Seth's trust and *way* overstepping her boundaries as an aunt.

Every second that ticks by while I'm crawling along at two miles an hour feels like an eternity. I glance in the rearview mirror, catching sight of my crazed reflection, eyes wide and panic stricken. Calm down, Jade. Penny is fine. Sacha probably just took her back home. She hasn't kidnapped her.

But... maybe she has. Maybe she *has* kidnapped my daughter.

My thoughts keep inching to the worst. Deep down, I've always known there was something very wrong with Sacha, something more than just her wild, irresponsible actions and general jackassery.

I remember that night in the woods, that loaded look she gave me. To this day, I still can't shake that look from my mind. That night, everything changed. And it all started with that look.

I try Seth again but after three rings I hang up in frustration. He's probably finishing up his meeting about now, oblivious to the fact our daughter has been abducted. I feel like I'm suffocating in this car, and I just wish either Seth or Sacha would answer their damn phones so I can breathe again. I press the gas pedal harder, narrowly avoiding rear-ending the vehicle in front of me before hitting the brakes and trying to calm myself down.

"Just breathe," I say out loud, but the words feel useless.

How can I breathe when I have no idea where my daughter is? I feel a red-hot anger festering inside me. First Sacha leaves the balcony door open this morning, and now this. I don't know what kind of twisted game she's playing but what I do know is once I find her and get Penny back into my arms, that woman is gone. She's packing her bags tonight. I don't care where she goes, she can find a nice cardboard box down a dark alleyway for all I care but she's not staying with us anymore.

When I get to our building, I slam the car door shut, the sound echoing around the gated parking lot. I hurry toward the entrance and rush through the doors, wishing I could teleport straight to wherever my daughter is. The lobby sits empty, and I jab my finger at the button for the elevator impatiently, hoping it will open straight up, but see it's on its way down painfully slowly. I glance over my shoulder, hoping to see Sacha walking in with Penny in tow, but I'm all alone.

Finally, I hear the soft ding of the elevator arriving. As the doors slide open, a woman I've never seen before comes into view. She's strikingly beautiful, with long blond hair that melts in waves over her shoulders, makeup that looks like it's been applied professionally and a perfectly tailored pantsuit that hugs her every curve. She looks more like a model for a high-end business-wear brand than one of the everyday people who might actually be buying their clothing.

I stare at her, momentarily frozen as I mentally shuffle through the faces of my neighbors. No one comes to mind. She must just be visiting because she definitely doesn't live here.

"Excuse me," I murmur, rushing into the elevator as she steps out.

She smiles as she walks away, her gaze lingering just a moment before the doors close, sealing me inside. As the elevator lurches upward, I watch the numbers light up one by one, seemingly counting slower than they ever have before. Why didn't I just take the stairs?

It eventually jolts to a stop on my floor, and I can't get the doors open fast enough. I step out and begin to sprint, hoping more than anything in the world that when I open our apartment door, I'll see Penny standing right there, unharmed. But I'm only halfway down the hall when I'm stopped by Mrs. Morris who stands just outside her door, a palette of floral patterns and mismatched accessories.

"Jade, dear! There you are!" she chirps. "I've been meaning

to catch you. I saw Penny the other day, such a sweet girl. She's getting so big, don't you think?"

Her burnt-orange cardigan clashes painfully with the rose-print skirt that swirls around her knees, and the tight gray curls on her head look to be spring loaded.

While Mrs. Morris is sweet and friendly, she's also our building's resident gossip, and right now I don't have time for that. I force a smile, trying to dodge past her. "Yeah, she's growing like a weed. I really need to–"

"And I couldn't help but notice you have a lady living with you."

Nothing gets past this woman.

I take another step, hoping to slip by her. "That's my sister-in-law. She's been staying with us while she finds her feet."

Though not for long. Sacha will be lucky if she's still breathing by the time I kick her ass out tonight.

"Hmmm." Mrs. Morris shudders a little, her expression shifting to one of concern. "You know, sometimes I get a feeling about certain people. And she seems... off."

This may well be the understatement of the year.

"She just went through a bad break up and she's still adjusting. Nothing to worry about. Now, I really have to go."

"Well, you'd be well advised to be cautious, because as my Ricky used to say–"

"I'm really sorry, but I've got to go!" I cut her off before she can regale me with another one of her late husband's many mottos.

I dart past her, wrestling with my keys before crashing through the door and slamming it behind me. The sound echoes in the silence of the apartment and I run toward the living room, half expecting to see Penny playing on the floor. But she's not there.

"Seth!" I shout. "Seth!"

Seth comes rushing out of the kitchen, wiping his hands on a towel.

"What's going on? Is something wrong?" Then his eyes move to the empty hall behind me and his expression changes. "Where's... where's Penny?"

"She's gone! Sacha's taken her!"

CHAPTER SEVENTEEN

Seth has been pacing the length of the hallway now for nearly ten minutes as he holds his phone to his ear, repeatedly dialing Sacha's number. Every time it just calls out, unanswered.

"We need to call the police," I say, not able to hold the words back anymore. "What if Penny's in danger?"

Seth waves this idea away with his free hand. "We're not calling the cops. Sacha just needs to pick up her damn phone!"

I keep quiet and hug my arms around myself, avoiding Seth's fury as he moves back and forth in front of me, mumbling angrily.

"I knew she was up to something. I knew it. It's one thing to manipulate her way into our lives again but–"

Seth stops mid-sentence as the door opens and Sacha walks in with a visibly bouncy and unharmed Penny. I didn't even know Sacha had a key to our apartment. She must have taken our spare one from the bowl in the kitchen; another thing I don't remember her asking about before doing.

"Mommy!" Penny runs toward me. She's holding a helium balloon and has the telltale smudges of chocolate around her lips.

I scoop her up and press her close to me. "Penny, honey. I was so worried!"

Sacha closes the door and pulls off her shoes casually, as though she didn't just kidnap our daughter. Seth clenches his fists, his jaw tightening as his sister breezes in.

"What. The. Hell. Sacha?" He spits. "You can't just take Penny from preschool without telling anyone. Do you even understand how serious this is?"

Sacha tosses her hair over her shoulder with a nonchalance that makes my cheeks flame with heat. "I was close to her school and figured I'd save you both the trouble. Plus, I texted Jade."

I pull out my phone, shaking slightly as I scroll through the messages. There it is, nestled among the many banal notifications:

> I'm near Penny's preschool, I'll pick her up and bring her home.

I must have missed it in my frantic attempts to call her. I show Seth, but he pushes my phone away.

"Seriously?" He glares at Sacha, his voice rising. "You think a text is enough? You don't just go picking up someone's kid because you feel like it! We're her parents. You need to confirm things with us first!"

"I can't believe this," Sacha scoffs. "I can't do anything right, can I? I do you guys a huge favor by collecting Penny and keeping her busy while Jade's at work and you have your precious little meeting, and do I get thanked? No. I get shouted at!"

Penny begins squirming in my arms, her face scrunching up with confusion. I feel her warmth, her small heartbeat against me, and I'm just so thankful she's okay.

But Seth doesn't let up. "What are you not getting? A text

isn't enough, Sacha! You can't just assume it's okay to take her without waiting for a response. It's reckless and stupid!"

"God, give it up!" Sacha crosses her arms defiantly. "Penny was fine with me. She had a great time, didn't you, Penny?"

Penny's worried eyes dart between us, sensing the tension. She opens her mouth to talk but only a squeak comes out before tears spill from her eyes and giant sobs rack her chest.

"Oh, sweetheart, it's okay," I say gently, trying to soothe her. "Come on, let's go play in your bedroom."

As I lead Penny away, I glance back at Seth, who's still locked in an intense stare down with Sacha. I can see the muscles in his jaw twitching and his hands digging into his sides as though he's holding himself back from launching at her.

In the bedroom, I guide Penny to the pile of toys strewn across the floor. "Look! Your dolls are waiting for you!" I say, trying to sound cheerful.

I close the door behind me to block out the sounds of arguing but it's no use, I can still hear their raised voices spilling into our daughter's bedroom. At least Penny seems to have calmed down a little, though her chest still rises every few seconds with sad little hiccups. I try to distract her by asking her about her day, but she's obviously still worried about what she just witnessed between Sacha and her father in the hall.

"Why is Daddy angry?" she asks quietly.

I swallow hard, my throat tight. "He's just upset that Sacha didn't tell us she was going to collect you from preschool. He's not mad at you at all, sweetie."

"But it was fun!" she whines. "I like her picking me up."

My heart aches as I watch her little four-year-old mind try to comprehend how something that seems like such a good thing to her could make us so upset.

"Oh, I'm so glad you had fun! What did the two of you do?"

Penny's face instantly brightens. "We got chocolate ice

cream! And I got a balloon, and we went to a shop and Auntie Sacha got me a new dress!"

"Wow!" I say, smiling. "All that in just one hour? It sounds like the two of you had a lot of fun."

And it does. Truly. I'm so glad that Penny is not only okay, but she's also had a lovely afternoon by the sounds of it. If only Sacha could have arranged this with us in advance. If she had, then I would have been grateful to her for taking Penny out on a nice little trip around the city, treating her to chocolate ice cream and a new dress. I would have been thanking her for doing us such a favor on a day when Seth and I were both busy. But as it is, I don't think I can ever trust her with my daughter again. I thought Sacha would know that as her parents, Seth and I need to sign off on all decisions regarding Penny.

But assuming that someone thinks the same way as you do is a very basic error. And a dangerous one, when dealing with a woman like Sacha.

Five minutes later, when I've cleaned the chocolate remnants from Penny's face and we've built a small fort out of pillows and books for her dolls, I leave her playing in her bedroom while I quietly slip out the door.

I haven't heard Penny talk about her imaginary friend Izzy-Bella in a few days, but I wouldn't be surprised if she suddenly makes a resurgence after the stress of all this. If Penny created her as a coping mechanism for her separation anxiety when I'm not with her, it seems logical that she would show up at other stressful times, too.

I close Penny's bedroom door behind me and move down the hall. I imagine Seth is probably packing Sacha's belongings for her, ready to boot her out and leave her sitting on her ass outside our door. But as I get closer to the living room, I can hear them speaking in hushed tones.

I stop and flatten myself to the wall, out of sight.

"I'm not going anywhere, Seth," Sacha's voice comes out smooth and controlled. "And I already told you what'll happen if you try to make me."

I hear Seth's foot falls pacing. "For Christ's sake, Sacha. What do you want from me? What is your end game here?"

"I just want to get to know my niece. If you play nice, I'll be out of your hair by next week. And if you don't... well, like I said, I'm kind of tired of keeping your little secret for the last fifteen years."

My heart thuds so hard inside my chest it feels like the floor might start to vibrate underneath me. The conversation I heard Seth and Sacha having on the balcony yesterday comes flooding back to me. It was clear they were discussing what happened to Squeak that night in the woods. But when they came inside and told me about Roman's passing, I put it to the back of my mind. Now it sounds as though there's something more. But this doesn't make any sense. What secret is Sacha talking about?

"You're not the only one who has spent years keeping your mouth shut." I hear Seth's voice quietly strain through gritted teeth. "I've never said a word about what you did. I covered for you and you're just lucky none of the others ever figured out what you did that night, because you'd be getting to know your niece from inside a filthy visiting room by now if they had."

I suppress a gasp and hold my hand to my mouth. Is Seth implying that Sacha is responsible for Squeak's death?

CHAPTER EIGHTEEN

THEN

"Strip poker!" Brady shouts when Seth suggests playing something different.

It's a little after eleven thirty and the music is turned up high, pumping out a playlist of nondescript dance tracks.

"No thanks, my friend," Seth says. "We don't have any playing cards or poker chips. Plus, I've already seen you undressed more times than I ever cared to in the locker room."

"Don't lie. I know you love it." Brady blows a kiss his way before lifting up his shirt and running toward Seth, who ducks and weaves from his advances.

Sacha grabs hold of Brady and wraps an arm around his waist while Seth scuttles safely back to me. "I think a stripping game is a great idea, Brady. Only problem is," she pats the back of her jean shorts, "I forgot to put anything on under these."

"If only I had a time machine so I could go back and unhear that." Seth lets out a nauseated groan beside me and turns away from his sister in disgust.

Brady, to his credit, laughs Sacha's comment off and ignores her desperate seduction tactics, untangling himself from her arms before sitting down by Roman.

I doubt Sacha has ever had to work this hard to get the attention of a guy before. Usually all she has to do is click her fingers and they'll come running, but Brady seems to be wholly unimpressed by her not so subtle attempts to lure him in. This must be killing her. I suppress a little smirk that's trying to break through at the thought.

Roman, halfway through his next joint, passes it straight to Brady who gratefully accepts it.

"Don't you have anything better than this?" Seth points to the sound system on the ground before getting up to look through Brady's selection of music.

Sacha grabs one of the battery powered lanterns and excuses herself to go duck behind a tree. Roman does the same, but lurks off in the opposite direction to Sacha.

I cradle my warm, nearly empty beer can in my hands and lean back on my log, the rough bark pressing into my thighs as I let the cool night air wash over me. The trees above begin to swirl and dance in my vision and I laugh for no reason at all. I might be a teensy bit drunk. But I'm still very much aware of my surroundings and I tip my chin back down to see that with Roman and Sacha now gone, and Seth preoccupied with the music, Brady has taken this chance to get closer to Squeak.

I listen to them talking softly and I subtly lean forward, trying to hear what they're saying. For a moment they both just laugh together before Brady bites his lip, like he's thinking of something.

"Hey, Squeak?" he says, a smile playing on his lips.

"Yeah?"

"Have you ever had a blowback?" He holds up the joint in his hand.

Squeak looks confused and shakes her head. "What do you mean?"

Brady looks a little nervous, but he's smiling. "Come here."

I stifle a quiet laugh as I watch Brady turn the joint around in his hand and put it between his lips, the hot end inside his mouth. This is every stoner boy's number one smooth move: a quick way to get up close and intimate with a girl.

I watch Squeak do as she's directed, moving in close to his face as he cups his hands around both their cheeks. A few seconds later she pulls back coughing and laughing, and Brady takes the joint from his mouth with the biggest smile I've ever seen on his face.

I look away quickly when I see him glance my way, not wanting him to know I was watching their cute exchange. But when my gaze reaches the treeline, I see Sacha hovering in the shadows, as still as a statue. Her eyes are glued to Brady and Squeak, and even in the darkness I can see the glow of jealousy in them.

"Yeees!" Seth calls out from his crouch by the sound system and 'Seven Nation Army' begins to thump out into the night. "I *knew* there had to be something good hidden in here!"

Roman is back now and Sacha seems to have been broken from her trance. She's placed herself in the middle of our circle and as the beat of the song starts to kick in, she begins dancing, her arms up high, hips moving back and forth in a controlled swaying motion.

I have to give it to Sacha, she's a great dancer. Confidence oozes from her as she shakes her hips back and forth before leaning down low and snapping back up, flipping her hair dramatically.

Everyone watches intently as she launches into an entrancing show. She moves around the inner perimeter of the circle, stepping to the beat of the music, stopping briefly at Roman and Brady to let them get a better look at her. Her hips glide as smoothly and effortlessly as river water flows, and their eyes are transfixed on her body as it moves in perfect tempo.

Then she moves right into the center of the circle and slowly lowers her fingers into the back pocket of her shorts, her hips never pausing or missing a beat. Her hand stays in there as she turns in a circle, still moving back and forth as though controlled by the music as she looks into each of our eyes in turn, wiggling her eyebrows, before she finishes off her theatrical display by taking her hand from her back pocket, producing something small and holding it up into the air. She waggles it around like she's trying to attract a puppy with a strip of bacon, and it takes a moment for me to clock that it's a little clear plastic bag containing white powder.

Brady laughs and Roman joins in before the two of them jump up and begin hollering and howling up into the night sky like wolves.

"Sacha showed up tonight!" Roman plucks the bag from Sacha's hand, plants a big kiss on her cheek and doesn't waste any time getting straight to business, reaching down and rifling through his rucksack, finding various items to help him set up a space to lay out the powder.

Sacha's face beams proudly at the reaction she's elicited from the guys. "Well, a party's not a party without a little... candy."

Seth rises from beside me and grabs his sister's arm, quietly pulling her aside. "Is that cocaine? Where did you get that?"

"None of your damn business, brother dearest," she says, playfully squeezing his chin before roughly pushing it aside.

Seth casts a disapproving look at her before sitting back down next to me. "Don't take any of that, Jade. Please."

"I won't. I promise," I say, learning just this second that this is where he draws the line.

He has nothing to worry about. I'm not interested in joining in with Sacha, Brady and Roman as they take turns lowering their heads to the cracker box on Roman's lap with a rolled up twenty-dollar bill.

Squeak sits alone, quietly watching the others. I'm glad she's also abstaining. She seems to have a good head on her shoulders.

Sacha, having firmly reinstated her value with the guys tonight, stands up straight and rubs at her nose before extending her arms to the sky above and releasing a gleeful scream.

CHAPTER NINETEEN

NOW

"So, what is this event anyway, some kind of art show or what?" Sacha picks at her popcorn as we stroll past the reptile enclosure.

Penny runs on ahead, overstimulated and a little hyper from the bucket of cotton candy she's been slowly devouring. It's a beautiful day at the zoo and I'm trying to just forget about what happened the other day and enjoy this amazing weather.

Seth didn't kick Sacha out for taking Penny from preschool, after all. And I still don't know why not. But when he came to me after their argument and told me he was going to give her a second chance, I knew that whatever it is she's hanging over his head must be big. But Seth has been so angry since then that I haven't figured out how to bring up what I overheard without risking aggravating him. He seems on edge at all times right now. I don't even know if I should bring it up at all. I mean, what would it achieve? What happened all those years ago was terrible, and I wish I could go back in time and change it, I wish we'd never even gone into the woods that night. But it happened, and none of us can take it back now.

Squeak isn't coming back. Brady isn't coming back. And now Roman isn't coming back, either.

If there's more to what happened in the woods that night than I know, then maybe I'm better off never finding out, because all I want to do now is move on with my life and forget every single horrible detail that has haunted me for so long. But I know that's impossible. At least once a week I still see her face in my dreams: her blank expression, her mouth gaping open, her glassy eyes.

Cool tendrils grip my spine just thinking about it and I shake myself, pulling my focus back to the present and the question Sacha just asked me.

"It's a gala. There's going to be art pieces for sale, live performances, things like that," I say, having no real idea myself of what to expect from the event our team will be catering a week from today.

"Sounds kind of like a bunch of rich snobs getting together to pat themselves on the backs if you ask me." Sacha places another piece of popcorn onto her tongue, then chews it without closing her mouth.

Well, nobody asked you, Sacha.

But I can't deny it sounds a bit like that to me as well. But money is money and not only is Darina offering me a big slice of the metaphorical pie she'll be baking that night, but she's also scored two tickets so that Seth and Penny can attend it, too.

My daughter is going to be *cultured*.

Seth trails several paces behind us, tapping away at his phone. I'm not sure he's seen one animal since we got here. He's been glued to his phone the whole afternoon and any time I've asked him what he's doing he just says 'work stuff,' which is confusing because he doesn't even have a job. I guess he's working hard with the Vanguard Career Group to score something big.

I've established that the second chance he mentioned giving Sacha doesn't involve actually interacting with her because I haven't seen him utter so much as a word to her since then. Sacha did, however, apologize to me the following day for not checking with me first before picking Penny up. Well, maybe she didn't *apologize* exactly, but she said the next time she does it she'll make sure we know about it first. I didn't tell her that there absolutely and categorically will not be a next time, but I chose to take her words as a gesture of goodwill. And when she suggested we all go out to the zoo today, I decided to take it as a sign she wants to try to work on her relationship with our family.

I think she really does care about Penny, and I guess if creating a close auntie–niece bond relies on us all trying to get along, then that's something we've got to do.

Sacha's being uncharacteristically friendly with me today, which I'm trying not to be suspicious about, but it's like she's suddenly had a change of heart since her big blow out with Seth. Maybe it's a sibling thing and they both just needed to let off some steam after not seeing each other for a while. It seems to have worked wonders on Sacha, but not so much on Seth. I look back at him, his head's still hung low, hunched over his phone like it's his lifeline. I wish he'd just look up and enjoy the day. Enjoy the sunshine.

Sacha is waffling on about something but I'm having a hard time keeping up, so I just nod and smile when it seems the right time.

"...that was literally the most drunk I've ever been," she continues, before second guessing herself on such an important fact. "Actually, no, the drunkest I've ever been was probably my thirty-first birthday party—which I'm pretty sure is still going on somewhere—but I basically haven't touched a drop of hard liquor since then, because it knocks me out for days. I mean, literally, I'll be on the couch, dead. Unable to work or do anything."

I use her brief gap between breaths to try to broach a subject I've been waiting to ask her about.

"Speaking of work, have you been looking for a job? I don't know how you'll afford to get a place of your own without one."

Hint, hint.

"Ugh," she groans. "I don't know, Jade. I mean, what am I supposed to do? Work at a café for sixty cents an hour and live off tips? No, thank you."

"Well, you have to do *something*. Surely you've got some kind of skill set that could get you a decent job?"

Sacha is quiet for a moment as she watches Penny skipping on ahead. Then she rakes her fingers through her hair and sighs. "My father used to say that when you're born, you're given a bag of tricks. And as you go through life, you open up the bag every so often and pull out a new one when you need it. Sport, music, math, what have you. Everybody always has something to pull out. And one of those things will set off a spark that makes you want to refine it, until it eventually gets you somewhere in life."

I stay quiet as I watch her speak. Her eyes seem to cloud over, troubled.

"But the problem for me was, while everyone else's bags seemed to be overflowing mine always felt kind of light. I mean, it pretty much felt empty. And my parents must have noticed this too, because when Big Boy Seth took straight to baseball in middle school and then academics in high school and then ended up being awarded that scholarship he got into college with, they rewarded him with special trips out, or the latest games console he'd been asking for, or even that car they gave him on his eighteenth birthday."

Sacha's face drops and I think I can see tears glistening.

"Well, Jade, that was *my* eighteenth birthday, too. And do you know what they got me? A goddamn bottle of perfume and two fifty-dollar bills stuck inside a card."

My heart sinks. I remember when Seth got that car. His parents were so proud of how he did in his final year of high school, and they rewarded him with something he'd wanted for a long time. It seemed like such a huge deal to me, but Seth was always complaining that the car they gifted him was old and beat up. I remember thinking about how privileged he must have been for that to be his number one complaint. But now I realize that I never even considered the fact that Sacha didn't get a car that year. That she was still catching rides around with friends while Seth got his own vehicle to drive.

As I walk beside Sacha now, I see pain in her eyes. The pain of a young girl who was never treated as equal to the brother she literally grew alongside from the very point of conception.

"At some point along the way, my parents gave up on me. The cement had dried," she says quietly. "I was who I was. And I've never apologized for who that is, no matter how much it disappointed them. But I guess the joke's on me, because now I have no tricks left in my bag. And I have no skills or talents to fall back on."

She swallows hard, visibly choking back emotion, and for the very first time in the many years that I've known Sacha, I feel a sudden surge of sympathy for this girl who never seemed to get a fair chance in life.

CHAPTER TWENTY

"And these are petunias, and these are geraniums, and these are marigolds," Penny lists off as she drags her aunt along the rows and rows of flowers growing on our communal rooftop garden.

She's getting most of the names right, but I chuckle under my breath at the adorable way she's mispronouncing them. All her 'r's still come out as 'w's.

"Wow, Penny! That's amazing, how do you know so much about flowers?" Sacha's eyes are wide and impressed.

"Mommy learned me them. We even have some over here, look!" Before I have time to correct her grammar, she pulls Sacha's hand and drags her over to the zinnias we planted together this spring.

It's a glorious Sunday afternoon and the sun beams down on us, warming the rooftop garden and bathing the many plants in its nourishing glow.

After a full day at the zoo yesterday, it's nice to slow down and just enjoy a day at home. I close my eyes for a moment, soaking in the earthy, sweet smell of the flowers and herbs. I still can't quite believe that just a few years ago, this place was nothing but a graveyard of dead plants and dry soil. Apparently, it had once thrived under the care of Mr. Morris, who, from what I heard, had a magical green thumb before he passed away a few years back. Mrs. Morris has a bad back and couldn't keep up with the gardening after her husband died and it ended up being abandoned entirely.

The day I first stepped onto this roof, I was lugging an extra thirty pounds around, pregnant with Penny. Maybe it was the nesting phase controlling me, but I felt a sudden determination to turn this forgotten space into something beautiful. And somehow, I succeeded. It even inspired some of the other residents to come up here every now and then and plant their own vegetables and flowers.

"Look, Auntie Sacha! I found a ladybug!" Penny's tiny fingers point at the ground.

"Wow, kiddo. Don't scare it off. Just watch," she says, hands on hips, but I can see the corners of her mouth twitching into a smile.

I glance at the garden beds, proud of the little sanctuary I've made up here on the rooftop. The basil is thriving, and the tomatoes are finally starting to turn red; I've got the beginnings of the perfect marinara sauce growing here. As Sacha and Penny follow around the ladybug, I get down to my knees and begin to prune a few weeds from around the herbs.

I have to admit, I've been really impressed with Sacha over the last few days. Between the relaxed trip to the zoo yesterday and the fact she tidied up her lotions, creams and makeup in the bathroom last night, and now her willingness to let Penny show her all around the garden up here, I feel like she's turning over a new leaf. She's even been making a point to keep the balcony door closed and locked up after she goes out there to smoke.

Don't get me wrong, I still want this woman out of our hair and far away from us so that Seth and I can relax and get back into our beloved routine that I miss so much. But for now, I'm okay with just enjoying this afternoon outside in the sunshine as she lends a hand keeping Penny occupied.

I look back to see if the two of them have caught that ladybug yet, but I inhale sharply when I see them. The weeds I'm holding drop from my grip to the soil below.

"Hey! Get away from there!" I shout.

Penny and Sacha are standing dangerously close to a section of broken railing at the edge of the rooftop and my stomach tenses at the thought of the sixty-foot drop just beyond it.

"Sacha, get her away from there!" I call again, waving frantically. "The railing is broken, she could fall!"

Penny begins to run back toward me, her eyes wide with fear, but Sacha stays, lingering a bit too close to the edge. She's inspecting the rail like she doesn't believe me. I've already asked the building manager to fix it about ten times, but he's been dragging his feet and the rail still dangles down, weathered and rusted away.

"You have to be careful, Penny." I kneel down in front of her when she gets to me. "No more playing near the edge, okay?"

"Okay, Mommy." She nods obediently, her innocence melting me.

Sacha finishes inspecting the broken railing and returns to us. She brushes a stray hair behind her ear and shoots a thumb back at the railing behind us.

"Well one thing's for sure, nobody in the world could survive a fall like that." She leaves the words hanging in the air strangely.

I hug Penny a little closer to me before she scuttles over to the herbs to continue where I left off digging up weeds. I don't take my eyes off her.

"Relax, Jade. She's fine," Sacha says dismissively.

I feel my chest tightening, my protective instincts kicking in. I suddenly want to yell at Sacha that it's not fine at all, and that since she arrived less than a week ago, I've had to worry for my daughter's life a total of three times now: the incident with her getting out onto the balcony, the abduction from preschool, and now her straying too close to the edge of the rooftop. And every single one of these things happened because of Sacha's carelessness.

I take a deep breath and push it down, not wanting to ruin the effort we've both been putting in the last couple of days over a simple mistake.

"Yeah, well, I don't want her falling off the roof. Just watch her closely when you're caring for her, please."

We both take seats on the old wooden folding chairs left out here from Mr. Morris's gardening days and watch Penny picking a bouquet of herbs.

"Jade, there's something I've been wanting to talk to you about." Sacha leans my way, out of earshot from Penny.

My thoughts immediately go to the conversation I overheard between her and Seth the other night. Does she want to talk about that night in the woods? I don't think I can take that. What good could it possibly do to dredge it all back up to the surface now?

"I don't think—"

"This is serious," Sacha interrupts me. "It's... it's about Izzy-Bella."

"Izzy-Bella?" I almost laugh with relief. I'd been expecting the worst, but she just wants to talk about my daughter's imaginary friend? That I don't mind doing. "Sure. What about her?"

Sacha wrings her hands together on her lap as though she's nervous. That's not like her at all. "When did you say Penny started seeing her?"

"Not long before you got here," I say, remembering the first day I came home to an excited Penny ready to tell me all about her new friend. "With Seth out of work, he began collecting Penny from preschool and bringing her home for the afternoon and I guess she got bored and imagined up a little friend to keep her busy until I got home from work."

"Right..." Sacha says quietly.

I can already see from the doubtful look in her eyes that she feels the exact same way as Seth does about this. Rather than seeing it as Penny using her vivid and creative imagination as a healthy way to help her in adjusting to a new situation, she thinks it's weird and some sort of sign that Penny is troubled.

I was a little upset when I overheard Seth one night at bedtime, telling Penny not to keep on talking about Izzy-Bella anymore, but I'm not at all surprised that Sacha sees an imaginary friend as some kind of cry for help. She hasn't spent any time around children before, and she couldn't possibly understand the complexities of a child's mind. As far as I'm concerned, Izzy-Bella is a healthy and normal exploration of Penny's imagination, and I won't ever make her feel otherwise.

"Look, Sacha," I say. "I know some people have a problem with the idea of imaginary friends, but the thing is, it's actually a very norm–"

"Jade, that's not the problem," Sacha cuts in and I stop mid-sentence, confused.

"Well, if that's not it, then what exactly is your issue with Penny having an imaginary friend?" I ask in frustration.

"Well... that's just the thing, Jade." Sacha pauses. "I don't think that Izzy-Bella is imaginary at all."

CHAPTER TWENTY-ONE

THEN

The breeze gently blows through my hair as Seth pulls me deeper into the woods, away from the laughter and music still echoing from the clearing behind us. While those guys are sniffing and rubbing their noses and dancing around, unable to hear anything over the thumping volume of the music, Seth and I have taken this chance to sneak away for a little fun of our own.

I'd been having a good time before Sacha went and pulled out that little bag. I don't know why she felt the need to turn up the heat on this party, but I get the feeling it had something to do with her witnessing Brady and Squeak getting closer.

I glance up at the trees looming above us like giants and I stumble slightly on the uneven ground.

Seth glances back at me. "You okay?"

If I were to answer him honestly, I'd say I don't know. Some little part of me wants to be right there in the action with those guys, letting my inhibitions and my hair down and dancing. And it's not like I don't know how to have a good time, it's just the alcohol is already doing its job just fine without me needing anything more potent to enjoy myself.

Seth is still waiting for an answer.

"Yeah, I'm just..." I don't want to say drunk. "I'm just happy to get away from those guys for a while."

"It's just you and me now," he murmurs in my ear, leaning close to me.

Suddenly, he stops walking and his hands clasp around my waist, guiding me until my back is up against the rough bark of a tree. The cool surface sends a shiver through me, but Seth is warm, his body pressing against mine. He leans in, his lips brushing against my neck. We start to kiss but my mind is wandering.

Was Sacha telling the truth? Has Seth really been staring at Squeak all night, as infatuated with her as Brady seems to be?

I know I should just relax and enjoy this. And I really try to as Seth presses closer against me, his hands traveling the bare skin under my T-shirt, his breath becoming more and more ragged. But I can't seem to concentrate when the image of him watching Squeak fills my mind. Would he rather he was here with her?

As he begins to unbutton my jeans, I shake my head, trying to dispel the creeping thoughts invading my mind. I try to focus on the smell of his skin, the feel of his tongue against mine. And when he begins to guide me down onto the carpet of pine needles below, my heart is racing, but not from excitement.

Even your idiot boyfriend has been staring at her all night.

Sacha's words echo in my mind, twisting like vines around my thoughts. Seth has me pinned down, his lips on mine while he reaches to unbutton his own pants. This is what I want, or at least it would be usually, but I suddenly feel like there are eyes all over the woods watching us and I snap my head back and forth trying to see out into the darkness.

"Jade," Seth murmurs, breathless, pulling back just enough to look into my eyes. "What's wrong?"

I swallow hard, forcing a smile that feels more like a grimace. "Nothing. Just... we're a little exposed out here."

He tilts his head side to side, his brow furrowing. "There's nobody around. Everyone else is back at the clearing."

"I know, I just..." I stammer.

He pulls back further, catching my hesitation. "You're not fooling me. You know I can tell when something's wrong. What is it?"

He gets up and sits next to me, the moment officially dead. I push myself back up until I'm sitting against the tree. Should I ask him? Will I just sound whiny and insecure? Of course I will, but what else can I do? We're in a relationship and it's totally wrong that he would spend the night staring at another girl.

"I... it's just, Sacha said... I mean, you know how she is, she's always watching everyone... and I..." I can't seem to get a full sentence out.

Seth laughs nervously. "What are you trying to say, Jade?"

I take a deep breath to steady myself, thankful he can't see my cheeks glow radioactive pink in the darkness. "Is Squeak... hot?"

Seth scrunches up his face. "Why are you asking me that?"

"Sacha said you've been staring at her all night."

For a moment, his expression freezes, and I can almost see the gears turning in his head. "What? Squeak? Come on, that's ridiculous."

"Is it?" I challenge him, feeling the tension crackle like static in the air. "Because Brady is all over her like he wants her, and he hasn't even given a second glance to Sacha. And I mean, come on, I know she's your sister, but you've seen how most guys look at her. No male with an active heartbeat turns down a girl like Sacha."

He leans back, his arms crossed. The tiny distance between us suddenly feels like a deep chasm.

"You believe Sacha? The girl who lies about literally everything? The girl who made up a story about me hanging out with my ex-girlfriend when I haven't so much as seen her face since we broke up?"

This is true. Sacha lies like the rest of us breathe. And I know she loves nothing more than stirring the pot just to watch everyone squirm, but something about what she said has really hit a chord with me. And after seeing how Brady has been acting around Squeak tonight, I can't help but feel like Sacha might be telling the truth this time. Seth is shaking his head, clearly annoyed at my sudden burst of jealousy. But I can't seem to stop.

"Is it true though? Do you find Squeak attractive?" I bite my lip.

"Squeak?" he says, trying and failing to look confused by the question. "I mean... she's not like... I don't know... I guess I haven't really thought about it."

My heart sinks. That molasses-like response sure sounded like a big fat yes to me.

"Look, Sacha would say anything to get between us," Seth says, frustration creeping into his voice. "Can we just go back to having fun?"

But as he leans in again, his body over mine, I can't shake the feeling that something is shifting in the shadows. And when we hear the sound of leaves crunching nearby, we both turn our heads to see Sacha pop out of nowhere like a jack-in-the-box.

"Jesus, Sacha!" Seth nearly jumps out of his skin. "You've come to watch us? What the hell is your problem?"

Sacha ignores him and just stands there, her eyes moving over the two of us, a smirk playing on her lips.

"Hey there, lovers," she teases. "Sorry to interrupt your special moment, but it's time to get back to the circle. We've got a game to finish playing."

CHAPTER TWENTY-TWO

NOW

Izzy-Bella is real. Sacha's words on the rooftop yesterday are still spinning round and round in my head as I put together Penny's lunch for preschool.

Sacha confided in me that she overheard Seth on the phone one morning last week, talking to someone he was calling Isabella.

Isabella.

I mean... what are the chances?

I spent the whole of yesterday evening mulling this over in my mind and the image that kept forcing its way inside my head was of the woman I saw exiting the elevator the day I was rushing back to the apartment. After the shock of being told Penny was collected from preschool by her aunt, my mind was firmly on finding my daughter in that moment. If I hadn't been so distracted, I might have realized that this beautiful woman—this stranger with her designer pantsuit and expensive shoes—was leaving the building around the same time Seth had just wrapped up his meeting. A meeting in our home. A meeting for which he'd specifically requested to have the apartment empty that day, sending Sacha off to go shopping.

Was the woman I saw Isabella?

If she was, and she's one of the team at the Vanguard Career Group who has been working with Seth over the last few weeks, then that would line up suspiciously closely to when Penny began telling me stories of Izzy-Bella coming to visit. Stories that I overheard Seth telling Penny not to talk about anymore.

At the time, I thought he was just uncomfortable with the idea of our daughter playing around with her imagination, but now I'm wondering if there was another reason for him wanting her to keep her mouth shut.

When Penny first told me about Izzy-Bella coming over to play and described her long blond hair and her beautiful pink dress, I pictured a little girl, maybe a princess or a ballerina that Penny had plucked straight out of a book and conjured up in real life, to play with and keep her company. I think I might have even done things like that when I was a little girl, an only child who didn't have any siblings to keep me occupied at home during the long summer days. But now I remember the woman in the elevator; her long blond hair, thick and shiny, cascading over her shoulders, almost like she was a fully grown princess—a goddamn Rapunzel in a pantsuit.

While Penny sits on the floor putting on her socks, I test out my little theory.

"Hey, Penny?"

"Yes?" Her face is deep in concentration as she tries to line up the toe-seam of her sock properly.

"How old is your friend Izzy-Bella?"

"Um... well, she's a big girl."

My heart sinks. "A big girl?"

"Yeah. Like... eight."

My shoulders sag with relief. Of course, a big girl to Penny could be eight. Not a fully grown woman. But the relief is short lived when my mind starts ticking over.

"Hey, Penny?" I continue.

"Yeah?"

"How old do you think I am?"

Penny thinks about this for a few seconds. "Um... ninety-two?"

This isn't good. "And how old do you think Daddy is?"

Penny finishes putting on her socks and taps her chin in thought. "Daddy... is... eleven?"

Okay, so it's clear that my daughter does not have a secure grasp on the fact that age usually correlates directly to height and looks.

"Good morning." Seth wanders into the kitchen and pours himself a coffee.

Penny runs off to the living room, where Sacha is watching a morning TV talk show. Seth kisses me on the cheek and I notice he's got a new suit on and smells great. I think he must have sprayed on the expensive stuff this morning.

Is he planning on meeting Isabella today? I don't want to jump straight to assuming he's having an affair, but now that I think about it, it all seems to add up. He's constantly distracted, always on his phone or making calls, he's been to more meetings and interviews in the last two weeks than I can count on both hands (if that's where he's actually been going) and now it looks like he's begun having meetings in our home with a woman named Isabella, who our daughter seems to think has been coming to visit while I'm at work, and never seems to appear when Sacha is here either. *And* Seth doesn't want Penny talking about her. I mean, if that's not enough to give me warrant to be suspicious, I don't know what is, exactly. And to top that all off, Seth and I haven't even made love in the past week, which is almost unheard of for us. But that could be down to the fact that Sacha is staying here, her presence having thrown everything in our lives off course.

I thought that my and Seth's roots had grown underground together, and there was nothing that could shake our foundation. But I barely slept at all last night lying next to a man who I'm beginning to wonder if I really know or not.

"You look nice, another job interview?" I ask casually as I put away Penny's medicine bottle.

Seth starts patting his pockets, pulling out his phone and tapping at the screen, like he hasn't heard me.

"Yeah..." he eventually says, absent-mindedly. "But I'll be back in time to collect Penny from preschool–"

"Jade!" Sacha's urgent voice cuts Seth off and pivots both our attention before we make a dash for the living room.

"What is it?" My eyes dart around when I reach the door.

"Over here," Sacha says, pointing at Penny, who sits on the couch, the front of her dress wet with a viscous substance. "She vomited."

"I'm sorry, Mommy." Penny's eyes brim over with tears and my heart breaks.

"Oh, no, sweetie, don't apologize! It's okay. What happened?" I say, pulling her dress over her head carefully so as not to get the vomit in her hair.

"I don't know." Penny sniffs.

"She was just sitting there next to me and–" Sacha crudely mimes barfing rather than finishing the sentence.

"Okay, um..." I glance at the clock on the wall, trying to think on my feet. "Well, I guess she can't go to preschool today in case it's something viral."

Seth tucks his phone into his back pocket. "Well, what are we going to do? You have work and I need to leave in ten minutes. I can't cancel this interview."

"I'll call Miss Carol and tell her Penny won't be in today." I sigh. "And I guess I'll just have to call Darina afterwards and tell her I can't come in to work today."

"What?" Sacha gives me an insulted look. "I'm going to be here all afternoon, why don't you just leave Penny with me?"

Seth and I exchange a glance and I'm sure he's thinking the same thing as me. Sacha spending time with Penny while we're here to keep an eye on things is one thing, but leaving our daughter with her unsupervised? My gut says it's a bad idea.

"Penny might have some kind of a stomach bug and she could end up vomiting multiple times today," I say, hoping this is enough to scare her off the thought.

Sacha waves this away as though it's no big deal. "I once shared a house with six guys, and they partied *hard*. I had to clean up vomit all the time. Trust me, I can handle this."

I glance at Seth, who shakes his head slowly.

"I don't know..." he begins.

"Oh, come on, Seth!" Sacha turns to him. "I'm not going to let anything happen to her. Why do you *always* think the worst of me?"

Seth opens his mouth, likely to begin a lengthy and detailed speech breaking down his many reasons why, citing dates and references, but I give him a sharp look and he closes his mouth slowly.

"Look," I say. "If you're here all day anyway, then maybe it makes sense. I mean, you can just let Penny crash out on the couch watching movies all afternoon, so long as you keep her clean and hydrated."

I don't feel entirely comfortable with this decision, but I really can't afford to take the day off work. Besides, if they're inside cuddled up on the couch, what's the worst that could happen?

CHAPTER TWENTY-THREE

My morning consists mostly of choux pastry and whipped cream, and if I hadn't already built up a monk-like ability to resist the many temptations I'm faced with each day here at the Crumb Cottage, I'd probably shovel two of the delicious éclairs I've been preparing into my mouth whole.

With each swing of the kitchen door, I've seen the queue wrapped all the way out the front door most of the morning, but by early afternoon things have slowed down and I finally get a chance to call Sacha to check up on Penny.

"She's fine, Jade," she assures me, her voice cheerful over the phone. "I found some old *Bear in the Big Blue House* episodes streaming and we're watching it together. I think I'm more into it than she is though."

I smile at the image. I'm relieved to hear Penny's on the mend, and glad that Sacha is both enjoying auntie duty and taking good care of my little girl.

I get that Seth was wary of leaving Penny alone with her today, but to me it seems like Sacha is really beginning to mature. It's as if getting to know her niece has given her a new perspective on life, a sense of responsibility that I've always hoped would blossom in her one day. But despite this, I can't shake the nagging doubts about her intentions.

Was Sacha lying when she told me she overheard Seth talking to someone named Isabella on the phone? I mean, it wouldn't be the first time she's planted a seed of distrust in my head, only for it to turn out to be a lie. There was the time she told me she saw Seth hanging out with his ex when we were teens. But Seth said he hadn't even seen her. Then there was the night in the woods, when she claimed Seth had been making eyes at Squeak all night. He denied that, too.

And now there's this Isabella.

Is it possible that Sacha has actually been telling the truth all along and it's Seth who's been lying to me this whole time?

He told me he has another interview today but for all I know he could be at this woman's apartment, his mouth on hers right now. I picture her long blond hair draped over the bed, his face hovering over hers, his suit jacket tossed carelessly on the floor in the heat of the moment. My chest burns with anger at the thought.

We've worked harder than most to build the perfect life together. The perfect family. Why would Seth risk losing it all over some passing fling?

But I have no real reason to believe that the woman I saw coming out of the elevator that day was Isabella (if there even *is* an Isabella). She could have been visiting someone else in our building. Maybe she's a friend or a relative of Mrs. Morris. Or maybe she was just a saleswoman going door to door, trying to peddle some new product. Sure, the timing looks suspicious, since Seth had finished up a meeting just before I saw her. But am I just letting my imagination go to the worst possible place? I don't know. But I get the horrible feeling that Sacha might actually be telling me the truth.

By the time I get off the phone with Sacha, the afternoon

lull I'd just begun to enjoy is shattered as customers flood in, ready to pick from the mouthwatering selection of goodies that line the display counters. I'm still hung up on my suspicions about Seth, but I'm too preoccupied to focus on it.

Stocking the display, I scan the bakery floor. The usual crowd is here: Charlene Henderson from the jewelry store next door, always opting for her pumpkin scone; the man who comes in most days with his husky twin boys for their powdered donuts; and then the college students, stopping by to fuel up on caffeine and pastries.

For the next two hours it begins to feel like any given day. My mind is free of all the drama at home and I can just enjoy this little compartment of my life.

But my bubble is popped when it's time to go home.

I arrive back at our building, the heavy glass doors sliding open as I step inside the lobby. I spot Seth leaning against the wall by the elevator, his arms crossed. I should feel a burst of happiness at seeing my husband after a long day but instead a cold knot tightens in my stomach. He sees me and smiles, but it almost feels like a mask he's wearing just to please me.

"Hey," he says.

"Hey." I force a warm tone, but my throat suddenly feels dry.

Did he just get back from spending the afternoon with Isabella? The thought sends fire through my veins and I shake my head slightly, trying to clear it.

The elevator doors open and a man who lives one floor down from us steps out, nodding a hello. I watch him walk away, my mind snapping back to the other day, the woman stepping out of the same elevator; her long blond hair, her trim frame and her polite smile seared into my mind.

I step in next to Seth and the doors slide shut.

"How did your interview go?" I ask, my voice steadier than I feel.

He shrugs, his gaze fixed on the numbers above the doors. "Not sure. I mean, I prepped a lot with my career counselors, but there were some unexpected elements. So... I don't know."

"Unexpected elements?" I echo, sharper than intended. "Like what?"

He hesitates. "Just... things I wasn't ready for."

I don't get this—it was never this complicated before. Job interviews shouldn't require a labyrinth of preparation.

"So, explain to me again, who exactly are these career counselors?" I quiz him.

His eyes avoid mine and I sense a hint of caution. "I told you before, the Vanguard Career Group. They help with high-end job placements. We discussed this already, it's worth the cost. It just takes time."

"What are the names of the people you're working with specifically?" I press, unable to let it go. "Do you work with them one on one, or as a group?"

He fidgets with the cuff of his shirt, avoiding my gaze. "What's with all the questions? I'm exhausted, Jade."

"Are they male or female?" I ask.

Seth squeezes the bridge of his nose. "What?"

I say nothing more, letting my question hang in the air uncomfortably.

"They're professionals, Jade. What does it matter?"

"You didn't answer my question," I say, my voice firmer now.

Seth's features darken as he stares back at me, the atmosphere in the elevator feeling like it might suffocate us at any moment. I can almost see the wheels turning in Seth's mind, a moment of realization crossing his face as if he knows I'm onto him. But before I can say more, the elevator dings, and the doors open, releasing us onto our floor directly in front of an agitated looking Mrs. Morris.

"Oh, Jade! Seth! You have to come quickly. I just heard screaming coming from your apartment!"

The words have barely left her mouth before I'm running, my feet hitting the carpeted hall so hard it shakes all around me. I grab the keys from my pocket, Seth right at my heels and we burst through the door, both our eyes darting around the empty entranceway.

"Sacha!" I call out, but there's no reply.

We don't stop to take off our shoes or jackets as we run straight to the kitchen, but there's nobody there. Visions of Penny falling from the balcony fill my mind, and my heart is thudding wildly inside my chest by the time I reach the living room. To my relief the door to the balcony is safely closed, but that relief lasts only a moment, turning to terror as I look to the floor and see Penny struggling furiously under the crushing weight of Sacha, who sits atop her little body, hands wrapped tightly around her neck.

She's trying to kill my daughter.

CHAPTER TWENTY-FOUR

THEN

The warm air clings to my skin as Sacha leads the way back to the group, her presence as overbearing as the music that filters through the trees.

I stick close to Seth, who's been quietly stewing since Sacha barged in on our time alone. I still don't know if I believe that he wasn't staring at Squeak, but since I can't prove otherwise, I guess I'll just have to take his word for it.

"Aw, Seth, are you mad your fun with Jade is over before it even started?" Sacha prods him in the side.

"How do you know we weren't just warming up for round two?" Seth spits back.

I don't know if I can stand any more of these two tonight. I'm sure once they're older and no longer living together under their parents' roof, they'll get along much better. But for now, it's excruciating to be around their constant bickering and name-calling. If it's like this for me, I don't even want to know what their parents had to deal with when they were small kids.

The moon lights our way back to the clearing, beaming a glow over the patch of forest we've claimed as our own for the night. The sounds of our footsteps and the crackling of leaves as we emerge from the trees are muted by the thumping bass of the music blaring from Brady's speaker.

Squeak is still perched like a woodland creature on the exact same log she was on when we left. Brady and Roman are in the middle of the circle, both shirtless and wrestling each other playfully—an eventuality that I've noticed every gathering of young men seems to culminate in. Squeak appears to be mildly amused by their horseplay, her lips curled up slightly, almost undetectable. Sacha seems less impressed.

"Guys! Quiet down!" She waves her arms in their direction. "We're about to continue our game of Truth, Truth, Lie!"

Roman and Brady part ways, fists still up and bobbing before they mutually concede, then grip each other's hands and bump shoulders. Sacha rolls her eyes, her irritation visible just beneath the surface.

Why is she so dead set on getting everyone to play this stupid game?

Seth tenses up next to me. "Aren't we done with Truth, Truth, Lie?"

"No, we just took a break," Sacha retorts, tossing her hair over her shoulder. "Come on, we've barely scratched the surface on the secrets we know about each other. What do you think, Squeak? Ready for round two?"

Squeak raises an eyebrow, her expression somewhere between bemused and scared. "Um... sure?"

"Hey!" The corners of Sacha's mouth twitch upwards in a crooked smile. "Well, if our girl Squeak wants to play, then we've got to, right?"

"Fine," Seth says, giving up.

We all make our way to the logs of our makeshift circle while Sacha mixes more rum and colas for the group. I take one when she offers and am a little surprised when even Squeak accepts one. I wonder what number drink this is for her. She's so small that she's got to be wasted by now, but you'd never know it.

Sacha claps her hands. "Okay! Who wants to go next?"

Brady stands up, pulling his shirt back on. "I'll do Jade."

"The hell you will!" Seth jokes, seemingly making an effort to relax back into a more lighthearted mood.

Brady just waggles his eyebrows suggestively at his friend before grabbing his drink and moving to the center of the circle. "Seth, you can't join in on this one. You'll already know which facts are true."

I'm not too worried. I know Brady has no good dirt on me. At worst, Seth might have shared a few mildly embarrassing details with him that he knows about me, but nothing that I can't handle the group finding out about.

"Do your worst!" I dare him.

As the game kicks off again, I can see Sacha's eyes on Squeak, and I don't like it. It's the same way a hawk watches its prey, calculating and assessing its weaknesses. I glance at Seth, who seems oblivious, but I can't shake the feeling that Sacha's insistence on playing this game means something. I just don't know what the real game she's playing here is.

"Okay, number one," Brady shouts before changing his voice to a gushing coo. "Seth was Jade's veeery first."

This is true and I don't really care who knows it, so I say nothing.

"Two," he continues. "She doesn't shave her legs. Like ever. It's au naturel, all the time."

Everyone looks at me but I keep my poker face going strong, not giving anything away.

"And three." Brady looks around the group conspiratorially before lowering his voice. "She and I once made out, about a week or so before I started seeing my ex."

Sacha's eyes snap to me, and her death stare is unmistakable.

This is obviously something that Seth hasn't shared with his sister because it looks as though this is the first time she's finding out about it.

"It's the legs," Roman says. "That's the lie. I saw her wearing shorts last week and I'm pretty sure I'd remember if she was part yeti under there."

I nod my head affirmatively, vindicated. "Thank you, Roman."

"Wait, so... you two actually made out?" Sacha points a finger between me and Brady in disbelief. "Wow, Brady. You must have been really desperate."

My jaw drops. I'm beginning to think Sacha's favorite pastime is baiting me. I open my mouth to retort, but I don't get the chance.

"I'm joking! I'm joking!" Sacha sings, but I don't think she was joking at all.

I'm so tired of her little put-downs and her lies aimed at stinging me and driving a wedge between me and Seth. But rather than just sitting back and leaving myself defenseless, I decide it's finally time to fight back. I'm not going to let her win this round, whatever her game is.

"Okay, my turn!" I jump up and walk confidently into the circle. "I'll do Sacha."

I've spent enough nights sitting in Sacha's room as I waited for Seth to finish work, listening to her ramble on about what she and her friends get up to, and all her little secrets. It's time to give her a dose of her own medicine.

Sacha smiles and crosses her arms defiantly. "Go ahead, Jade. I've got nothing to hide."

Well, let's just see about that, shall we?

"Number one." I jump straight to it. "Sacha once stole two hundred dollars from Seth's wallet."

Seth's face snaps toward where his sister sits, but she intently avoids eye contact.

"Two," I say, charging on with purpose. "She and Erica Thorpe were the ones who scratched that giant dick on the side of Mr. Rashford's car."

This elicits a round of shocked but amused faces from the circle, as Sacha shoots her steely glare straight at me.

"And three," I declare. "The reason she did that was because he turned her down when she made a pass at him."

There's quiet all around before Seth finally breaks it. "If you stole money from me, Sacha, you're as good as dead."

Sacha doesn't answer him, and she doesn't take her eyes off me.

"The lie has to be Mr. Rashford, right?" Brady's eyes are wide. "He's like forty-something and balding. You wouldn't..."

Sacha shrugs. "Wouldn't I?"

"Ew." I hear from Squeak, and it's so unexpected that I laugh out loud.

"Oh, get over it," Sacha says. "I probably wouldn't have actually done anything with him, I just wanted to see if he was tempted. And don't worry, brother dearest, I never stole any money from you."

Seth seems equal parts relieved and disgusted by the outcome of this round.

"Okay, let's move on," he says, clearly wanting to change the subject from his sister's bizarre brand of promiscuity. "I think it's about time the quiet one joins in for once. Squeak? Since nobody's done Roman yet, what kind of dirt have you got on your cousin?"

CHAPTER TWENTY-FIVE

NOW

The room feels like it's spinning, the walls closing in on me as I watch Sacha squeeze the life from my daughter.

I should have never left her alone with Penny today. I've always known there was something desperately wrong with my sister-in-law—something I have seen rear its ugly head many times over the years—but I couldn't have anticipated this. She's attempting to kill a child. Her own niece.

I dash straight toward them, and I'm a split second away from lunging at Sacha to pull her away from her perch atop Penny, when she turns to me suddenly.

"Jade, help! I don't know what's happening!" She screeches in a tone I've never heard from her before.

It's only now that I see Sacha's eyes are filled with tears, her expression frantic.

That's when I realize she isn't trying to strangle Penny, but holding her down firmly, squeezing the tops of her shoulders and pinning her to the floor as her little body thrashes and convulses, her eyes rolling to the back of her head. She's having a seizure.

"Sacha, get off of her!" I shout, pulling her away from Penny. "You need to stop holding her down!"

She does as she's told but I can hear her panicking as she hovers behind me.

Seth hasn't wasted a moment and is already on the phone with Penny's specialist, Dr. Cross, as I assess the situation calmly, just like our doctors have trained us to do. I look around the floor to see that there are no objects around that could hurt Penny, before pulling a pillow from the couch and placing it underneath her head. I then roll her to onto her side, listening closely to make sure that her airways aren't obstructed in any way. She's okay. She's still breathing.

I can hear the muffled voice of Dr. Cross on the other end of the phone, as Seth nods his head, taking in every detail and answering his questions. Penny's small frame is still tense, her limbs flailing wildly. But a moment later the violent movements begin to subside. My heart is pounding against my ribcage, and the heat of the apartment isn't helping. I'm starting to sweat underneath the jacket I haven't yet had a chance to remove. Sacha is still behind me, her panicked breaths louder than anything.

"When did it start, Sacha?" Seth asks, placing his hand briefly over the mouthpiece of his phone.

"Um... uh..." Sacha is flapping about helplessly, her wide eyes not moving from Penny.

"Sacha, breathe," I say firmly. "Penny is going to be fine. We just need to know when this started."

"It... um... like a minute ago, maybe two? I don't know!" Her voice trembles. "Is she going to be okay?"

Seth gets back on the phone with Dr. Cross, and I remain by Penny's side as her convulsions slow and she's left lightly shaking.

"Sacha, sit down," I say forcefully, turning briefly to face her. "You need to be calm for Penny."

This is true. I was taught this in countless sessions with therapists and specialists. Even in this state, Penny is absorbing the emotions of those around her. If we let panic seep in and don't remain calm, it could inadvertently make this worse for her.

"She's going to be okay, but there's nothing we can do right now. She's nearly out of it, we just have to let it run its course," I say, my voice sounding miles calmer than I feel inside.

In reality, it doesn't matter how many times we've gone through this, it's utterly terrifying. But panicking is the worst possible response, and I've trained myself to do exactly as the doctors have told me to, which is to make sure Penny is breathing, while giving her body a safe space to get past the seizure.

Seth's voice is quiet behind me. "Dr. Cross said he'll stay on the line with us. Just to be safe."

He looks at me intensely and I can feel the weight of our shared worry. Seth and I have been through this more times than we ever should have, and I'm so relieved that he's here right now. Every bit of doubt I'd been having a few minutes ago about his commitment to this family comes temporarily screeching to a halt as I watch him focus on making sure Penny's okay.

"He says if it lasts more than five minutes we'll need to bring her in," he says gently.

"I think it's subsiding now," I say, still perched firmly next to our daughter, who is pale and trembling on the floor. I brush a damp strand of hair from her forehead. "Penny, sweetie, I'm right here."

Her eyes flutter.

"Is it over?" Sacha asks, her voice just a whisper. I can see the tears pooling in her eyes and for a moment I feel an unexpected surge of compassion for her. She's clearly never witnessed a seizure before and she's visibly terrified.

"We just have to wait."

It takes another minute or so for us to be sure Penny's okay before Seth ends the call with Dr. Cross, his expression relaxing. "He said we need to monitor her closely for the next twenty-four hours, but that she should be fine."

"Is that it?" Sacha's voice rises, a fresh wave of panic washing over her face. "What kind of a doctor is he? Shouldn't we take her to the emergency room? What if it happens again?"

"Sacha, please! Just breathe. Penny is going to be okay. We just need to stay calm and focus on keeping her relaxed." I return my attention to Penny, who is slowly starting to regain some semblance of awareness.

"Penny, sweetheart, can you hear me?" I ask, my voice softening. "You're safe. Mommy's right here."

Her eyelids flutter again, and I can see the fight in her begin to return. She cuddles into my lap, and for the first time since I stepped inside our apartment, I allow myself to just breathe. But as I slowly begin to relax, a creeping thought slides into my head. One that I can't shake.

Just moments ago, I thought Sacha was trying to kill my child. I thought that she was squeezing the breath from her body, ready to end her tiny little four-year-old life. And the worst part, the part that really scares me, is how easily I believed it could be true.

CHAPTER TWENTY-SIX

The kitchen is cluttered with empty takeout cartons from our lazy dinner, their greasy contents now eaten up. I didn't have time to cook tonight, Penny needed me close. So we ordered in and I ate my vegetable kung pao while she snuggled up on my lap at the table.

After talking with Dr. Cross again, we concluded that the seizure was probably a result of Penny having vomited up her medicine this morning, and the fact she was under the weather likely didn't help. I don't ever want to get used to this but unfortunately these were the cards we were dealt. For now, I just want to focus on making sure she's okay, and thankfully, she seems to be doing a lot better now. And up until her seizure, she must have been having a pretty great day with her aunt, because after dinner tonight she insisted that Sacha be the one to be there with her for her night-time bath.

I can hear the muffled sounds of Penny splashing about in the tub as I wash and stack the plastic cartons, ready to recycle tomorrow. I'm trying to ignore the light tremor in my hands. I know I should just be grateful that everything turned out okay, but all I feel is a lingering sense of unease. I wipe my palms on the rough fabric of my jeans.

I know that Sacha did nothing wrong. What happened was in no way her fault, she didn't know how to react when she saw Penny begin to convulse. But seeing her there, on top of my daughter, holding her down, is a sight that keeps coming back to my mind. The one good thing that came of this, if nothing else, is that Sacha's reaction proved to me that she really does care about Penny. She was terrified for her niece's life. I think it's the only time I've ever seen her genuinely scared.

There's a side of Sacha that I really don't care for. The one that always seems to float through life with a selfish, entitled attitude. But today, with Penny's seizure, I saw a glimmer of the deeper emotions she keeps hidden. It turns out that deep down, she has a heart tucked away there somewhere.

I wipe down the countertop, the sticky remnants of soy sauce and sweet and sour glaze smearing about on the sponge, before stepping back to admire my handiwork. It may still reek of Chinese food in here, but at least it's tidy.

I glance down the hall and hear faint sounds of talking from within the bathroom. I move slowly down the hall, trying to listen in but the bathroom door is only slightly ajar, and I can't quite hear what they're saying. I can't resist peeking in.

Penny, pink and happy, is sitting in the tub, surrounded by a mountain of bubbles as she pours water from one cup to another. Sacha is sitting on the floor with her back to me, her knees up to her chest as she chats with Penny, unaware of my presence.

"But I wasn't so lucky," Sacha is saying quietly. "Because I had a brother. And let me tell you, that's the worst."

Penny doesn't seem to be listening but Sacha continues anyway. "Brothers are like a shadow that always stands over you. They block out all the sunlight. They get all the applause, all the validation... sometimes even a car. And what does a sister get? Nothing. Ever."

It seems Sacha has been reflecting on this a lot lately. Was it really that traumatizing growing up with Seth for a brother? I guess it's hard for me to see it, since he's always been good to me. But now that I think back, maybe I overlooked a lot of the horrible things he said and did to his sister when we were younger.

I remember the time Seth and I were driving back to his parents' house after a stop to get burgers. It was pouring with rain and when we passed Sacha walking home, Seth slowed to a crawl and rolled down the window to ask if she wanted a ride. When she went to get in, he just rolled the window back up and laughed. He kept on driving, leaving her to walk home in the rain.

Another time, while Seth was rummaging through Sacha's bedroom looking for a CD she'd borrowed but had never returned, he found her stash of weed and took it for himself, but not before leaving a small bag of it in the pocket of her jeans, ready for their mom to find when she did the laundry. Sacha spent the next week grounded, staring up at her bedroom ceiling, while Seth and I spent each night lying out on the grass of an empty sports field, staring up at the stars as we got high.

Since I grew up as an only child, I figured this was normal sibling rivalry. Now I'm wondering if it went beyond the usual squabbling antics of most brothers and sisters. Maybe the reason Sacha turned out the way she did is because Seth made her life a living hell since day one. That, coupled with the fact that their parents always favored him—and did a monumentally poor job of hiding it—how could anyone blame Sacha for being bitter about her younger years?

"But you know what? None of that will matter soon enough." Sacha reaches into the tub and runs her fingers gently through the water, still unaware I'm standing nearby. "Things are going to change. Just wait and see, Penny."

There's a strange faraway tone to her voice, but the fact that she's saying things will change strikes me as a great thing. Maybe she's planning on getting a job and paying her own way in life for once, show her brother she's not a loser, after all. At least, I hope that's what she means, because it's coming up on two weeks since she arrived at our home and as much as I'm impressed by her emotional growth, I still want her gone. Badly.

I quietly slip away, leaving them to it and get Penny's pajamas folded and ready on her bed.

Seth would usually do this, but he's working on his laptop in the kitchen. I've given up asking what it is he's doing. We haven't addressed the unfinished conversation about who it is he's working with at Vanguard, and I don't know whether or not I should bring it up again. I usually feel comfortable talking about anything with Seth, but recently it's like every time I've asked him about what he's doing, where he's going or who with, he shuts down completely. For a while I put this down to him being so stressed in this strange limbo he's found himself in between jobs, but now that Sacha has introduced the whole Izzy-Bella/Isabella thing, I'm really beginning to think there's something more going on.

I try to put it to the back of my mind once Penny is out of the bath and as I tuck her into her bed, I give her a kiss on the head. She pulls the covers right up to her chin and grins as Seth comes in holding her favorite book about a tired llama. I slip out of her room as they begin their night-time stories and join Sacha outside on the balcony.

It's a still night and I try to position myself on the end furthest from the cigarette smoke, but it seems to be clouding the entire area.

"Sorry." She waves at the space between us, clearing the air. "Didn't realize you were coming out."

"That's okay." I lean against the railing and look down at the street. "I just wanted to come and say thanks."

Sacha raises a quizzical eyebrow as she exhales a fresh cloud of smoke.

"For looking after Penny today," I clarify. "I know what happened was scary, but you stayed right by her side. It touched me to see how concerned you were for her."

Sacha nods slowly. "She's my flesh and blood. She's the only family that actually matters to me."

I scoff at this. "Well, that's not true. You've got your mom, and Seth."

Sacha throws down her cigarette and presses the toe of her shoe to it, extinguishing its glow. "Why should I care about my mom when she's made it clear she couldn't care less about me? She doesn't even want me to visit her at her stupid retirement community. She's probably embarrassed to think of anyone seeing her with me. And Seth... there's no love lost there."

"That's because the two of you never even try to get along. If you'd just give him a chance, you'd see that–"

"Seth only cares about himself. You of all people should be able to see that."

"What does that mean?" My hand shoots to my hip defensively.

"Wake up, Jade! The man is lying to you!" Sacha's eyes flash with anger. "I saw her, okay? I saw Isabella drop him off in her flashy car, is that what you need to hear?"

I feel like she just threw a brick at my chest. "When?"

Sacha sighs as she pinches the bridge of her nose. "I... I didn't want to tell you this. But I was out here having a cigarette earlier, just before Penny's... thing started."

"Her seizure?" I ask.

"Yeah. That. And I was looking down at the street and saw some blond woman pull up in a red car. Seth got out and walked around to her side, then he leaned in through her window and... I'm pretty sure he kissed her."

The air on the balcony seems to condense, now far thicker than the smoke that just finished dissipating.

I can't believe it. Seth is having an affair.

CHAPTER TWENTY-SEVEN

THEN

I sip my drink slowly and lean back on the log, letting the ever-climbing buzz of the alcohol wash over me. Our circle has been infused with a refreshed atmosphere and I find myself joining in with the others as they beckon Squeak on, chanting her name.

Roman is on his feet, tugging at his cousin's arm to no avail. "Come on, Squeak! Everyone has to take a turn and you're the only one who hasn't played yet."

Squeak casts a look around as she holds her own, refusing to get up. "Why? I don't even have any interesting facts about you to share."

"Oh, gee, thanks." Roman clutches his chest, pretending to be hurt.

"You know what I mean." Squeak rolls her eyes. "You haven't vandalized anything or slept with any teachers, that I know of."

Unsurprisingly, everyone but Sacha laughs at this thinly veiled dig at her expense. I'm beginning to see that Squeak has a little fire hiding behind her usual subdued demeanor.

"Who cares? Anything will do," Roman dares her.

"Childhood stuff, personal stuff. Go ahead and embarrass me, you have my full permission."

Squeak stares at Roman with an apprehensive expression but much to the surprise of everyone in the group, she concedes and slowly rises to her feet.

But now that she's fully vertical, the effects of the alcohol she's consumed tonight are much more visible than before. She sways a little as she walks, and when she reaches the middle of the circle and comes to a stop, it's as though she's trying hard not to lean at an angle. She fidgets with the hem of her cardigan as she pauses, thinking of what to say about her cousin.

A quiet stillness creeps all around as we look on. The collective gaze of our group is firmly glued to Squeak. Ten steady eyes, all staring directly at her. I can sense her discomfort at this turn of events, and feel a little sorry for her, knowing she's not one for being the center of attention, or even at the perimeter of it, for that matter. Squeak bites her lower lip gently and shifts her fragile weight from one laced-up black boot to the other.

It's impossible not to notice the distinctly fascinated kind of look in everyone's eyes, and I'm sure if a mirror were held up to my own face right now, I'd see it too. I can't pinpoint an exact reason, but there's a sort of power that resides in the fact she's usually so quiet and reserved, yet she's agreed to partake in our silly little game that has us all waiting with bated breath for her to start.

I take a glance at Seth and see that he's smiling as he watches her think. Brady is, too. I guess Sacha really was right about Squeak's appeal.

The weird thing is, for all anyone else knows, Squeak could be as brash and self-centered on the inside as Sacha is on the outside. But there's something about a person who spends their life choosing silence over unbridled noise—who sits back, subdued, and watches wordlessly rather than putting themselves out there—that makes them seem wise. Controlled. Mysterious. Basically, everything that Sacha isn't. And I think that's both the reason for her hold over the guys as they watch her right now, and for Sacha's barely concealed animosity as she sighs and rolls her eyes, letting everyone know she's tired of waiting.

When Squeak finally speaks, her voice is soft and airy. "Alright, here goes. One: Roman once got lost in a department store for two hours as a child. Two: His first pet was a dog called Rambo. And three: he knows how to juggle flaming torches."

She bites her lip again when she finishes and wraps her arms around her narrow midsection. I can't help but let out a silent laugh at how tame these glimpses into Roman's life are when everyone else decided to prod some ribs with their picks.

Brady is the first to share his thoughts on these choices and raises an eyebrow. "Flaming torches? That's a bold claim. If he could really do that, I feel like I'd know about it."

"Is that your guess? You think that's the lie?" Squeak challenges him.

"Is it?" Brady grins up at her, and for a moment I can see they're both getting a little lost in each other's gazes.

Squeak smirks, seeming to suddenly enjoy this attention. "You'll never know unless you guess."

Sacha is crossing her arms, completely unimpressed by this round. I think it's obvious that since the first moment she suggested playing this game, she was hoping we would all uncover some deep, dark juicy secrets about each other. But so far, it's only her who has parted with anything more than trivial offenses. She blows a piece of hair from in front of her face and bobs her feet on the ground impatiently.

"It's the flaming torches, then, final answer," Brady settles.

"Ooh, sorry." Roman elbows his friend gently. "That one is a hundred percent true."

"What? Since when can you juggle with fire? No, scratch that... since when can you even *juggle*?"

Roman doesn't answer. Instead, he searches around the clearing for a moment before finding three small rocks then proceeds to throw them up into the air in turn, sending them flying back and forth between his hands. An impressive feat, given he's several drinks, two joints and at least one line of coke into the night.

"Clown school," Roman says, catching the last rock and throwing up jazz hands. "Well, clown summer camp, age ten."

Brady raises his beer to Roman. "Just when I thought I knew the enigma that is Roman Shwartz, you go and throw another curve ball."

"Or three of them," Squeak adds.

The gusto with which Brady laughs at Squeak's joke is tediously exaggerated, and Sacha looks on, anger etched into her features.

"So, which one was the lie, then?" Seth asks Squeak.

"His pet dog's name," Squeak says. "It wasn't Rambo."

"What was it?" Seth looks back and forth between Squeak and Roman.

"Sprinkles," Squeak smirks and her eyes light up.

"Man, I miss Sprinkles." Roman sighs before throwing up the rocks again to juggle.

Sacha seems to have truly had enough of this PG rated round and shoos Roman and Squeak back onto their logs.

But just as Squeak is about to sit down, Brady grabs her and pulls her onto his lap. I watch as she plays it cool, smiling coyly, but allowing him to make this ballsy move. He nestles his chin onto her shoulder and anyone with working vision can see where this will be going tonight.

Immediately something burns in Sacha's eyes, and the heat of her glower makes my skin prickle.

"Final round," she announces, her tone determined. "And since Squeak is the only one who hasn't been the subject of our game yet, I think *I'll* do her."

CHAPTER TWENTY-EIGHT

NOW

A thousand deafening questions roll through my head as I stand in the bedroom getting ready for the gala, each one fighting to push its way to the forefront of my mind.

Two weeks ago, my life was blissfully uncomplicated. My days were mapped out in a predictable but comfortable pattern, my nights spent wrapped in the arms of a man who I trusted with every fiber of my being to do right by our family. We had left our stained past firmly behind us. We'd done everything we could to move on with our lives and create a wholesome and nourishing environment for our daughter. But something has changed. It's clear from Seth's disengaged demeanor, his hesitancy to answer my questions, his quiet phone calls and the pronounced distance that's fallen between us. And now Sacha says she saw him exiting another woman's car, leaning inside to kiss her goodbye.

I want to believe she's lying, that her words are just poison in my ear and I'm letting them spread through me, unrestrained. After all, she's tried to contaminate our relationship with her lies more times than I can count. But I can't deny that something about this feels different. All the clues are there: Seth being so distracted, that woman in the elevator, Penny's stories of 'Izzy-Bella' visiting on afternoons I'm not home. It all adds up to the obvious. My husband is having an affair.

But then the wheel of doubt begins turning in my mind again. Even if Sacha did see him with another woman, there are many reasons he could have been leaning into her car. He could have been grabbing his papers, or leaning in to shake hands, or countless other totally innocent explanations that Sacha overlooked in her quest to turn me against her brother. And that's if she even saw anything at all. She could have completely made it up.

I just wish Sacha would find a place to go and leave us alone already. Every bit of peace I once knew has been turned on its head since she arrived, and as much as I'm happy to see the relationship between her and Penny blossom, I have to wonder what her endgame is. What does she want from us? Because I have a hard time believing that her only motivation for coming to stay with us is to get to know her niece better.

Sacha can't stand Seth, she's never made any secret of that, and there's no way she'd elect to spend any more time around him than she absolutely has to unless she has an ulterior motive.

Does Sacha really hate her brother enough to insert herself into our lives with the aim of splitting us up?

This isn't the only thing on my mind as I pull on my tight black jeans and tuck my white shirt inside the waistband. I've been living in a state of silent dread since the news of Roman's death. But maybe there's nothing to worry about. The cops haven't shown up at our door thus far, so I'm beginning to feel quietly confident that my gut instinct was right and even if Roman were to have confessed all in a farewell note, he wouldn't have thrown the rest of us under the bus on his way out. I glance at the mirror, adjusting my hair, trying to distract myself from the relentless worry.

"Jade?" Seth's voice pulls me from my spiral, and I turn, forcing a smile, but I can see the hint of concern in his eyes. "You okay?"

"Yeah, just finishing up," I say.

"You've got this." He leans against the door frame, crossing his arms. "The gala is going to be amazing. I'll bet your team's catering will be all anyone talks about afterwards."

I laugh at this, but I hope he's right. I was at the Crumb Cottage until late last night, pitching in to get everything ready. It was after two in the morning by the time I climbed into bed next to Seth, and even then I lay awake half the night, my mind racing around and around in circles.

I bite my lip nervously now as I turn to Seth. I know I need to confront him about what Sacha told me, or these nagging thoughts will never release me from their death-like grip.

"Who's Isabella?" I ask, frankly.

A flash of something passes over Seth's face. "Izzy-Bella? She's Penny's imaginary friend. You know that."

I try again, but slower this time. "No. Who is *Isabella*?"

Seth swallows, a telltale sign that he's nervous. The thing about being in a relationship with someone for well over a decade is that you get to know all their little ticks and tells, and Seth probably doesn't know it, but he is exhibiting every single one of them right now. The lack of eye contact. The sweat above his top lip. The shifting feet. If I ever needed more proof that he's hiding something from me, this is it right here.

"Uh... there's someone called Isabella who works for the Vanguard Career Group, if that's who you mean?" he suggests.

I cross my arms and fix my gaze squarely on him in an intimidating glare. He tries to match it but fails within seconds, when his eyes flash down to his watch. I'm not going to let him off easy this time.

"Isn't it a bit of a coincidence that around the same time you started working with someone named Isabella, our daughter started telling me about an Izzy-Bella coming to our house while I was at work?"

Seth's Adam's apple bobs in place for a moment before he speaks. "I... Wh-what are you implying?"

He looks like he's under a heat lamp that's turned up full. I wish more than anything that this wasn't his reaction. I wish his response was carefree. Because now I know. I know he's having an affair. After all, what innocent man would ever act like this if he had nothing to hide?

"Izzy-Bella isn't imaginary at all, is she?" My voice comes out small.

Seth blinks rapidly. "What? What are you talking about?"

"Stop!" I cry, tears flooding my eyes. "Just stop. An affair is one thing, but how heartless can you be, having this woman in our home while Penny's here? She thinks she's her *friend* now. I can't believe this, Seth! How could you do this to us?"

Suddenly he's by my side, gripping my shoulders tightly. "Jade, what are you talking about? How could you think that? Where are you getting this from?"

I'm sobbing uncontrollably as I pull away sharply from his grasp. "I can't take any more lies! I saw Isabella leaving the building after your *meeting* with her, and Sacha even saw you get out of her car and lean inside to kiss her!"

Seth's face darkens as he grabs the back of his head with both hands. "Sacha!"

"Oh, yeah, blame Sacha for outing your lies! Don't bother taking personal responsibility!" I spit, raging now.

I take a breath and try to calm my nerves, aware that Penny and Sacha are nearby in the kitchen. I don't want them to overhear this.

Seth's face is deep red with a fury that looks as though it could burn straight through metal. "No, Jade. Can't you see what this is? She's trying to turn you against me! This is what she always does. She's done it since the moment we started dating, don't you remember? She likes to play games. She always has. She's feeding you lies!"

I want to believe him, but it just doesn't add up. "Why does Penny's imaginary friend share the same name with this woman you're working with, then?"

Seth rubs his hands down his face, groaning. "I don't know. I... I mean, maybe she heard me mention her name on the phone and just liked the sound of it. You know how kids are. It's a very common name. There's probably even an Isabella in her preschool for Christ's sake."

I sit down on the side of the bed and wipe the tears from my cheeks. "So... Penny has never met Isabella?"

"No! Of course not. All my meetings with Vanguard are at their offices. Well, except for that one here, but that was just because there were renovations being done in their office that day. Both Isabella and David came here and we talked for about an hour before David left to take a call and Isabella went over a few last details with me before following him down soon afterwards. Penny never saw either of them. And I most certainly never kissed anyone!"

My heart gradually begins to slow down to a more normal rhythm. Seth makes a convincing case. He sits down next to me and holds my hand in his, this time maintaining eye contact.

"Do you believe me?"

I search his eyes and find myself melting with relief. "Yes."

He holds me close, and I rest my head on his chest. I should never have doubted him. Of course Sacha was lying, it's what she does. This is just another one of her sick little games.

The problem is, I know how deadly Sacha's games can be.

CHAPTER TWENTY-NINE

I stand back and look myself over in the bedroom mirror. Black jeans, white shirt, slicked back bun and only a hint of mascara and lip gloss. The perfect look to blend nicely into the background as the collectors and high rollers do their thing this evening.

If I'm being honest, I'd rather be on the other side of the fence. But since I promised Darina I'd be front and center tonight making sure the attendees are happy and well fed, I'll grin and bear it. Events like this are incredibly exclusive anyway, and I still can't believe Darina managed to score two tickets for Seth and Penny, mere mortals.

"Is that Penny's dress for tonight?" Sacha asks as I walk into the living room holding a clothes hanger.

Sacha looks ready for a quiet evening at home. In one hand she's clutching a half-full bag of microwave popcorn, in the other a TV remote. Her hair is in the same messy bun she styled yesterday, and she's visibly wearing no bra under her worn T-shirt.

I'm in no mood to speak with her. I feel utterly betrayed (though hardly surprised) by her efforts to insert distrust between me and Seth. We're all adults now, she shouldn't be playing these games anymore. Thankfully, learning of her lies was the final straw for Seth, and he's assured me he's going to talk with her before he leaves for the gala this evening. He's going to tell her that she has three days to find somewhere else to stay, because come next week, she's out on her ass. I'm glad I'll already have left by the time he begins this conversation, because I don't feel like having her bitter attitude aimed my way.

"It's just the dress seems a little drab, you know, for such an *upscale* event." Sacha says the word 'upscale' with her tongue hanging out, I'll assume to emphasize how unimpressed she is by my getting to cater it.

The dress in question is a classy linen A-line in a neutral oatmeal color. It has a black silk sash, and is a timeless piece that Penny will no doubt look absolutely beautiful in.

"There's nothing wrong with the dress and Penny likes it," I say, hanging it on the door for Seth to put her in later.

"If you say so." Sacha stares at it a little longer. "But the color of it looks like the smell of feet. Don't ask me to explain it."

My mouth hangs agape at this, but I'm saved from any more of her bizarre observations when Seth walks in holding something in his hands.

"What's in the box?" Sacha asks him, readjusting the couch cushion behind her.

"First prize trophy for minding my own goddamn business," Seth retorts without hesitation.

I stay quiet, determined not to get involved in this sibling quarrel as Seth walks over to me and places the box in my hands.

"What's this?" I ask, hoping not to get the same answer as Sacha did.

"Well." He smiles. "I figured just because you're working

and can't dress up for the event tonight, it doesn't mean you can't sparkle in your own way."

I open the small black box and inside is a delicate silver pendant necklace with three tiny letters hanging from it. *J*, *S* and *P*: Jade, Seth and Penny. I take it out and dangle it from my fingers. "Oh, Seth, it's beautiful. Thank you!"

A little ball of guilt punches me directly in the gut for having doubted him earlier. This is exactly the kind of thing I've come to expect from Seth over our years together. He's always thinking of me and surprising me in touching little ways like this. He's not a cheater, he's a good man and I never should have let Sacha make me doubt him.

Seth takes the necklace from my hands and spins me around to clasp it behind my neck before standing back to look at me. "Perfect."

I'm still clutching the tiny letters as I arrive at the venue. And forty minutes later, as guests begin piling in wearing luxurious dresses and snazzy tuxes, any drama with Sacha is the farthest thing from my mind as I weave my way through the crowd, tray in hand, balancing an assortment of goodies.

Before long the room is buzzing with laughter and conversation. I silently watch a woman in a shimmering emerald-green dress and a chic professional updo chatting animatedly with a man in a tailored navy suit. They're gesturing toward a massive abstract painting as though there's a lot more to it than just splats of color randomly dotted around. A guitar is being strummed gently in the corner, and the scent of sixty or so different expensive perfumes blend together in the air.

I plaster on a smile and offer lemon tarts to attendees who barely glance my way as they whisk them off the tray before continuing their conversations. And when I bring out the mini raspberry éclairs, I'm confronted by a fridge of a man in a suit so tight it looks about to burst, who takes six of them at once without even bothering to pretend they're not all for him.

I linger close to a group of art collectors and listen in as they debate the merits of a large canvas depicting a shattered bottle of wine with as much heat as if they were discussing politics. I'm not really into the whole art thing, but I do enjoy getting a bite-sized glimpse into the world of the ultra-wealthy who—devoid of the perspective us lesser people still hold—scramble to find meaning and value in seemingly insignificant objects.

I stifle a laugh when a woman in a stunning white gown drops a piece of our dark chocolate ganache tart on her dress and scurries off to the lady's restroom in a state of fevered panic.

I'm just wondering where Seth and Penny are when I see something that makes me stop in my tracks. A woman hugged tightly by a floaty red dress clutches a drink by the bar, her head thrown back as she jokes with a man in a sharp burgundy blazer. He leans in close to her and whispers something that makes her laugh even harder, her head turning my way before she locks eyes with me.

Oh no. No, no, no.

What the hell is Sacha doing here?

CHAPTER THIRTY

THEN

An unpleasant shudder passes over me as I watch Sacha slowly pace the circle. Every time the mood lightens up and we all start to have a good time, she feels the need to step in and make sure everyone is paying attention to her.

But this time, she's putting the focus squarely on Squeak.

Squeak seems about as confused as the rest of us. But there's something else in her eyes, something not quite right. She looks shaky and unstable.

Sacha presses on. "We've all taken our turns to be put on blast. It's only fair that somebody does Squeak. And I happen to know a thing or two about our girl here."

Roman and Seth exchange glances and I see a question pass silently between them, the same question going through my own head right now: What is Sacha up to?

I doubt she knows any more about Squeak than I do, which is practically nothing. I know that she's Roman's first cousin, and she went to our high school. I know she likes Coldplay, because I once saw her scribbling in a notebook covered in stickers of their album covers. And I know that she, like Roman, is an animal activist of sorts, having attended an anti-fur protest with him last year.

Other than that, I can't say I have any other insights into her life. She's always kept to herself, stayed quiet and gotten on with whatever she's doing. Frankly, it's a miracle that Roman convinced her to come with us at all tonight because she's about the furthest thing from a social butterfly I could imagine and it's obvious from the look on her face right now that she'd like to be anywhere but on that log while Sacha stalks around in front of her like a lion waiting to pounce.

The group quiets in anticipation before Sacha raises her voice. "I'm going to tell you two truths and a lie about Squeak. Let's see if you can guess which is which."

Squeak jitters a little where she sits, and the undercurrent of anxiety I see in her movements worries me. Brady is beside her, seemingly oblivious to the tension brewing, his attention fixed on Squeak as if she's the only other person here; something Sacha has noticed too, by the looks of it.

"Let's see... First," Sacha taps her chin, "has anyone else ever wondered why Squeak is so damn thin? I used to think it was an eating disorder, until I found out that her family can't afford to feed themselves. My mom told me she and her friends take it in turns to leave care packages on the Bernottis' doorstep every month just so they don't starve."

Squeak's face pales and her mouth opens.

Whether this is true or not, this sort of fact is not at all in the spirit of the game and Sacha knows it. I don't know what's worse, the fact that she's potentially exposing something so private or that she clearly knows what it's doing to Squeak.

"Um, Sacha," Brady says, his voice uncertain. "That's not... you know... this is supposed to be fun."

Sacha waves his concerns away. "Who's not having fun?"

An awkward silence falls over the circle as the trees creak

and strain above us. Sacha smiles, feeding on our discomfort like a parasite.

I wait for someone to reach out and say something to her, to tell her to stop, but she quickly carries on.

"Second: Why does Squeak always wear cardigans, even in the summertime? That's because she used to cut herself in high school. I know this because she once forgot to lock the bathroom stall, and I found her inside there with a pink disposable razor ripping up her arms like she was carving a roast turkey."

A blanket of silence remains over the group. I can see Squeak's breath hitch, her eyes darting to mine. I want to scream at Sacha, tell her to shut up, but the words stick in my throat and when I glance at Seth beside me, he's too busy trading glances with Roman, who looks as though he's ready to get up at any moment and rip Sacha's throat out. Seth would let him, I'm sure. He'd help out, even.

Squeak's face has frozen. She's staring at the ground, her fingers fiddling with the hem of her cardigan like it's the only thing holding her together. She doesn't say anything, but I can see the way her lips tremble.

"Sacha, stop," I finally snap, unable to hold back anymore. "You need to stop."

She turns to me, a carnivorous grin on her face.

"Oh, lighten up. It's just a game. And I only have one more fact to go."

I can't look at Squeak. I can feel her shame radiating through the space between us, and I wonder if Sacha knows just how much damage she's doing.

But when I look at Sacha, her eyes are practically glowing in the darkness, like she's savoring the moment, and I can see she knows exactly what she's doing. In fact, I'm beginning to wonder if she's been planning this the whole time. In Sacha's eyes, Squeak is a threat. Someone standing in her way of Brady. This was never a game. It's Sacha's own sick brand of torture.

"And third," she continues, before anyone can stop her. "Remember when Roman told us that crazy story about his uncle robbing the drugstore with a hatchet? Well... turns out that's not the real reason he's in jail for the next twenty years. *That* sentence came after he kidnapped his own daughter when she was ten years old and kept her locked in his car for a week, dirty and starving." Sacha finishes, locking eyes with Squeak.

I feel bile rise in my throat, Sacha's callous tone making me sick to my core. Squeak's face is as white as a sheet.

Sacha watches her hungrily, her smile never faltering until she suddenly holds up a finger and pouts. "Oh, wait... I was supposed to add in a lie, wasn't I? Silly me. Those three facts were all completely true."

Roman jumps up, fists by his side. Brady shifts where he sits, clearly uncomfortable now, his eyes darting to Squeak, who looks as though she's just been punched in the chest. Her mouth opens and closes, but no sound comes out. I don't know what to do. I want to grab her, hug her. But I don't think anything can help her feel better after what Sacha has just done.

Sacha sits down again, knowing she's hit her mark. And when I see the look of satisfaction on her face, I realize I'm no longer looking at the person I once thought I knew. Sacha's not just a rebel or a wild child or a loudmouth bitch, she's something much worse.

And she's not just trying to put Squeak down. She's trying to destroy her.

Before anyone can stop her, Squeak rises up and flees the circle, stumbling unsteadily as she runs for the trees, her shattered cries swallowed by the darkness of the woods beyond.

CHAPTER THIRTY-ONE

NOW

The blood-red dress hugs Sacha's body like it's been stitched into her skin.

I can't deny that she looks incredible, her auburn hair flowing gently around her shoulders like a waterfall of silk, her dress hugging her curves like a vise grip. But it looks completely out of place as she stands by the bar, trying to blend in with the classy high society types.

I blink, hoping I'm mistaken, and Sacha hasn't really just shown up here unannounced. But no, it's definitely her.

How the hell did she get in? This gala's supposed to be exclusive, the kind of event where you need an invitation and a trust fund to even think about stepping through the door, and I'm pretty sure she doesn't have a ticket. I don't know what kind of strings Darina had to pull to score tickets for Seth and Penny tonight, but I do know Sacha isn't the type of person who has the connections needed to get into an event like this.

Maybe she slipped past the staff somehow or conned her way inside. But she must have just arrived, because there's no way I would have missed her earlier. I've been working the floor for the last hour, busy as hell, but not nearly busy enough to overlook her being here. A dress like that is not the type to go unnoticed.

My eyes scan her, taking in the details. It looks like she spent hours getting ready, but I know that's impossible. Only two hours ago, she was sprawled on the couch in our apartment, wearing that ratty old T-shirt of hers, yesterday's unbrushed bun still perched atop her head. How did she go from couch potato to this so fast?

And if she did get a ticket for tonight, why didn't she mention it to me? She had every opportunity. She didn't say anything about coming to the gala, and it's definitely the sort of thing she would have reveled at flaunting in my face. She'd have wanted me to know all about her plans to rub elbows with the high rollers while I'm stuck serving hors d'oeuvres to people who wouldn't even notice if I tripped over their feet. But she never mentioned it. Not once. Instead, she just showed up and parked her ass at the bar, like this is a regular Saturday night for her.

The only explanation is she's here to stir up trouble. And I'm not in the mood for her antics tonight.

I wish Seth would hurry up and get here. Maybe he could explain why his sister has suddenly materialized here, dressed up like she's about to hit a red carpet when she's supposed to be in our apartment, packing her bags before he kicks her to the curb.

I don't know what to do. If I confront Sacha and ask her how she got in, she's going to make a scene and I'm not supposed to be seen speaking with guests, let alone arguing with them. The last thing I need right now is for Sacha to get me fired.

She's talking with the guy in the burgundy tux, his laughter echoing across the room as she flashes him a grin that could charm anyone and everyone, except the people who really know her.

I want to scream at her to leave, to go back to the couch and the sweats and the takeout containers and the belongings strewn around our living-room floor. She doesn't belong here. My grip on the tray tightens and I can feel something ugly stirring inside me.

I spot Darina talking with a tall woman in a sleek black dress who I recognize from a photo hanging below a piece of work displayed here. Hopefully she'll be distracted for the next few minutes because I need to call Seth and see what's going on without Darina noticing and calling me out over using my phone.

I keep my head low and make my way to the back of the room, ducking behind a large ficus plant before pulling my phone from my back pocket. But just as my finger is hovering over Seth's number, I spot him and Penny—nearly eclipsed behind Mr. Six Éclairs—inspecting a large glass bird.

I glide through the crowd, trying to shrink into the background before pulling Seth aside. He turns, a glimmer of surprise crossing his face, quickly replaced by a huge smile.

"Jade! It's incredible here. And the food is unbeliev–"

"What the hell is Sacha doing here?" I cut him off, forcing a smile in case Darina happens to look over. "She wasn't invited."

An irritated look clouds his face. "She insisted on coming, I couldn't stop her."

"Where did she even get a ticket?"

"She used Penny's. She said she'd tag along and chance that they'd allow Penny in without a ticket since she's so small. Unfortunately, she was right. I was hoping they'd say no, and Sacha would be forced to go home."

"Why would she even want to come?" I press, my voice low, trying to keep it between us. "I thought she'd be mad at you once you told her you're kicking her out next week. You *did* tell her, right?"

"Yes! Of course I did. And she agreed to leave by the middle of next week. But then she started going on about wanting to spend her last few days here with Penny and that's when she had the idea about the ticket."

I glance down at Penny and suddenly it hits me: she's wearing her floral poly-blend dress with the tutu skirt—a tacky piece I picked up at a chain store one day after she begged me for it. Not the classy oatmeal linen dress with the black sash that I'd specifically selected for tonight.

"What happened to the dress I picked out for Penny?"

"Oh." He looks down at Penny, who is now poking at the glass bird. "Sacha was the one who got her ready. I guess she picked this dress instead."

My mouth hangs open. I can't believe this. She knew I wanted Penny to wear the linen one tonight. I'd hung it up specifically, ready for Seth to dress her in before leaving. But Sacha purposefully took over that job so she could make the switch at the last moment. She made no secret that she didn't like the outfit I'd picked out, and she's put my daughter in a dress that's better suited to a children's birthday party than an evening at an upscale art gala.

From across the room, Sacha's eyes meet mine. The look of satisfaction behind her smile is infuriating. Suddenly I feel unmoored, like I'm standing on a cliff edge and Sacha is the wind that threatens to push me right over the edge to the jagged rocks below.

Ever since she arrived at our apartment, she's been playing a game. A game she's enjoyed playing for years. The rules of which are simple: she sprinkles seeds of doubt into my head, tries to turn me against her brother, and pushes all my buttons before she sits back and watches on with glee as my discomfort and paranoia grows.

I'm sick of this game. And I'm sick of her.

I try to catch her eye again, to show her that she can't shake me, that I'm not going to let her mess up the life I've built with her lies about Seth having an affair, about Izzy-Bella not actually being imaginary, and with her feeble attempts to undermine my parenting by making clothing decisions for Penny. But she's already turned her back to me, leaning in to talk again with the guy in the tux. She's right up close to him, flirting like a pro, and I'm sure it's all fake. Because clearly this isn't about her wanting to come to the gala, or about spending time with Penny. She's trying to push my buttons. Make me feel like I don't have control. But why?

What does she stand to gain?

CHAPTER THIRTY-TWO

The gallery is filled with an air of grandeur, everyone's milling about, mingling and making sure their faces and names are being noticed among the many more notable ones, but all I can see is Sacha.

She's attracted a crowd of about six men who all appear to be enthralled by her apparent confidence at critiquing something called *Elysian Echo*: a large, unremarkable stone piece in a soulless shade of gray. It's the kind of thing that looks like you'd find it by the bushes in a parking lot but has now been plopped onto a pedestal triumphantly. I half expect it to start rolling away like a rebellious donut.

Sacha knows nothing about art; of this I am entirely sure. She once said that most modern art looks like someone covered their eyes at a hardware store and taped whatever they found themselves pointing at to a watermelon. So, I'm a hundred percent sure that as she entertains these men now, she's either talking out of her ass and somehow making sense, or these particular guys would still be hanging on her every word if she were merely reciting the lyrics to 'Gangsta's Paradise'. She has that effect on men. She makes absolutely sure of it.

I've only ever seen one guy dare to defer his attention from her on to another female, and that girl ended up dying within hours.

I shudder thinking about that night. Sacha's cold-hearted stare. The look of betrayal on Squeak's face. Her limp body dangling from Roman's arms as he wept for his cousin.

I've worked hard to move on from what happened that night. Seth has, too. But Sacha appearing back in our lives now —spreading her toxic venom and leaving chaos in her wake—has dragged me right back to that part of my life. The part where I couldn't ever seem to find stable ground. And right now, it feels like the floor could begin to crumble underneath me as I walk about the room, offering up tiny pastries and smiling politely while gripping the tray so hard I'm sure it could snap any moment.

The sound of clinking glasses and soft murmurs fill the air, but I'm not really hearing it. I can barely focus on anything other than the throbbing headache at the back of my skull that's starting to roll through me in waves.

I've only just ducked into the office that's doubling as our prep area to refill my tray when the door opens behind me and Sacha floats in as though she owns the place.

"Jade, we need to talk," she says, an urgency in her voice.

"What are you doing in here, Sacha? I'm working."

She looks around as though checking to confirm we're alone, before taking the tray from my hands and placing it down on the table.

"What are you–?"

"This is serious," she says gravely, grabbing my arm. "It's about Seth."

"Don't bother." I shake her hand off my arm. "I already know the truth. I talked to him earlier and he explained that everything you told me was a lie. He never kissed Isabella, he never took her home to meet Penny and he's not having an affair. Penny probably overheard her name while he was on the phone and used it for her imaginary friend—who is, in fact, entirely imaginary."

Sacha purses her lips, her eyes brimming over with a look of pity. "You're wrong. He's lying to you. He's been lying to you for years."

Here we go again. I cross my arms and wait for the lies to start pouring from her mouth.

"Jade, you've always been so desperate to hold on to him that you've become blind to what he's doing. What he's always done. And this time, it's going to be the thing that breaks apart your family." Her tone is somber now, and if I weren't already hardened to Sacha's melodramatic performances, I might be taken in by her empathetic gaze and serious tone.

"He *is* cheating on you. I know he is. And now I have proof. Before we left tonight, I asked Penny to describe her friend Izzy-Bella to me in detail." She sighs. "She described the woman I saw Seth with exactly. And there's more."

I say nothing as she pulls a piece of paper from her sequined clutch and unfolds it before shoving it into my hands.

"What's this?" I ask, looking down.

"I asked Penny to draw a picture of Izzy-Bella."

My eyes scan over the colorful crayon drawing in front of me. The long yellow hair. The black clothes. The red shoes. All crudely drawn in the messy scribbles of a small child, but telling, nonetheless. If I didn't know any better, I would say this is the woman I saw leave the elevator that day.

"You made Penny draw this. You told her exactly what to draw," I say, swallowing hard.

My face feels like it's burning, but I don't want her to see how badly this is eating at me. I don't want to give her the satisfaction.

"I didn't," she replies quietly. "I'm sorry. I know it's not what you want to hear."

I can't just blindly believe her. She's lying again. She's trying to get back at her brother who just told her he's kicking her out. That's why she wanted to come here tonight. Everything about her reeks of desperation. Even her dress with its vibrant red material flashes like a warning sign.

"Do you remember all those years ago when I told you I saw Seth talking with his ex at the mall? Well I lied. They were actually making out. I just didn't have the heart to tell you what I'd seen."

I let this bounce right off me. I've let her lies penetrate my mind for too long. I won't let it happen again.

"And remember when I told you he couldn't keep his eyes off Squeak that night in the woods? Well... there's something else that I didn't tell you. Something that Seth begged me not to share with you. In fact, it's the only reason he hasn't kicked me out before now. Because I told him if he did, I'd finally tell you what really happened that night."

At the sound of Squeak's name on Sacha's lips I snap out of the quiet spiral of doubt she's sent me into. I've had enough of this. I'm not waiting around for her to spew any more vile lies from her mouth. I have a job to get to.

"No. Leave me alone, Sacha. I mean it."

I grab the tray and load it up, determined to get back out into the crowd and do the job I was hired to do tonight.

"You deserve to know," Sacha pleads as I head straight for the door, ignoring her.

Before I leave, I turn back to her one last time.

"I'm done letting you play games with your brother's life.

With *my* life. And I'll be damned if I'll ever let you get close enough to our daughter to play mind games with her, too."

I don't wait for her response as I push my way through the door and back out into the crowd.

CHAPTER THIRTY-THREE

THEN

Everyone sits in stunned silence as we stare in the direction Squeak ran off. Everyone but Sacha.

"Talk about an overreaction." She blows air through her teeth.

Then all of a sudden, it's like someone has hit the play button. Roman lurches forward and grabs Sacha by the arm, his fingers biting into her flesh. "What the hell was that? What exactly were you trying to do?"

"Get off of me!" Sacha pulls her arm away from him. "I was just playing the game. It's not my fault Squeak can't take it on the chin like the rest of us."

Seth scowls at his sister before directing his attention to Roman. "We need to go find her, it's dark and she could get hurt out there."

Roman nods, already moving in the direction Squeak disappeared, his eyes scanning the darkness.

I'm so angry at Sacha that I can barely hear anything over the thudding of my pulse in my ears, but I know they're talking about setting off in different directions, figuring out how best to find her.

"Brady, stay here with the girls," Seth orders his friend, and Brady nods in return.

Seth and Roman each grab a lantern and head out into the darkness surrounding us, leaving me, Sacha and Brady sitting in silence.

I turn to Sacha, who tips back a beer like she doesn't have a care in the world, and I just can't hold it in anymore. "What is wrong with you? Why would you do that to Squeak?"

Her eyes flick up and for a split second I see something defensive in her expression, like she's thinking of a way to turn it all around. But then it's gone, replaced with a cold, vacant look.

"Just a little fun." She shrugs.

"Fun for who?" I shake my head. "None of the facts you shared about her were anything like the ones in the other rounds."

Sacha holds up a finger. "Excuse me, Miss Righteous, but weren't you the one who told everyone about what I did to Mr. Rashford's car? And about him rejecting me?"

"Those aren't even nearly on the same level!" I shout, standing up. "You just exposed her family's struggles, her depression. And she's not in a good state right now, Sacha. Did you see her? She could barely even stand straight."

Brady sits quietly. He hasn't said a word since Squeak fled.

"She'll be fine," Sacha mumbles. "She's a big girl. If she can't handle a little game that's hardly my problem."

I can't breathe for a second, the anger in my chest rising to my throat, sharp and hot, and I can feel my fists ball up at my sides. "You seriously don't care, do you? You don't care that you just broke that girl, right in front of everybody. You don't care about anyone but yourself!"

Sacha looks bored. It's like she's deliberately trying to provoke me. I want to scream at her. I want to tell her how vile she is. But instead, I push it all down and take my seat on the log again, waiting for Seth and Roman to find Squeak and bring her back safely. The party is over. I don't want to stay a minute longer, and I doubt anyone else wants to, either.

Sacha, clearly done with our conversation, sits down on Brady's lap, draping an arm over his shoulder and flashing a smile like nothing just happened.

"Want another beer?"

Brady shrugs her arm off roughly before standing up, sending Sacha tumbling to the ground below. He looks like he's set to explode, but he keeps his voice low and steady.

"Just stay the hell away from me."

He grabs a lantern, then stalks off toward the treeline and merges into the dark after the others, leaving me and Sacha alone in the clearing. So much for him staying with us like Seth had asked him to.

The rejection seems to slam into Sacha like a physical blow, and her bravado falters. She stares after him for a moment, her mouth agape. Finally, she gets up from the ground and brushes herself off. She sits down and takes a long drink of her beer before wiping her lips with the back of her hand and staring out at nothing.

All I wonder as I look at her tired face is if she's really as empty as she seems. Empty and cruel.

I don't think I've ever hated anyone more than I hate her in this moment. Nothing matters to her. Not her brother, not Squeak, not her reputation. Nothing. I turn away, disgusted by how utterly detached she is from everything except herself.

But a moment later, she says something that surprises me.

"I screwed up, Jade. I... I think I've done something really bad."

I don't know what to say to this. It might be the first time I've ever heard Sacha acknowledge that she's anything less than entirely perfect, and not wanting her to get defensive again, I decide to go easy on her.

"The guys will find her soon, I'm sure. And maybe you can apologize to her then."

Sacha doesn't seem to hear me as her hand runs through her hair, pulling it back tightly to her scalp.

"I... I wasn't thinking. I forgot about what Roman said..." She stops, then stands up suddenly. "I need to go help find her."

I don't know what's gotten into her all of a sudden—an awakened sense of morality roused from its lifetime of dormancy, possibly—but when she grabs the last lantern and rushes for the trees, I have no choice but to follow behind her or be left in the darkness alone.

I expect Sacha to head straight for the path, but to my horror she runs directly into the dense overgrown woods and doesn't slow down as I attempt to keep up with her.

"What are you... Sacha, wait!" I yell.

We're rushing through the trees, not any of them distinguishable from the next and I'm scared that if she keeps up this fevered pace, we won't be able to find our way back to the main path. I'm not concerned for Seth or Roman or Brady, who have been coming here to ride their bikes around since they were ten years old and know these woods like the backs of their hands, but this is my first time here, and I'm pretty sure it's Sacha's first time, too. If we get lost out here in the dark, I don't know what we'll do. We could be wandering around until morning.

The densely wooded area she leads us into is even darker than I expected at this time of night. Even with the moon and stars shining down on us, everything is still bathed in a thick blanket of blackness that presses in from all sides.

"Hey," I call to Sacha. "Slow down, I can't keep up!"

She's clutching the lantern tightly, its faint glow flickering unevenly as it swings about, causing our shadows to move about on the ground.

I've got no lantern, no flashlight, and even my phone is back in my bag at the clearing. I have no choice but to keep following Sacha as she calls Squeak's name out into the night. My chest feels heavy and the beer in my stomach begins to churn as we run, but Sacha seems to have laser focus as she rushes ahead, her head darting this way and that.

"Squeak! Are you here? Squeak!" her strained voice calls out and I want to help shout her name, but my chest is already huffing up and down and I can't seem to catch a breath.

Sacha's voice suddenly sharpens as it bounces off the trees. "Squeak! Answer me!"

Something's wrong. Sacha's acting weird.

This isn't like her. It's like she's not just worried about Squeak anymore, but something else, something bigger. And I can't make sense of it. One moment she was cutting Squeak apart with her razor-sharp words, the next she's frantically scouring the woods in the darkness, desperate to find her. It's like she suddenly grew a conscience in the last ten minutes. Like she suddenly realized that what she did went beyond the standard ribbing and teasing expected in that kind of game and her words could cause irreparable damage for someone as sensitive as Squeak.

But for some reason, I don't think that's what this is. Is it possible there's something else on Sacha's mind? Some other reason she's so desperate to find Squeak?

The trees are packed so tightly now, they swallow what little light leaks from the lantern Sacha's swinging.

"Sacha, can we please slow down? The guys have probably found her already. They're probably all back at the clearing by now."

Either that or they're all back at the trailhead and Squeak is crying into someone's hoodie while we're out here chasing shadows for no reason. Or maybe the guys are still out here like us, looking for her. Squeak could have reached the road and run halfway back home by now, who knows?

Suddenly I'm feeling like this is a useless endeavor and I just want to turn back, go and collect up my things and leave. But I'm stuck following Sacha, since without her I don't have a light to guide me. I try to keep up with her, but the uneven ground trips me up, my sneakers slipping over roots and loose stones, causing my shoelace to come untied. I stumble and nearly fall, my voice catching in my throat.

"Stop! Can you just stop, please? I need to tie my laces."

Sacha finally slows down and swings the lantern out toward me.

"Thanks," I say, reaching down to tie my shoe.

I kneel, fumbling in the dark, my fingers clumsy and hot. "Listen, can we just turn back now? She's not out here, or if she is, she obviously doesn't want to answer us."

I don't blame her, either. Squeak didn't ask for any of this tonight. She didn't even elect to come. Roman brought her along and I'll bet he's regretting that decision more than anyone else right now.

"Can you shine the light over here? I can't see my laces."

There's no answer.

"Sacha?" I look up, but she's not there.

My heart begins thudding so hard in my chest that I'm sure it will echo, but all I can hear around me as I get up and turn in circles is the rustling of my footsteps and the sound of my own ragged breathing.

"Sacha!" I scream, my eyes darting frantically as I spin around, squinting to see through the trees.

A deep ache spreads through my chest as I realize I have no idea which way we just came from. I have no sense of direction, no light to guide me, and Sacha seems to have been swallowed up by the dense thicket. It's just me, alone in this suffocating blackness. I can't see beyond a few feet in front of me. I clutch my arms, trying to calm myself, but panic courses through me.

"Seth! Brady! Roman!" I yell out, my voice cracking.

There are six of us out here tonight, somebody has got to hear me, surely? But there's nothing other than a horrible silence broken only by the rustle of leaves and branches creaking.

For the next ten minutes, I walk slowly back in the direction I think we came from, but it's impossible to be sure. The woods feel different now and it takes everything in me not to sink down to the ground and weep like a child separated from her mother in a grocery store. Suddenly, I hear voices just beyond me, and I finally spot a shallow beam of light in the distance.

CHAPTER THIRTY-FOUR

NOW

The tray is too damn heavy, and my arms are already starting to ache, but I keep moving about offering samples of our baked goods to men in expensive suits and women dripping in jewelry, who barely feign interest as they make their selections.

There's about an hour left until I can go home and rest my legs, soak my feet, and maybe even convince Seth to massage them. But for now, I'm stuck gliding around in flats that are scraping the backs of my heels as the music swells through the gallery.

It's live jazz now. Three young men playing drums, double bass and sax, the soft sounds drifting through the air as people stand around, their heads nodding, their eyes always scanning. For what, I don't know. I just know I don't want to be here, or around these people any longer.

I spot Sacha again, her red dress standing out like a drop of blood on white paper, and watch as she lifts a glass from a passing tray, before she turns and I see that she's holding hands with Penny. I look around, but Seth is nowhere in sight.

Before I know it, Sacha swoops Penny up into her arms and my daughter squeals, her legs kicking with glee, arms thrown around her aunt's neck like this is the best night of her life. And maybe it is. She's four and it's well past her bedtime, a real adventure for someone her age. One that I can't even share with her because I'm working.

They spin around to the rhythm of the music and when Penny laughs, people turn to look, smiling at them as they dance as though they're the most adorable mother-daughter duo. Of course, Sacha beams and laps it up. She probably wouldn't correct anyone if they asked.

I should be the one holding Penny, spinning her, making her laugh like that. But I'm stuck wearing black and white, sweating under these lights, dodging art snobs and their wine-soaked opinions. I'm the one picking up dropped napkins and plastering on a fake smile while Sacha slips about the room like they threw this party just for her.

She doesn't care that she's slowly been poisoning my mind. Whispering lies, planting ideas in my head—about Seth, about what he's really doing when he's not with me—trying to turn me, twist me into someone who doubts the man I love. And maybe she sees the cracks. Maybe that's all she ever wanted. To pick apart her brother's life bit by bit, knowing the best way to get to him is through me.

But I don't believe her lies anymore. And once she leaves our apartment next week, I won't ever let her return. Seeing how much Penny adores her stings my heart, because I know what Sacha does to people. How she pulls them close and cloaks them with her charm just to turn around and burn them later. I've seen it. I've lived it. And no matter how much Penny loves her, no matter how much it seems like Sacha loves her too, I can't let it go on. I can't let her get her hooks into my daughter.

I keep my head down, tray in hand, weaving through clusters of clinking glasses and murmuring conversations. As I wipe down a tray, I watch Penny wave as Seth exits from the bathroom and makes his way back to them, her fingers still clutching Sacha's neck.

As I work my way around the room, I try to just ignore it, but every time I catch sight of Sacha holding my daughter I feel like snatching her up and running out the doors with her.

Soon, the music stops and someone clinks a glass. Everyone turns to stare as an older woman in a deep-green tweed jacket and matching pencil skirt taps her glass and holds it up, waiting for the crowd to hush. When her voice begins to rise above the chatter, praising the artists, their talent, something about the wonderful turn out tonight, the importance of supporting the arts, I stand to the side of the room, out of everybody's way and scan the crowd absent-mindedly. My heart nearly stops when I spot a face I've seen before.

She moves through the crowd, her long blond hair draped delicately over her shoulders. She's wearing a silver sequin dress and has the kind of smile that belongs in a magazine. I recognize her immediately.

Isabella.

I don't understand. Why is she here? Is she an artist? A collector?

My eyes flick to Seth, and for a second I forget to breathe. He's spotted her too. He looks surprised when she approaches him, but the smile on his face says everything when she stops beside him to talk, standing close enough that I can see their body language, the way he's leaning in and the kiss he plants on her cheek. It feels like a blow to the stomach.

But nothing in the world could prepare me for what happens next.

A sudden burst of noise cuts through the room, an unmistakable, delighted shriek, and my breath catches as I turn just in time to see my daughter break free from Sacha's arms and bolt across the gallery in her little patent shoes.

"Izzy-Bella! Izzy-Bella!"

A cold numbness spreads through me as I stand, rooted to the spot, watching in horror as the moment unfolds. The glittering art, the gleaming smiles, the distant voices, they all blur around me. All I see is Penny, her little legs pounding across the polished floor with all her might.

She throws herself at Isabella, wrapping her tiny arms around her waist like this has happened before. Like they know each other. Like this is far from the first time she's ever seen her.

The tray in my hands tilts. A few tarts slide to the edge and teeter threateningly before my hands slip and the whole thing goes clattering to the floor.

CHAPTER THIRTY-FIVE

I push open the door and throw my keys into the bowl on the stand, the clink of metal echoing through the hall.

It's after midnight and I'm so exhausted I can barely even stand. It feels like every bone inside me has been stretched to breaking point but the strain on my body pales in comparison to the aching feeling sitting deep inside my heart.

Of course, Seth had heard me drop the tray earlier. He'd rushed over to me, abandoning Isabella and leaving Penny with Sacha. He bundled me into the privacy of the prep room, trying to explain it all away but I couldn't even listen. His words felt like white noise and all I could hear was Penny's delighted voice calling out that woman's name.

I pushed him away. I told him to take Penny home. To leave me alone.

Darina had walked in, her face clouded in concern after the scene I'd made with the tray, asking if everything was okay. I'd made my excuses and rushed to the staff bathroom to straighten myself up before getting back to work. By that point, Seth and Sacha had left with Penny, and I spent the next hour desperately avoiding looking in Isabella's direction.

Had I caught that woman's eye, I don't know what I would have done. Ruined both my and Darina's careers most likely. I doubt she'd ever be hired to cater for an event again after one of her staff members pulled every last strand of shiny blond hair from the head of a guest and stuffed it down her throat.

Somehow, I managed to make it through to the end of the night without making another scene, but every single moment was another torturous reminder that I've been blind this whole time.

Sickeningly, Sacha was telling the truth. I've allowed myself to be lied to and manipulated by Seth.

It didn't help that two of the catering staff bailed early, leaving only a few of us to clean up the mess, lugging crates of leftover supplies back to the bakery. Now I'm tired, upset, and all I want to do is collapse into bed and sleep for twelve hours, though that's a joke. Penny's going to be up in six hours, demanding breakfast. And anyway, I can't bring myself to sleep in a bed next to Seth tonight, my skin crawls just thinking about it.

Every time I close my eyes, all I can see is Penny's beaming face, her little hands clutching on to the legs of the woman she's come to know as Izzy-Bella. A woman who was never in her imagination at all. A woman who was always very real.

And Seth tried to dismiss it, tried to make me believe there was no connection between the Izzy-Bella our daughter couldn't stop talking about and the Isabella he's been working closely with these past few weeks. But it couldn't have all clicked into place faster, witnessing Penny's reaction to her arrival.

My husband has been having an affair. Tonight confirmed that for me with a clarity so bright the image is still burned into my eyes. Not only has he been lying to me, but he's been attempting to shut Penny up, trying to keep her from talking about Izzy-Bella in case I figured out she wasn't really imaginary, but a frequent visitor to our home. And it took Sacha, of all people, to help me see the truth.

A painful thought hits me. Maybe Sacha has always been telling the truth. Maybe she did see Seth kissing his ex-girlfriend all those years ago. Maybe he did spend that night in the woods staring longingly at Squeak before everything went so horribly wrong.

I guess I'll never really know.

So no, I won't be sleeping next to the man who has spent weeks lying to me, and maybe years betraying me. And since the couch will still be occupied by Sacha for the next couple of nights before she leaves, I guess I'll be sleeping on Penny's floor.

I quietly grab a spare blanket and a pillow from the cupboard in the living room, careful not to wake Sacha, and begin for Penny's room. Her floor won't be comfortable but at least I won't have to see him lying next to me.

I hear the soft hum of the refrigerator and the distant sounds of the city outside as I creep past the couch, trying not to make a sound.

"Jade?"

My shoulders slump and I turn slowly to see that Sacha's not asleep, but getting up, as our eyes catch in the dim light. She's still wearing tonight's makeup, now smudged around her eyes, but her hair is back in the messy bun she always ties it up in when home and she's sporting that ratty old T-shirt again. Nothing like the glamorous look she had at the gala earlier.

"You believe me now, don't you?" she asks quietly.

I just want to sleep. I'm exhausted. And whatever this is, it feels like a trap I don't want to step into.

I let out a long sigh. "Sacha, it's late."

She shifts, tucks her legs underneath her and speaks again,

quieter this time. "Now you know why he's kicking me out. He's trying to keep the truth from you. And not just about Isabella."

I hesitate, my throat tightening. I know she's waiting for me to ask more. And maybe I want to, but I can't bring myself to do it yet. If this is about that night in the woods, it's probably best left for another time. I'm already hurting and I don't think I can take any more right now.

She keeps her voice low. "Everything I told you tonight was true. Everything. He's just really good at hiding the truth from you. He always has been. But... you do believe me now, don't you?"

I do. But I don't want to say it out loud. Then it'll all become real.

"I don't know," I whisper. "Maybe."

She looks down at her hands, then back up at me. "Are you going to leave him?"

I don't have an answer. I can barely even think right now. I want to curl up and forget about all of this. I want to go back to pretending everything's fine. But I know I can't.

"I don't know," I finally say. "What do you want from me, Sacha? You want me to divorce him? You want me to–"

"I just want you to finally see who he really is, after all these years. Who I've always known he is. I want you to believe me." She lowers her gaze for a second, then looks back up at me with something almost longing in her eyes. "I've been trying to tell you for so long but you were too in love to see it. Seth is not a good person. He never has been."

I swallow, my throat tight. I can't have this conversation with her tonight. I need to sleep. I need to think. I say nothing more and start for the door but Sacha calls to me quietly as I'm leaving.

"Just think about how he acted when he arrived back to the

clearing that night, Jade. When he said he couldn't find Squeak... I could see you didn't believe him."

I stand there for a long time, the memory flooding back to me uncomfortably. Finally, I turn away and walk down the hall. But when I reach Penny's bedroom door, Sacha's words keep ringing in my ears.

Seth is not a good person.

CHAPTER THIRTY-SIX

THEN

After what feels like an eternity of walking around blindly searching in the dark, I finally find my way back to the clearing, my whole body sagging with relief. But the relief doesn't last for long when I see that the only other person here is Roman, pacing back and forth, phone pressed to his ear. He spots me and pulls it away, locking the screen.

"Was that Squeak?" I ask, pointing to his hand.

"No." He shakes his head, eyes flicking to the screen as if expecting it to light up any second. "I keep trying to call her but her phone's off. Where's Brady? I thought Seth told him to stay here with you and Sacha."

"We all went off separately, to look for Squeak."

Roman eyes me skeptically. "But you don't have a lantern."

"Sacha took the last one, then ditched me."

His brow creases. "You okay?"

"Yeah," I lie, knowing he's got bigger problems than worrying about me right now.

The silence stretches between us and the only noises I hear are the tree branches swaying in the night. It sounds like doors creaking open all around, and suddenly the clearing feels more like a trap than a safe haven.

"You know Sacha was wrong about Squeak," Roman says quietly. "About her dad. My uncle. He didn't kidnap her. He just took her away for a few days. He knew the cops would find him after he robbed that store, so he picked her up outside of school one day and asked her to come with him down the coast. They spent the days playing at the arcades and eating fast food before the cops caught up with them and took her home. She told me it was the happiest she'd ever been. That's not how the lawyers spun it though. They said he'd abducted her, kept her away from her family."

Roman looks sad for his cousin. I wish I could say something to help, but nothing seems to come to mind. I finally break the silence, my voice low. "I'm going to start packing up everyone's stuff. Once we find Squeak, we should really get out of here."

I begin collecting up discarded bottles and putting them into the nearly empty cooler before gathering everyone's scattered belongings and placing them inside their bags, searching the ground to check I haven't missed anything.

Everything's gone wrong tonight. Sacha ruined everyone's good time. Squeak ran off. I got lost in the dark and now... well, now I just want to go home.

We came out here to have fun, to party, to unwind. But it's turned into a nightmare.

I hear a noise and turn to see Sacha bursting into the clearing, her eyes avoiding both Roman's and mine as she sinks down onto a log and hugs her arms tight. I glance at Roman, who looks at Sacha with a mix of worry and irritation.

"Did you see Squeak?" he asks.

She shakes her head in a quick, jerky movement. She's calmed down since I last saw her, the urgency she had earlier at trying to find Squeak now gone. She's probably just coming down from whatever she took. Her eyes are tired, not worried or frantic like before. Maybe she's sobered up enough to realize she doesn't care about where Squeak is, after all.

I watch her for a second longer, trying to read what's going on behind her glazed eyes. She looks about as ready to go home as I feel.

Roman's shaking his head. "If my mom and aunt find out I lost Squeak, I'm dead. I was supposed to be looking out for her tonight."

"She's not a kid, Roman," I say. "But I get it. I'm sure she'll be back soon."

Before we can figure out our next move, Brady appears. He stops abruptly, taking in the scene; me, Sacha, Roman, the woods stretched out behind us.

"Anyone find her?" he asks.

"No," Roman says. "And my aunt's going to kill me if she finds out about this."

"Where's Seth?" Brady looks at the three of us, but nobody answers.

"Has anybody seen him since he left to go look for Squeak?" Roman asks.

The weight of this question hangs in the air and I spot Sacha's gaze flick toward me, something hiding behind her eyes before she looks away again.

"I didn't see him," she finally answers.

I say nothing.

Everyone is here except Seth and Squeak, and Sacha's earlier words play back in my mind.

Even your idiot boyfriend has been staring at her all night.

But before I can begin torturing myself over it, Seth walks back into the clearing alone, looking disheveled, his shoes covered in dirt.

"Did you see her?" Roman asks him.

Seth looks slowly around the group. "No."

That's when I hear it in his tone. The tremor in his voice. I know he's lying.

Roman's fists clench at his sides. Something in the air feels weird. And the look of disgust that Sacha gives Seth only adds to my worry.

Everyone's back now. Everyone but Squeak.

"She probably just went back to the cars," Brady suggests. "Maybe we should all head back and see if she's there."

Roman stares out into the night, his expression is blank. "Okay. Let's do that."

A sobered silence falls as we gather our things and get ready to leave, none of us much in the mood to talk. When Seth tries to catch my eye as he passes me my bag, I look away. And when he tries to take my hand as we set off for the main path, I shake it off, putting my hands in my pockets.

CHAPTER THIRTY-SEVEN

NOW

The waffle iron hisses with a satisfying sizzle as I pour the batter inside. Penny is waiting eagerly at the table, legs swinging back and forth like little pendulums while she tries to be patient.

It's Sunday, and that means waffles for breakfast and pajamas until midday. This morning she's wearing her pink cotton sleep set with unicorns, and despite having been bundled off abruptly from the gala last night, she seems blissfully unaware of the fact that life as we know it is about to come crumbling down around us.

I haven't spoken to Seth since he left the gala, but the same question has been swirling around inside my head since I lay down to sleep on Penny's floor last night: How did we get here?

Just two weeks ago, I couldn't fathom us having marital issues. We never fought. We never shouted. We never let things fester between us. I even looked down on the couples we knew who couldn't find a way to make their relationship work. I thought they just weren't trying hard enough. What a sanctimonious fool I was.

Seth and I never had the perfect marriage, after all. And I could put all the work in the world into trying to save our relationship, but what would it count for when all I get in return is a man who lies, cheats and then lies some more just for good measure.

I open the lid of the waffle iron and lift two perfectly golden waffles out onto a plate, drizzling a generous helping of my homemade blueberry syrup on top before serving it to a squealing Penny.

"Waffles!" She claps her hands excitedly.

I smile, gripping on tightly to this feeling and storing it safely away inside my heart. I'm going to need it.

I watch as she dives in with gusto, her fingers gripping the fork tightly as she attempts to shovel adult-sized bites into her tiny mouth. I laugh at her enthusiasm, and just for a moment try to pretend like everything's normal. This is just a regular Sunday morning. But that fantasy gets swept away when I hear Seth's footsteps.

He walks into the kitchen, and I purposefully avoid making eye contact with him, instead focusing on wiping down the waffle iron.

"Hey, princess. Those look delicious." He kisses Penny's head.

Penny mumbles something back in reply, her mouth too full to make out what, but in my peripheral vision I see Seth turn to me.

"Jade, can we talk alone?"

His familiar Sunday stubble shadows his chin. The dark circles under his eyes are new, though. His pleading gaze is fixed on me, but I don't feel in any rush to talk to him about what happened at the gala last night.

"I'm busy," I say dismissively as I swipe the cloth over the grill. I can see him standing there, waiting, but I don't move.

He steps closer, his voice dropping to a quiet plea. "Please, Jade. Just for a minute. I need to say something."

I abandon what I'm doing and step back, leaning against the counter and wiping my hands dry on a towel. "I don't want to talk."

Penny doesn't seem to notice the tension. She's busy using her fork to put lumps of blueberries into each pocket of her waffle.

"Please, we can't do this. This isn't us." His voice cracks a little on the last word and it's enough to make me pause.

I nod silently, because if I don't talk with him now, he might keep up these quiet pleas and eventually Penny will sense that there's a problem.

"Mommy and Daddy need to go talk for a second, okay?" I say to a blueberry-stained Penny. "You just stay here and finish your breakfast."

Penny nods happily before shoveling another forkful into her mouth, her mind on waffles and waffles only.

It's so unfair that we all have to outgrow that kind of unburdened innocence we have in childhood. Especially when the weight of its absence is so crushing.

I glance at Seth on our way to the bedroom and see deep lines of worry carved into his face.

Good.

I want him to suffer. I want him to experience just as much pain as I'm going through plus more. And truthfully, as much as I don't want to hear anything he has to say, I'll be happy to watch him squirm as he says it.

I walk into our bedroom where the familiar smell of Seth's cologne still lingers in the air, the suit he wore to the gala now slung over the back of a chair. The bed is unmade only on his side. My side is still tucked in neatly, and for some reason this of all things is what brings tears to my eyes. But I quickly swallow down my emotions before turning to Seth.

"So you want to talk? Talk."

He closes the door behind him, and for a moment I stare at the bed, wishing I could just bury myself under the covers.

Seth runs a hand through his hair and begins to pace around the room, unable to stand still.

"Okay. I've thought about what happened last night every which way," he says, his voice low. "And... I don't get it. I don't understand what happened."

That's all he's got? That's the elaborate excuse he's had all night to come up with?

I cross my arms tightly over my chest, trying so hard to hold my tears inside. "What *happened* was your girlfriend showed up to the gala and our daughter was happier to see her than she's ever been to see me."

He stops pacing for a moment and for the first time he looks directly at me, his eyes pleading. "I swear to you, Penny doesn't know Isabella. She can't. I don't know how it's possible. She–"

I cut him off before he can go any further. "How much time has Isabella spent here while I've been at work? Have you even been working with the Vanguard group to find a job, or has that just been one big lie as well?"

"Of course I've been trying to find a job." Seth's jaw tightens, and I watch him swallow, the muscles in his throat working like he's trying to hold something back. "I just... there's a lot going on, I'll explain it soon. But you have to believe me that any meeting I've had with Isabella has been on a strictly professional basis. And David is always there with us. Even if I was the kind of lowlife scumbag who would cheat on you, I'd hardly do it with him right there, would I?"

I have no reason to believe that this is true. I only have his word that this David is present at all of their meetings, and that directly contradicts what I know about Penny's 'friend' Izzy-Bella, who apparently visits our home all by herself.

Seth runs his hand through his hair, pacing again, but slower this time. "I didn't know Isabella was going to be at the gala last night. Why would I? We've never discussed anything other than business. But I can't make sense of why Penny thinks she's her friend. All I know is that Sacha must have had something to do with it."

I scoff. "Are you serious? You're going to try to pin this one on Sacha? I swear the two of you are the most dysfunctional siblings I've ever met! Any time something goes wrong in either of your lives you blame it directly on the other. It's time to actually take some responsibility, Seth. This has nothing to do with Sacha."

He's shaking his head like I'm not getting it, but I am. I'm seeing things clearer than I have in a long time. Sacha was right. I've been blind all these years to Seth's lies and I'm just waking up to see that my 'perfect husband' is anything but.

"Let me ask you this." He holds up a finger. "What made you first question whether Penny's friend Izzy-Bella was actually imaginary or not?"

I think back. "Well, Sacha said that–"

"Yeah, Sacha. The woman who Satan himself has to check under his bed for each night," he says sourly. "I figured. So, she fed you lies and then she somehow convinced Penny of the lie, too."

"I'm not listening to this anymore." I begin for the door, but he catches my arm.

"Sacha has been trying to turn you against me for years with her lies. You have to believe me!"

I'm quiet for a moment. I want to believe him, of course I want to. But the more he talks, the more it feels like he's trying to convince himself, not me.

"I don't know why Sacha showed up here when she did," he continues, his voice tight with frustration. "But I do know that she knows exactly how to get inside your head. Just think about it, everything was fine before she arrived!"

I feel a twinge of doubt, the tiniest thread of uncertainty in my mind. I can't deny that he's right. The biggest concern clouding my mind before she showed up was how soon we'd get back to being a two-income household. Now it feels like my life is in tatters.

Maybe Sacha really is just playing some kind of sick game with us. She's always loved mind games, that much is true. But... that doesn't explain how Penny knew Isabella.

"Jade." Seth clutches my arms and looks deep into my eyes. "You have to believe me. She set this up. She's playing us! Sacha is not a good person."

I pause at his last words, Sacha's voice last night coming back to me like a boomerang. *Seth is not a good person.*

Why does it feel like these two are reading from the same script?

CHAPTER THIRTY-EIGHT

I rub at my neck, trying and failing to ease the stiff cramp before giving up and cutting the crusts off Penny's sandwich.

Somehow the couch was even less comfortable to sleep on last night than Penny's floor, which makes me wonder why it's taken Sacha this long to leave. Not that she's gone entirely, all her stuff is still here. But she texted last night to say she'd be back sometime to collect her things, and I didn't care to ask where she's gone. Maybe she's found a friend to stay with, or maybe she's holed up in some random guy's bed. It sure wouldn't be the first time. Either way it freed up the couch for me, and even though my neck is sorely paying for it this morning, it's still better than sleeping next to Seth, who spent most of yesterday desperately trying to convince me of his innocence.

I pull a pink plastic container from the cupboard and place the sandwich, a yogurt pouch and a granola bar inside it before clipping the lid on top as the sound of cartoons drift in softly from the living room. I don't normally let Penny watch TV on a weekday, especially before preschool, but I haven't got the energy to entertain her myself right now and our routine is messed up beyond all recognition anyway.

I contemplate the prospect of life as a single mom. It's a terrifying thought. Lonely and exhausting, sure, but maybe easier than all this guessing. Maybe easier than pretending I don't feel like I'm losing my mind.

Part of me wants to believe that Seth's telling the truth, because the alternative is that I've either been duped this whole time, or I've been so desperate to keep the life we've built together that I've subconsciously remained blind to it.

"Has Sacha come back to collect her things yet?" Seth's voice breaks through my thoughts and I glance up.

He's wearing a suit and tie, but he's still got that stubble along his jaw and his eyes are sunken. He resembles a man who's just come off of a twenty-four-hour bender, not someone preparing for a job interview.

"No," I say quietly, picturing her wrapped up in some guy's sheets, avoiding the mess she left in her wake.

"She'd better come back for them soon." Seth runs a hand through his disheveled hair. "Or I'll be throwing everything she left in the trash tomorrow. I'm done putting up with her crap. Look at what she's done to us."

I bite my tongue to keep from snapping at him that if it weren't for his betrayal in our marriage, Sacha wouldn't have had any ammo to divide us with.

"Are you working with Isabella today?" I ask, seeing no point in skirting around the issue.

"No. I'm meeting David in preparation for a final stage interview I've got later this morning." There's a glimmer of hope in his voice. "I can't say too much yet, but I'm really hopeful this is the one. I'll know by the end of the week."

I study his face, trying to figure out if this is yet another lie, and this 'final stage interview' with David is actually a secret rendezvous with Isabella. He catches me looking, and his expression softens.

"Look, Jade, things are going to get better. Sacha's gone, and maybe this new job—if this interview goes well and I get it—will be the thing that helps us get back to normal. That's all I want. Our life back."

I look away because I can't promise him that. I can't promise anything, not when I still don't believe him about Isabella. I catch his flicker of frustration at my hesitance, his hope dimming. But I don't care. Above all else, I have to protect myself and Penny.

Penny runs in, her bag bouncing on her back and I bend down, wrapping my arms around her tiny frame and kissing her forehead. "You ready for preschool?"

She nods and I spin her around and zip her lunch and water bottle into her backpack before she toddles over to Seth, who takes her hand and picks up his own bag.

"I should be done in time to pick her up from preschool, but if not, I'll call to let you know," he says.

"Okay."

"Okay, well, uh... we'll see you later." He turns.

"See you later. Bye, Pen, have a great day," I call, my tone softening for her.

This is the most stilted goodbye Seth and I have ever had, and I can only hope Penny doesn't notice how awkward our exchanges are all of a sudden.

"Bye, Mommy!" she calls back, pulling Seth's hand toward the door.

Seth gives me a tight-lipped smile, then slowly follows our daughter.

I watch them leave and wait until the door has shut behind them before letting out a shaky breath and downing the last of my coffee in one gulp. But rather than grabbing my bag and heading out the door to work, I pick up my phone and dial Darina's number.

"Hi, Jade. Everything okay?" she answers on the second ring.

"Hey, Darina. Everything's fine, I just wanted to let you know I'll be in a little late this morning." I massage my neck with my free hand.

"That's no problem. Is everything okay at home? It seemed like there was something going on with you and Seth the other night at the gala. I know it's none of my business what's happening inside your marriage, but... I've been worried."

I've come to really care about Darina since starting work at the Crumb Cottage, but she's one of the biggest gossips I've ever met and if I don't want my marriage woes shared far and wide, I need to keep all the juicy details of my turbulent marriage to myself.

"We're fine. Just a lot on our plates, is all."

"Hmm." She sounds unconvinced. "Well, if there's anything I can do to help lighten the load, just let me know. And don't worry about coming in late today, take as much time as you need."

"Thanks, Darina."

I end the call and grab my keys from the counter, my fingers trembling slightly. I can't believe I'm really going to do this. But Seth's secrets are eating me alive, and if all this talk of meetings and interviews is just a cover for him hooking up with Isabella, I want to see it for myself.

I glance at the clock, my resolve hardening. I'm going to follow my husband. I don't care if it's crazy. I want to find out where he's really going.

CHAPTER THIRTY-NINE

THEN

I walk alone behind the others, my footsteps muffled on the carpet of pine needles and twigs as the wood's shadows encroach from every direction.

Roman and Brady are leading the way back to the cars, though they're so far ahead now that they seem to disappear into the darkness beyond.

Seth and Sacha are silent as they walk on opposite sides of the path, avoiding each other as usual. I walk a few paces behind them, not far enough to lose them but far enough that it feels like I'm utterly alone.

Something is definitely off between them. More than usual. It's clear to me from the way Seth walks, his shoulders tense, attention fixed ahead, while Sacha is quiet for possibly the first time in her life, her body language closed off. My skin crawls, like I've got pins and needles all over. I wrap my arms around myself as I walk.

I saw the way Seth looked when he got back to the clearing. I saw him stare into the woods like he was waiting for something to emerge from the darkness. I know he has a secret.

But the woods have a way of making your mind fill with

shadows and whispers, and right now, I can't tell what's real from what's just my imagination. I think of all the secrets that must be hiding inside these old woods. All the things that have happened here on quiet nights like this, in the cloak of darkness, not too far from the city. There could be anything hidden around here: drugs, money... dead bodies.

The walk back feels longer than the way in. Like the path has stretched and the trees have multiplied. I keep the lantern held firmly out in front of me, but it doesn't do much to help. Everything's still dark. Not even regular dark. Forest dark. The kind of dark that crawls into your mouth and up your nose, trying to suffocate you.

Sasha's sharp inhale as she trips on a tree root snaps me out of my thoughts.

I watch as she steadies herself. She glances back briefly but her lips are pressed tight, and her hands are now clenched into fists by her sides. I can't be sure, but before she turns her attention back to the path ahead, I think I see wetness in her eyes, like she's barely holding back tears. I've never seen her like this before. She's always been so confident and controlled. But she's shown emotions tonight I've never seen from her before.

I wasn't thinking. I forgot about what Roman said...

I think back to what she said earlier before she rushed off in a hurry, scouring the woods for Squeak. I thought she was talking about the hurtful things she'd revealed during the game, but now I'm wondering if it was about something else. Though what that could be, I don't know, because what could be worse than the revelations Sacha made about Squeak's past and private life? No wonder Squeak ran away like she did, I probably would have done the same.

I glance upwards, but there's nothing to see except thick branches that seem to reach out like arms to the dark sky above. The wind picks up, rustling the leaves on the path, and I pull my arms tighter around myself, trying to stop my mind from creeping.

I try to focus on the sound of our footsteps, but they're getting quieter. Roman and Brady are so far ahead that they're nothing more than shadows. It feels like it's just the three of us walking through a void.

Then, something to the right catches my eye.

My feet stop moving and I'm rooted to the spot, but neither Seth or Sacha seem to notice as they continue their quiet march.

I don't call them back. I don't say a word as I stare at the shrubs just beside the path.

I almost thought I'd imagined it, but no, it's right there, unmoving. A splash of color that almost glows against the dark backdrop of the woods. My breath catches. It's something small and soft, like fabric.

I narrow my eyes, trying to see better as I move toward it, holding out my lantern. Standing close, it's unmistakable now—a light-pink garment, lying crumpled on the ground, half-hidden by the underbrush. I freeze, staring at it, my chest tight. I blink, trying to convince myself that I'm wrong, that the darkness is playing tricks on my eyes, but there's no doubt in my mind of what it is.

Squeak's cardigan.

The others are out of sight now, swallowed by the darkness of the path ahead and I'm all alone as I quietly step toward it. My hands tremble slightly as I push aside a branch and crouch down, picking up the soft woolen fabric.

I don't understand. Why is this here? My mind races with every possible explanation, but nothing makes sense.

I look all around, trying to find any other signs of her presence.

"Squeak? Squeak, are you there?"

I edge forward, the bushes brushing my legs, reaching out

like skeletal fingers. I should probably shout for the others, but there's a gut feeling gnawing at me, telling me not to.

"Squeak?" My voice is barely more than a whisper, swallowed up by the space around me.

I take another step forward, clutching the cardigan tight in one hand, the lantern in the other.

Nothing.

I can feel sweat sticking to the back of my neck as I take a slow step forward, craning my neck to see if there's anything there, any sign that Squeak might be nearby.

And then I see it. A shape just out of the corner of my eye.

I gasp and turn, my breath catching in my throat as I stare down in disbelief at the scuffed ground. The tangled braid. The pale face.

And for a long, agonizing moment, the woods go completely still.

CHAPTER FORTY

NOW

I lock the apartment door behind me and immediately begin to question if I should go ahead with this insane plan as I step out into the headache-inspiring lighting of the hallway.

If Seth catches me following him, he'll think I've completely lost it. But what choice has he left me? He insists that nothing's going on between him and Isabella, and this is the only way I can think of to find out if he's lying or not.

I feel queasy at the thought of him and Isabella secretly meeting up for a weekday passion-fest, but I shake the image from my head as I make my way to the elevator.

Before I can even press the button, Mrs. Morris materializes behind me as if from nowhere. I wouldn't put it past her to have been watching from the peephole in her door, ready to pounce the second I walked past.

"Jade, darling!" she cries, and I wince at the volume. "I saw Seth leave with Penny this morning. He doesn't look himself, does he? Not at all. When was the last time he shaved? Do you think he's alright?"

It's too early for this many questions, but Mrs. Morris has always had a knack for catching any changes in our routine and

I'm not sure why I thought this crisis of ours would sneak past her.

I spin around to face her, and take in her outfit: a floor-length caftan in patterns of neon oranges, lime greens and watermelon pink. A giant brooch shaped like a flamingo blinks at me from her shoulder. On anyone else I'd say this was an assault on the senses, but for her, it's practically understated. Her oversized earrings jingle as she leans in slightly, her eyes twinkling with the sparkle of a passionate gossip-hound.

"Seth's fine," I say, forcing a smile. "Just busy, you know how it is. Work stuff."

"But I thought he was still jobless?" she says, her voice dropping to the faux-concerned register she uses when she's fishing for drama.

"Not for long. He has a very promising interview today."

Or he's off to screw another woman. Who can say? There's a fifty–fifty chance of either of these things being true.

She nods approvingly before tilting her head. "You know I notice a lot of things. He walked right past me without even a good morning. That's not like him, is it? Trouble at home?"

I jab at the elevator button like it owes me money. I should have gone for the stairwell. I could have thrown myself down it.

"No, Mrs. Morris. Really, he's fine. We're fine. Everything is fine." I smile. Maybe if I say it a few more times it'll be true.

She frowns, clearly not buying it. "Are you sure? Just tell me, honestly, are you two getting a divorce?"

I bite back the instinct to snap at her and instead give her a tight smile. "I've got to get going, I'm already late for–"

Before I can finish, she clutches my arm, perfume and polyester closing in on me. "I just want you to know I'm here if you need to talk. I worry about you. About little Penny."

"I really have to go," I say, grabbing the elevator door and stepping inside before she can say anything more.

First Darina's pity on the phone this morning, now Mrs. Morris accosting me in the hallway, asking about divorce. As if I needed more confirmation that everyone in our life knows our marriage is hanging on by a thread.

The doors slide mercifully shut before I can say something I'll regret and I exhale, leaning against the wall. My reflection in the dull metal of the elevator doors looks pale and tired. Mrs. Morris was right—Seth does look like hell lately. But so do I. And I hate that everyone sees it.

The elevator jerks slightly as it slows. I straighten my shoulders, smooth down my shirt and try to look like someone who has their shit together.

A little late for that, I guess.

The sunshine drapes a dusty light over the cracked pavement of Maplewood Lane as I crouch behind a sparse, poor excuse for a hedgerow and begin to question my own sanity, playing detective.

Penny's preschool is just across the street, and thankfully Seth doesn't notice me as he stands outside with his eyes fixed on his phone, waiting to send her inside. When the teacher begins filing the children in one by one, Seth gives Penny a kiss on the head before waving goodbye to her and turning to leave.

The great thing about our apartment is that it's close enough to Penny's preschool that we can walk her to and from there. Meaning I can drive to work each day, and Seth can still collect Penny in the afternoons. And the hidden advantage of having only one car right now is that it makes it much easier for me to follow Seth today as he sets off on foot.

He looks over his shoulder before crossing the street but

doesn't see me. He's too busy watching for traffic, and when he finally crosses over and makes his way to the corner beyond, I hold my breath and step out from behind the bush, moving fast. My shoes glide over the cracks in the sidewalk as I try to catch up.

When I round the corner, I spot him up ahead, his back turned to me, heading downtown. I keep a healthy distance between us, trying to figure out what excuse I'd make up if he were to turn around right now and catch me stalking him. But I know he'd immediately see through anything I could say. Thankfully, he doesn't so much as throw a glance behind him and after fifteen or so minutes, he leads us to the street the Vanguard Career Group offices are situated on.

I stop inside a doorway to steady my breathing as Seth pauses in front of the building and pulls out his phone, tapping on the screen for a moment before slipping it back into his pocket.

So, he really is going for a meeting at Vanguard. At least he wasn't lying about that.

Maybe I have nothing to worry about. Maybe Sacha has just turned me into a paranoid mess. And a stalker on top of that. But the thought of Seth nuzzled up close with Isabella continues to circle in my mind. Her perfect blond hair, her brilliant smile, her smart outfits and high heels. And the fact that Seth has been so distant lately, never willing to share anything about what he's doing with these people, makes me wonder what exactly is going on if not an affair. Maybe I'm just underestimating the stress he's under from the endless interviews and job searching.

It's beginning to look like I've been overthinking this though, because he really is on his way to Vanguard, presumably to prepare for the final stage interview he has, just like he told me and I have just spent the morning stalking my own husband through the city like the world's most deranged wife.

When Seth enters the building, I quickly cross the street and stay hidden behind a bulky Range Rover. The Vanguard building has huge glass windows at the front that reflect the sky above while also allowing me to see straight inside. I can see the entire ground floor: an open space with high ceilings, a minimalist design, and a long reception desk that looks like it belongs in a fancy hotel. The furniture is all neutral colors, white, black, and gray. No wonder this job-seeking service costs a fortune, the place looks like a corporate headquarters, not the small-time agency I'd pictured. I guess this explains how Isabella can afford those high-end pantsuits and beautiful shoes.

Through the large windows I follow Seth with my gaze. He's shaking hands with a balding man in a deep navy suit, probably David. Thank God it's not Isabella. I breathe easier. The two men seem to be smiling, animated, gesturing as if they're discussing something exciting. Neither of them makes a move to sit down for this meeting, which I find strange, but I stay where I am and wait it out as I crouch low behind the Range Rover. The monotonous city noise—honking cars, chatter, the hum of traffic—drowns out as I keep my eyes fixed on them both.

A woman walks by pushing a chocolate-coated toddler in a stroller and throws me a strange look. A look that just last week I would have given to a woman hiding behind a huge SUV, spying on an office building. Nobody ever thinks they're the crazy wife until it happens to them. It's a sudden onset illness you don't see coming.

Barely a minute later, Seth pats the man on the arm in a businesslike manner before turning around and stepping out of the building again, alone.

My eyes narrow. Why was that so quick?

Seth said he was meeting David in preparation for a final stage interview, but they were only talking for two or so minutes. That hardly seems like much of a meeting. Did he just pop in there to cover his tracks in case I were to call the office and ask if he'd been in there today? That seems unlikely, but I suppose he is on high alert since what happened at the gala.

Seth is stalking off down the street now, fast, and all I know is that I have to follow him.

I watch him walk briskly down the sidewalk, disappearing around the corner. I keep my pace steady, slow enough so I don't draw attention, but fast enough to keep up with him. For a minute it looks like he's headed back in the direction of our apartment, but suddenly he takes a sharp right, cutting down an alleyway between two run-down buildings. As I round the corner after him, I spot a garbage truck parked nearby, leaking a rancid smell out into the warm morning air and I wince, putting my hand to my nose.

I keep my pace, following him as I try to think of a good reason he'd be going in this direction, but I'm getting more and more concerned by the second. The alleyway is quiet, with nothing but a couple of stray cats and some worn out, anatomically inspired graffiti on the brick walls. Nothing like the polished corporate office Seth left minutes ago.

He pauses ahead of me and glances around like he's looking for someone. I duck behind a dumpster and feel the panic at nearly getting caught constricting my chest.

I stay low, the stench of urine on the ground floating into my nostrils as I begin to quietly wonder if I've gotten this all wrong. Maybe it was never an affair I needed to worry about, but something even darker. Does my husband secretly have a drug addiction? Has he come here to meet his dealer?

I bite my lip, unmoving as I try not to leap to conclusions, and when I risk taking a peek, Seth is exiting the alley and turning onto the next street. I run to keep up and relief washes over me when I see him beeline straight for the Starbucks across the way.

He's just grabbing a coffee, that's all. He's not a cheater, or a drug addict or the kind of guy who hangs around dark alleyways, he was just taking a shortcut to the closest Starbucks for a morning coffee.

I suddenly feel very stupid and am poised to turn around and give up this ridiculous charade when I catch a glimpse of blond hair through the window of the coffee shop.

Seth approaches a woman, his face lighting up in the kind of smile he used to reserve only for me. And then, as if on cue, the woman turns, and I see her face.

It's Isabella.

CHAPTER FORTY-ONE

I wake up at 6am on Tuesday with a jolt, light filtering through the curtains of Penny's room and onto my face. I slept on her floor again, not because Sacha came back to take her previous spot on the couch—we still haven't seen her since Sunday, and good riddance—but because I wanted to be close to the only person I can still trust in my life.

I yawn and rub my throbbing head. I spent half the night curled into a ball next to Penny's bed, wondering what our future will look like. How the divorce will affect her. Because that's the only option now. I won't be taking Seth back, not after yesterday. When I saw him meet Isabella at that coffee shop, I felt like my lungs were collapsing as I struggled to breathe. I didn't wait long before turning away and accepting the truth. I saw enough. Enough to know that Sacha was right. He's been lying to me all along. All of it. All the meetings, all the job interviews, the excuses. They were all just cover-ups for this. For her.

Maybe if I were somebody else, somebody stronger, I would have confronted them right then and there. Told them what they've done to our family. The damage their affair has caused.

But I didn't. And when I got home from work to find Seth playing on the floor with Penny yesterday, I didn't mention what I saw or what I now knew. I didn't say a word. Neither did he. If Penny noticed our lack of communication, she didn't show any signs of it.

I'm just trying to keep it together for her now. And tomorrow, I'll be taking the day off work to go see a divorce lawyer.

The strange thing is, I'm not even angry anymore. I don't know what I feel. Just lost. My whole identity has been wrapped up in my relationship with Seth since I was a teenager. I don't even know who I am as an adult without him. But I guess I'm going to find that out in time.

As I sit on Penny's floor, feeling the weight of it all pressing down on me, I hear a strange noise, like a deep snoring, coming from somewhere down the hall. Seth doesn't usually snore. Something I've always been thankful for.

My father used to snore so loudly that my mother self-banished herself into the spare bedroom for several years until he began using a CPAP machine for his sleep apnea. Once she moved back in and they began sharing a bed again, it turned out they both liked having their own space much better and promptly parted ways again at night. They're in their late seventies now and have been happily living this way for over twenty years, their marriage still firmly intact. Nonetheless, I was relieved when Seth and I moved in together and I found that he never so much as snorts in his sleep.

So, what exactly am I hearing?

I stand up slowly, trying not to wake Penny as I tiptoe out of her bedroom and pull her door shut as quietly as I can behind me, pressing the handle down to keep it from clicking.

The hallway is dim, but from out here I can hear it clearly.

There's no doubt about it, it's snoring. I freeze for a moment, listening. It's coming from the living room.

Did Sacha sneak back in last night? I thought we'd finally gotten rid of her, but this would be just like her, returning to our home whenever she pleases.

This is it. I'm done. She can't do this anymore.

Seth made it clear to her days ago that we'd had enough of her. She can't just waltz back in like she owns the place, especially not in the middle of the night without so much as a text to ask if it's okay. She's not just crashing here whenever she feels like it anymore.

I stride down the hall, ready to wake her up and confront her. The curtains are drawn in the living room and no sunlight is making its way through yet. It's quiet except for the steady snoring that's much louder in here, like a gas-powered chainsaw. I reach the doorway and see a figure sprawled out on the couch, arms thrown over their face, legs stretched out.

"Sacha!" I hiss. "Get up."

The snoring continues. She's out cold.

"Sacha!" I say louder as I flip the switch by the door and watch the room flood with light.

But when I look at the couch, the figure comes into full view and I stumble back, clutching the wall, my eyes wide with terror.

It's not Sacha asleep in my living room, snoring. It's a man. A man I've never seen before. About mid-thirties, sandy colored hair, and splayed out buck-naked on my sofa like a crashed helicopter.

I let out a panicked shriek. "Seth! Seth! Help!"

The man begins to rouse from his unconscious state at the sound of my screams, and I hear the thudding of feet hitting the ground in the master bedroom as Seth responds to my frantic cries for help.

My legs finally start working again, adrenaline activating. I turn around and sprint back down the hall, my heart slamming against my ribs like a sledgehammer as I collide with Seth. His hair is messy from sleep and he's wearing only his boxer shorts.

"What's wrong? What happened?" His eyes dart around, scanning for danger. "Are you hurt?"

I frantically point in the direction of the living room before eventually finding my voice. "There's a... there's a naked man on our couch!"

A look of disbelief passes over Seth's face before he pushes me aside and storms off in the direction of the living room.

"No! Seth, what if he's dangerous?" I shriek, but there's no stopping him.

I have half a mind to go scoop Penny up into my arms and get us both out of this apartment, fast. I don't know who that man is. I don't know how he got in here. But I resist the urge to wake my daughter, as she's probably safest asleep in bed right now.

I follow close behind Seth as he barrels down the hall, our bare feet padding loudly on the wooden floor, and when we hit the doorway, sure enough, there he is. I didn't just imagine it. There really is a strange man standing right inside our living room.

He's halfway through pulling up a pair of wrinkled jeans, his eyes are bleary, and his sandy hair is sticking up in disorderly tufts. When he spots Seth he hops backward, his eyes darting around like he's looking for an exit as he rushes to get his jeans buttoned.

"Who are you?" Seth demands, his voice low. "And what are you doing in our apartment?"

The guy stops mid-button, both hands shooting up like there's a gun pointed at him.

"I, uh, I'm Eddie," he stammers, his voice hoarse. "I'm just leaving, I swear. I didn't know this was your place."

Seth takes a step forward, shoulders squared like he's ready to knock this man straight through the window. "And whose place did you think it was, exactly?"

From up the hall I hear the toilet flushing but I'm so distracted by the angry heat I feel coming from Seth at my side, I don't stop to question it. I'm pretty sure if this Eddie guy blinked too hard, my husband would jump on him.

"I, uh..." He glances past us, toward the hallway, and Seth and I turn just in time to see a figure lean casually against the doorway.

Her hair's a mess, eyes still puffy from sleep, but she's clearly enjoying the show unfolding in front of her, judging by the laugh she's trying to smother with her hand.

"You've got to be kidding me," I mutter.

Seth rounds on his sister. "Why the hell is this man in our home? No, scrap that. Why are *you* in our home?"

Sacha shrugs one bare shoulder, the strap of her tank top sliding down her arm. "We met last night. My friend Gina disappeared with some Portuguese guy in a Corvette and didn't leave me a key to her place, so I brought Eddie back here."

Seth's lips are pursed tightly as he lets out a breath through his nose. "Let me get this straight. You show up back here at my home after I kicked you out, and you bring a man you don't even know with you? Are you serious, Sacha?"

"Sure, I know him." She smirks. "He rents out cars for a living and he's a Sagittarius. Right, Ed?"

Eddie freezes. His eyes bore into Sacha's like he's hoping she'll rescue him. She doesn't.

Seth moves closer to Sacha, almost nose to nose. "He could've been anyone. He could have killed us all in our sleep. We have a child here, Sacha!"

"Oh my God, calm down," she says, stepping back. "We had a few drinks and passed out on the couch. So, I forgot to ask you, big deal."

Eddie shifts awkwardly, pulling the collar of his shirt on over his head before fumbling for his socks on the floor. I step back to get out of his way, but something cold and wet squishes under my left foot and I look down to see a used condom lying discarded on our polished wood floors.

I yelp in disgust and jump back, nauseated.

Seth's gaze moves to the floor beside me, his lips curling downwards and his fists curl up, knuckles sharp. He makes a sudden dive for Eddie, who jumps out of the way and runs behind the couch.

"I didn't... look, I'm getting out of here now!" Eddie stammers as he grabs his shoes and dashes for the apartment door as fast as he can, probably wondering whether the hook-up was worth this much drama.

I shake my head then turn to Sacha, who's biting her lip as she watches him leave. My brain is still catching up, trying to make sense of the total absurdity of it. "You realize I nearly called the cops, right?"

Sacha looks set to fling some useless retort back my way, but before she can say another word, Seth picks up her bag and shoves it to her chest, hard enough to knock the breath from her.

"Get out," he snaps, his voice cold and hard. "Now."

She barely catches her bag before it hits the floor, her fingers clutching the strap. "Seth, stop. Just listen for a second–"

"Get out of our home." His voice is low and deadly serious. "And don't ever come back here."

Sacha's breath catches, and she quickly smooths down her wild hair. "Seth, listen, Penny's been so happy with me staying here. We've been bonding. She loves having me around. You can't just–"

"Don't." He cuts her off with a raised hand, voice sharp and final. "Don't you dare act like you've done something good here for our family. All you've done is try to break apart our marriage and fill our daughter's head with lies. You're done. I mean it. Penny is better off without you in her life and so long as I still have any say in it, you'll never see our daughter again."

"What?" Sacha sets her face to bewildered. "Are you kidding me? You can't just–"

Seth doesn't let her continue as he steps forward, shoving her hard toward the door.

"Get out," he spits.

Sacha struggles against his advances and turns back to point a finger in his face.

"You don't want to do this," she says, her normally unshakable veneer shattered, replaced with raw anger. "You really don't."

She grips her hand to the door frame, but Seth shoves it aside and pushes her out of our home, slamming the door shut in her face.

CHAPTER FORTY-TWO

THEN

I scream for so long and so hard that when I finally stop, the sudden silence rings in my ears.

The others continue to call out my name, searching for me as Squeak lies there in the dirt like a discarded doll, her body stiff, her eyes staring wide and empty into the night. I can't look away, though every inch of me wants to. Her blond braid lays beside her face, tangled with dry leaves and twigs. Her camisole, once white, clings to her body, now stained with dirt. From somewhere beyond, I hear Roman and Brady's voices calling out for me, responding to my screams, but I can't bring myself to answer.

My hands are trembling, and my throat feels raw, like it's been scraped with glass. I can't stop staring at her. Her lips are slightly parted, her eyes hollow and unseeing as her body seems to sink deeper into the earth, as though trying to disappear into it. Next to her, a small puddle darkens the ground, and I swallow down a gag from the acidic and bitter-smelling odor.

The trees around me are a blur through the tears that fill my eyes until I hear leaves crunching and the snap of branches close by, and I wipe at my face with my sleeve.

Roman and Brady crash through the bushes, out of breath from running, their eyes wide and both their gazes laser focused on me.

"Jade, what's wrong?" Roman huffs through gasps for air. "We heard you screaming from the–"

He freezes when he spots her.

He takes a step forward, then another, like he's unsure what he's seeing. His breath hitches when he kneels down next to her and his hands shake as he scoops her into his lap. He whispers her name softly in disbelief.

"She's..." I can't bring myself to say it.

"Squeak... wake up. Wake up!" His voice is suddenly desperate.

But Squeak doesn't move.

Brady's eyes widen, his face deathly pale as he watches Roman plead with someone who will never again be able to answer him. Roman may not have realized yet, but I can see that Brady does. He's wide awake in this nightmare.

Roman's hands shake as he cradles Squeak's head, her braid falling into the puddle of vomit beneath her. Tears choke me as I watch him embrace her so tenderly, and I can't stop the sobs that spill out of me. I clutch my hands in my lap.

Brady quietly kneels beside Roman, fingers trembling as he puts them to Squeak's neck, checking for a pulse. He's silent at first, before pulling them away slowly.

"She's... she's gone."

Roman's voice suddenly tears through the night. "No! No!"

His cries echo through the woods, and I can't bear to look at his face, so torn with anguish.

He's shaking her now, his hands pulling her lifeless body closer to him.

"Squeak! Come on, please!" He chokes back sobs before

looking up at Brady with wild eyes. "Do something! She's my cousin, man! You know CPR! Just do something!"

Brady's lips tremble, like he's trying to find words, but he can't. "It's... it's too late. She's already dead."

These words cut through the air with a sharp finality.

Roman's cries are quieter now, a broken sound that leaks out of him in pieces. All I can make out is the word 'no' whispered over and over.

From the corner of my vision, I notice movement nearby. That's when I see them.

Seth and Sacha are silently watching us. No shock, no tears, no screaming. Their faces are unreadable. And as I look at their unmoving postures, I notice something that I've never really seen before now; they may not be identical, but the DNA that binds them as twins is blindingly clear. Maybe they hate each other's guts, but nature has played an ironic joke on them by making them so alike. But their faces are too calm, and that's what unnerves me the most. It's like they're witnessing a scene they've already watched before.

Seth steps forward and locks eyes with mine. Without a word, he crosses the space between us and wraps his arms around me in a protective embrace but it feels hollow, like he's trying to shield me from something he's already accepted. His grip is firm, almost possessive, and I want to break free and push him away. But I don't. I say nothing.

Across from us, Sacha's vacant gaze is still fixed on Squeak's body. She clutches her arms around herself, rubbing them as if she's cold. Roman is still holding Squeak in his arms, his face twisted in disbelief as if he can't process it, like if he just holds her long enough, maybe she'll come back. Brady is standing a few feet away, pain etched on his face.

The whole scene feels like a bad dream that I can't pull myself out of, and all I can think of is how strange it is that neither Seth nor Sacha are reacting like the rest of us. Like they're immune to the grief, the shock. Like these emotions are already behind them.

The silence in the woods is thick now and no one moves, until Brady puts a hand on Roman's back and clears his throat. "Roman, buddy, we need to call for help. Pass me your phone, I'll do it."

Roman doesn't respond.

"Rome..." Brady shakes his shoulder, trying to break him out of the shock he must be feeling. "We need to–"

"We can't." A quiet voice floats through the air, and we all look up at Sacha. "We can't call for help."

I find myself clutching Seth's arms, feeling a cold dread seeping into me. Though somehow, I knew this was coming.

"We can't? What do you mean *we can't*?" Brady appears stunned. "Squeak is dead. We need to call someone. The cops. Her mom. Someone!"

I watch as Roman lays his cousin back on the ground and stares at the darkened patch beside her. "Sacha is right."

I never thought I'd ever hear someone utter those three words together, let alone when she's suggested something so despicable, so heinous that it's unthinkable.

Roman stands up and puts his hands to the top of his head. "Alcohol poisoning. It must have been. And I'm the one who let it happen. I brought my baby cousin here tonight and then let her die alone."

"What?" Brady's voice rises several notches. "No, Roman, this is not your fault! And *alcohol poisoning*? How does that even make sense? She just had a few beers, maybe a rum and cola, not nearly enough to kill her!"

He's right. It couldn't be alcohol poisoning. Squeak may have been small but she didn't drink enough to take her down. None of this makes sense.

I look at the vomit on the ground, Squeak's blue-tinted lips, and think of how loose and different she seemed right before everything went wrong. Suddenly, all I can think of is that little white bag that Sacha held earlier.

"Sacha, did Squeak take anything else tonight?" I ask.

"What? No. And don't try to pin this on me." Sacha glares at me.

"I'm not trying to pin anything on you. But you know, Roman said Squeak had that heart thing as a child." I pause for a moment, looking down at my hands. "And it might not take much to... you know."

"Overdose?" Roman asks, a crease forming on his brow.

"She just drank too much. We all saw her. She could barely stand up straight by the time she ran off," Sacha says defensively before changing the subject. "Roman is right though, the fault will come down on us. Do you guys want that hanging over your heads forever? This will put a black spot on our futures."

I notice that Seth doesn't speak up to set his rambling sister straight. And he doesn't take his arms from around me. But Brady seems to suddenly snap as he dives forward and jabs a finger straight into Sacha's shoulder.

"*You* did this to her!"

"What?" Sacha scoffs, but I can see fear in her eyes. "I didn't do anything."

"Didn't do anything?" Brady doesn't let up. "Are you kidding me? Everything was going great until you demanded that we all play your stupid game! You bullied Squeak, you spat out her deepest secrets to everyone. That's why she ran off, and that's why she died here alone without any of us here to help her!"

Brady is up in Sacha's face now and I feel Seth's arms slip away from my shoulders as he rushes forward and pulls his friend away from his sister. "Hey, just back off, okay? This wasn't Sacha's fault!"

This may be the first time I've ever heard Seth defend his sister. Brady just shakes his head and spits on the ground next to where Sacha stands, his point made.

"I was supposed to be looking out for her." Roman's words come out in a numbed tone. "My mom... my aunt... how can I...?"

Roman doesn't, or can't, finish this thought but we all know what he's saying. The burden of her death will come firmly down on his shoulders.

"Let's just think about this logically." Seth runs a hand through his hair as he paces. "We brought her out here, we supplied the alcohol, we let this happen. If the cops get involved... I mean, Brady's got that internship lined up, Roman and I have our scholarships. This could ruin all of that. And I'm not saying we don't care. Of course we care. But..."

I blink at him. "You're seriously suggesting we just leave her here?"

This doesn't seem at all like the Seth I know. Accidents happen all the time, and if nobody here is to blame for her death then why should we hide it?

Unless Seth knows something we don't.

My eyes move to Sacha and I see a brief look pass between her and her brother. What is it they're not saying?

"She's gone," Seth speaks softly. "She's not coming back."

"Maybe... maybe I could tell them she wasn't there when I went to pick her up tonight," Roman says, crouching down and holding his cousin's limp hand. "She tried to run away before, when she was younger. She just... I mean my aunt doesn't have to know she's dead. She's her only child. It would destroy her. I don't think she could survive without Squeak."

My stomach flips. This isn't like Roman. I get that he's

scared of his family blaming him for Squeak's death, but is this really what he wants for her? To rot in the woodlands, her disappearance forever unexplained?

"Brady?" I say, almost pleading. "You're not really considering this too, are you?"

Brady is crouching down now, his head in his hands, hair covering his face. He says nothing.

I shake my head, trying to understand what's happening. It's like something has suddenly taken over their ability to reason. Their shock and fear guiding them into darkness. I want to speak up and tell them we can't do this, it's not right. But I'm so shaken that when I open my mouth, only a strangled choke exits it.

"So, it's decided." Sacha's steadfast voice floats through the still night air. "We leave her here."

CHAPTER FORTY-THREE

NOW

My shirt is glued to my front with a mixture of sweat and passion fruit curd and there's a smear of something sticky dried onto my forearm. I'm hot, exhausted, and despite not eating so much as a bite of the many desserts I made this afternoon, I feel like I'm slap bang in the middle of a monumental sugar crash.

I single-handedly made one hundred and fifty individual fruit tartlets today for a fancy heritage club just north of the city. My wrists still ache from shaping pastry like a machine, and all I want right now is to strip off, crawl into the shower and then spend the evening cuddled up reading storybooks with Penny.

I fling my bag down by the door and listen out for her usual clattering and singing, but the apartment is quiet. The kind of quiet that instinctively makes a mom raise an eyebrow. But a moment later I hear soft laughter from the kitchen followed by Seth's voice bouncing playfully. It sounds like they're in the middle of a game.

I'm so glad that Penny didn't witness this morning's drama; her mess of an aunt's stale vodka breath and selfish, entitled attitude; naked Eddie; Seth yelling at Sacha and tossing her out on her ass. But thankfully, we're done with all that now. Sacha's gone for good this time. I don't care that it turned out she was telling the truth about Seth and Isabella's affair, I'm sure I would have found out about it sooner or later without her being here to give me little shoves then watching on in glee at the downfall of our marriage.

Seth still doesn't know that I followed him on Monday, and we haven't even spoken to each other since the incident with Sacha this morning. I have an appointment tomorrow with a divorce lawyer downtown who specializes in family law. I want to discuss my options with him before I break the news to Seth.

I hear the sound of Penny's laughter floating out of the kitchen again, and it's like a balm for my tired heart. That sound, above all others, is my favorite in the world. I would burn everything down to protect it. I lean my head on the door frame, listening to them play a game they call 'rude wombat', and find myself smiling. Despite everything else, Seth's a great father. I'll give him that. He's always been good to Penny, and I know he always will be no matter what happens with us.

I'm about to walk in and say hi when I hear the tone of Penny's voice change suddenly. "Daddy, when is Auntie Sacha coming home?"

There's a long sigh. "I'm really sorry, buttercup, but we're not going to be seeing Sacha again."

"Why not?" Penny whines.

"Because..." I listen to him struggle to find the words to explain the situation to such a young mind. "Because Auntie Sacha is having a hard time learning how to be a grown-up. And it's not a good idea for us to be around her right now."

"Oh," Penny says, as though this makes perfect sense. "Will she be a grown-up tomorrow?"

"No, sweetie, I'm sorry." I hear Seth sigh again. "It's going to take a very long time."

I sit on the edge of Penny's bed, towel-drying her hair while she chatters at me, her arms swinging about as she narrates her day at preschool. She smells like lavender shampoo and she's wearing her bunny print pajamas with the too-short sleeves that she refuses to let go of. They ride up her arms and make her look like a delicious marshmallow trying to escape a s'more.

"...and then Joey put paint in his mouth, but Miss Carol didn't see, so I told her and Joey spit it out on the floor and then I made a cloud picture with glue and fluffy balls."

"Wow," I say, ruffling her damp curls. "It sounds like you've had a busy day."

She spins around and beams at me with her pearly-white baby teeth. I could squish her all over. Seriously. I could just fold her up and carry her around in my pocket all day to take out and squeeze whenever I like. It's ridiculous how much I love this little person.

Her cheeks are still pink and soft from the bath, and she's talking about her new friend, Nina, and the story they made up, giggly with the memory. I listen, nodding along, but something begins to itch at my brain.

It was an evening just like this when Sacha first arrived here. I remember getting Penny ready for bed after her bath and hearing muffled voices before finding Sacha in my kitchen, quietly conversing with her brother like they didn't want anyone to hear them. And then again on the balcony the following day, when they didn't know I'd arrived home. I heard Sacha say they'd both played a part in what happened to Squeak, but I'd managed to brush it off. After all, each one of us who was there that night felt we'd been responsible in our own way for what happened. It's the exact same guilt that led both Brady and

Roman to their untimely deaths. But now I'm curious if there was something more to her words.

I've often wondered what really happened that night. Why Squeak had seemed healthy—if a little inebriated—before she'd run off, only to end up dead by a puddle of her own vomit not long afterwards. I remember thinking that Seth and Sacha knew more than they were letting on, but I couldn't quite find a way to piece together why they wouldn't say more if they knew what happened to her.

I can still hear Penny's voice floating on, but I'm not even listening anymore. I'm back there again, in the woods. The earthy, sharp smell of moss and bile. The sound of the trees creaking all around, followed by the awful silence when I found her lying there. I remember Roman's painful cries as he held his cousin's limp body in his arms. Brady's face as white as a ghost at seeing the girl he'd been flirting with all night lifeless, vacant and cold. Seth and Sacha's steely faces as the rest of us grieved.

But the image I see most vividly, the one that stands out from the rest, is of my last glance at Squeak after we'd moved her into the deep undergrowth. I'd lingered just a moment longer than the others, looking down at her body by that stream before I hurried to keep up with the rest of the group, leaving her forever behind us.

We never talked about it after that night. That was the pact. Leave her, walk away, and never speak of it again. When the whole neighborhood was out looking for her, we looked, too. But nobody ever checked the woods. And the reason that nobody checked them was because when Roman was asked, he lied. He told them Squeak never showed when he went to collect her, so he gave up and hung out all night at the skate park on the opposite side of town from those woods. He never changed his story, and the rest of us were never brought into it.

Even Seth and I never talked about it again. And there was

a reason I didn't want to talk about it to him. But maybe I should have pushed, maybe I should have pressed him about what happened when he went off alone into the woods. Maybe I should have asked him about why he had been the last one to arrive back at the clearing. Why his hair was a mess. Why his shoes were dirty. Why his eyes were wild. But I didn't. I pushed it down. Because I wanted to protect our relationship.

Penny's voice pulls me back, still going strong. "Then Joey sneezed, and more paint came out of his nose and then–"

"Gross!" I laugh, kissing the top of her head.

Penny bites her lip, her face clouding over. "Mommy, why won't Daddy let Auntie Sacha come home?"

I force a smile, brushing her cheek softly. "She just has some growing up to do, honey." I echo Seth's earlier explanation.

Her big eyes look up at me and I think I see a hint of fear. "Is Daddy mad at her?"

I stop to ponder what the right thing to say is. "Well, you know sometimes when people have siblings—you know, brothers and sisters?—they can have disagreements. It's not a big deal."

Penny bites her lip again. "Is he mad about the little lie?"

My smile drops. I look at my daughter's concerned face, searching my mind to think of what she could mean by this, but come up blank.

"What lie, Penny?"

Penny goes quiet, looking down at her feet.

"Come on, sweetie, you can tell me. What lie are you talking about?"

A gush of air leaves her mouth before she finally musters up the courage to talk. "The little lie I told. About my friend."

My heart beats rapidly in my chest, but I try and stay calm. I have the sudden feeling that I know exactly what she's about to tell me, but I prompt her to continue in her own words, in case I've got it wrong.

"What are you talking about, Penny?"

"When we were at the big party with the paintings, I said the lady in the sparkly dress was my friend Izzy-Bella." She's frowning now, her lower lip jutting out like it always does when she's about to cry. "But she's not. I don't know that lady. That wasn't Izzy-Bella."

My heart is threatening to burst clean out of my chest. "Wh-why did you do that, Penny? Why did you lie?"

Penny's eyes are wide now as she sees my shock, and fat tears begin to spill down her cheeks. "Auntie Sacha said she'd give me candy if I did it. She said not to tell. She said it was a just a *little lie*."

CHAPTER FORTY-FOUR

I find Seth sitting in bed, a binder I don't recognize open in his lap. He blinks when he sees me, his surprise at my presence evident, before he straightens slightly and sets the binder down beside him.

"Hey," he says.

"Hey." I hesitate for a second before I step in, slowly.

The room smells of fresh linen and Seth's aftershave. It used to feel familiar and warm in here, but now it feels like a museum exhibit I'm not supposed to touch. It's crazy how fast a room can stop feeling like your own. A few nights on Penny's floor and now I feel like a guest in my own bedroom. I sit down on the end of the bed, keeping some distance.

It took a while for me to calm Penny down tonight and to convince her that she wasn't in any trouble for lying (while firmly explaining why she must never lie to me again), but we worked it out and she's now fast asleep, cuddled up with her stuffed bunny.

I took some time to think after Penny fell asleep and I've decided that if I still plan on seeing a divorce lawyer tomorrow, I need to talk with Seth first. No more avoiding the hard conversations, no more dodging hurt feelings. Just the truth. As awkward as I know it's going to be.

Seth watches me, as though wary that I'm suddenly initiating contact after days of avoidance. He knows something's coming but he's giving me the space to get there myself.

I clear my throat. "Penny told me something tonight."

He leans back against the headboard, watching me with a neutral expression.

I take a breath. "She said that the night of the gala, Sacha paid her in candy to pretend that the lady in the sparkly dress was her friend, Izzy-Bella."

"I knew it," he mutters quietly before exploding like a firework. "I knew it! I told you, didn't I? I mean, at first when I saw Penny run up to her and hug her, I thought maybe she was just confused. She'd never met Isabella before, I knew she hadn't. But she's just a kid. Kids do weird stuff. I thought maybe she was just messing around. But once I stopped to think about it, I knew, I just *knew* that Sacha was behind it. That woman is certifiably insane, Jade. You believe me now, right? This was all one big set up. Penny's friend Izzy-Bella was always imaginary, and the fact that she shares a similar name to someone I've been working with is completely coincidental! You know I would never cheat on you, right?"

His words hit me somewhere deep down. But I blink back my feelings and continue, my voice trembling a little. "There's something else."

Seth locks eyes with me. "What? What else did Sacha do?"

I sigh. "It's not about Sacha. It's... it's something that I did. I followed you. Yesterday."

Seth exhales and runs a hand through his hair. A smile almost touches his lips, but his expression is one of confusion. "You followed me? Where?"

"To the Vanguard offices. After you dropped Penny at

preschool. You told me you had a meeting with David, but I saw you leave there not long after you arrived. Then I saw you go meet Isabella, alone."

He rubs his hands over his face, then looks at me. "Oh, Jesus."

"Yeah. Sacha didn't need to make Penny lie, after all. I figured this one out all by myself. How long have you and Isabella been having an affair?"

"Wh–" Seth stops, looking like he's just been slapped. "You don't really still think that, do you?"

"I have an appointment with a divorce lawyer tomorrow." I cross my arms.

Seth jumps up from the bed, his feet hitting the floor. "Are you kidding me, Jade? Divorce?"

"I don't see any other choice." My voice cracks and I feel the wetness of uninvited tears rolling down my cheeks. "How could you do this to me, Seth? To Penny?"

"Do what? I've already told you a million times that I didn't *do* anything. There is no affair. There are no lies. All I've been doing is working my ass off for weeks on end trying to find a good enough job to get our family back on our feet, and I..." His tone softens. "Well, I guess this is probably the time to tell you."

I stare at him, not knowing what to expect. Denial? Anger? Some kind of confession?

"Jade, I've been wanting to tell you for a while now, but I couldn't. Also I... I didn't want to get your hopes up until everything was concrete. That meeting that you saw me at with David? Well, I was supposed to be going there to prepare for my final stage interview, but he told me right then and there that they gave me the job. I got it, Jade!"

His enthusiasm is evident from his tone, but I have no idea what he's talking about. "What are you talking about? What job?"

"Sentinel Dynamics!" Seth looks ready to burst with excitement. "It's a big deal, Jade. They're a cybersecurity firm, but not just any. They handle national security stuff, high stakes, that kind of work. I signed an NDA, and I couldn't talk to you about it until everything was final. Man, I'm telling you, the process was intense. There were layers of protocols, background checks, all that kind of stuff." He kneels down beside me and grabs my hands in his. "Jade, this is my dream job. And the salary is way more than I made at my last job. We'll finally be able to pay off our debt, start saving properly, maybe take a vacation once in a while! It'll be a fresh start for me, you and Penny."

I have to admit, this explains a lot. And I feel myself getting wrapped up in his excitement for a brief moment until the realization dawns that it doesn't exonerate him completely. "If what you're saying is true then why did you meet Isabella at the coffee shop?"

"Oh that?" Seth reaches behind him and picks up the binder I'd seen him holding when I came in just now. "She had my welcome packet from Sentinel. David told me where to go to collect it from her."

I put my head in my hands. I feel so stupid. That look I saw him give Isabella yesterday through the coffee shop window wasn't a look of lust, it was the look of a man who had just been told he'd scored the job of his dreams.

"I'm so sorry I couldn't share more until now. I was planning on telling you this morning, but then I woke up to you screaming about a naked man on our couch and..." He laughs. "You know, it just didn't feel like the right time. But you believe me now, right? I would never do anything to put our marriage at risk, I thought you'd know that. You and Penny mean everything to me."

These words make my heart soar. I never wanted to believe

that he would cheat on me, but between Sasha's toxic whisperings and the lie she made Penny repeat, I couldn't come to any other conclusion. Now I just feel guilty. Guilty for ever doubting my husband.

"Oh God, I've been so stupid."

"No." Seth takes my shoulders. "Jade, this wasn't your fault. This was Sacha. She did this. It's what she's always done. But we never have to worry about that again. I'm not going to let her back into our lives. Not ever."

I stare at him, feeling the tension crackling slowly as it dissolves between us. Then, for the first time in a long time, we embrace. All of the worries, all of the thoughts of fighting and separation and lawyers and custody battles disappear. I feel grounded. Like I understand my own world again. Like I have my life back.

Seth strokes the back of my hair. "Can we just start over? No secrets. No avoiding each other. Just us, as we used to be."

Right now, nothing could possibly sound better, and when Seth's lips move toward mine, I don't pull back. And when his hands begin unbuttoning my shirt, I reach for his. And when we lay down, every curve and dip of our bodies perfectly molding into one another's like they're two halves of a whole, like they always have been, I feel confident that our troubles are firmly behind us.

I lie still in the dark, listening to Seth's slow, steady breathing beside me. His warm body presses against mine as he traces his fingers up and down my arm. I reach out and pick up the clock on the nightstand. It's a little after midnight. After a few moments soaking in the comfort of being back in my own bed, I move to get up.

"Hey, where are you going?" Seth murmurs, clinging on to my arm like he never wants to let me go again.

"Just checking on Penny," I say, slipping back into my clothes. "I thought I heard her stirring a little while ago when we were... busy. I'll be right back, I promise."

The hall floor is cold beneath my bare feet, and I stop outside Penny's door, fingers brushing the frame. I could have sworn I heard her stirring and talking in her sleep, but as I peek into her room now, there's only silence. I guess she settled herself.

I stand in the doorway for a long moment, but in the glow of her dim nightlight it's hard to make out anything beyond the shape of her bed and the soft lump of her stuffed animals in the corner. Then my eyes fall to her blanket, which has slipped to the ground, crumpled and twisted. She has a habit of kicking it off herself in her sleep. No wonder she was stirring, she must be cold without it. I hurry over, kneeling down to pick it up, but when I go to place it on the bed, my fingers freeze. The bed is empty. Penny's not in there.

A flood of panic surges through me as I bolt from the room, my breath hitching in my throat. The bathroom door is closed. I rush toward it to check if she's in there, but when I switch on the light the room is empty.

A scream rips from my throat, raw and desperate. "Seth! She's gone! Penny's gone!"

I hear Seth stumble as he rushes to throw something on before his footsteps thunder down the hall, his eyes wide as he approaches. "What do you mean gone? Gone where?"

"Penny's not in her room," I cry. "She's not here. I don't know where she is, she's just gone!"

We both begin shouting her name, running from room to room, the panic between us rising. But there's no answer. Nothing. She's not here.

"You stay here and call the cops, I'm going to go door to door to check if anyone has seen her," Seth says, jumping into action.

I'm trembling as I grab my phone from the kitchen countertop where I left it charging, but when I hear the jingle of Seth's keychain I stop, frozen. "Seth!"

"What? What is it?" His voice is urgent.

My mind races and a cold dread clutches my chest as I think back to earlier today. "When you kicked Sacha out this morning, did you take back her key?"

"No." Seth shakes his head, then his face drops. "Oh, God."

I don't wait a second. I grab my phone and pull up Sacha's number, pacing as it calls.

She answers on the third ring, her voice calm and quiet.

"We're up on the roof. Come join us."

CHAPTER FORTY-FIVE

THEN

The weighted silence that has descended over our group is broken only by our hesitant footsteps and Seth and Roman's heavy breathing as they carry Squeak's limp body across their arms. We trudge through the dense trees in a crooked line, branches scratching at our arms like they're desperately trying to stop us from going any further.

No one speaks. There's nothing to say. I lower my head, trying to keep the tears from falling again, trying to push the gnawing knot in my stomach as far down as I can, but right now, it feels like all I'll ever see when I close my eyes is the image of Squeak's face when I first found her.

Roman's voice breaks through the silence. "Just a little further. She needs to be deep enough in, or we risk somebody finding her."

If anyone knows their way around here, it's Roman. He's always told us about his connection to the woods, his time here growing up, exploring. I glance over his shoulder, trying to gauge how deep into the underbrush he's going to take us.

Reality dawns. This is real. We're really going to do this. Not long from now, we'll go home, wash the dirt off ourselves and pretend we never saw Squeak tonight. To her mother. To Roman's mother. To everyone. We'll let them believe she just ran away again. That she chose to leave.

Roman has convinced himself that this is the only way to protect his family.

They never have to know. It'll be better this way. For everyone.

But what is this going to do to us? As people. As friends. Or in Seth and my case, as lovers.

I can already feel something tearing loose in my chest. A part of me trying to crawl out and run for the hills. But it's too late. I'm here. I said yes. Or at least, my silence constituted an agreement.

I think about Squeak, who always seemed so young and innocent, despite her age. I think about how her family will never know what really happened to her. I feel sick at the thought that we're making her disappear. Erasing her, like she was never even here with us.

I catch Seth glancing back my way and our eyes catch in the dark. I snap my head away. I can't look at him right now. It may have been Sacha's idea not to hide Squeak's death, but Seth had seemed all too ready to support it, like it was the only choice we had.

Every now and then I catch the two of them silently exchanging looks. They know something. I don't know what it is, but I have a feeling that it's the reason we're out here in the middle of the night, carrying a dead girl through the woods, along with a secret we'll all be forced to keep forever.

Even Brady has given up his protests. He walks stiffly with his hands in his pockets, having refused to help carry the body.

The sound of trickling water hits my ears, and I see Roman slow down.

"Just up here," he says.

A minute later we step out of the thicket and onto a wet bank. There's a small stream directly in front of us that reflects the moon above and the earth smells damper here, with decaying leaves and a rotten tang that sticks in my nose.

Roman signals to stop.

"Here," he says, and he and Seth drop to their knees, letting Squeak's body roll from their arms gently, face down right beside the water. Her loosened braid spills down to the dirt and her legs fan out unnaturally.

Roman stands, brushing dirt off his hands. I expect him to say some words. Maybe something about Squeak's life, what she meant to him, how much this hurts. But he doesn't. He doesn't even look at her.

"We should go." His voice is quiet.

No one argues, but Brady looks around at each of us in disgust, before shaking his head and stalking off. Sacha tries to keep up beside him.

Seth watches them disappear before taking my hand. "Come on, let's go. It's going to be okay."

What a lie. Nothing will ever be okay again. How can it be? How can we continue our lives with a burden so heavy, weighing down on us at all times? And who's to say that one of us won't break down and confess everything? Brady already looks ready to snap.

A secret is easy enough to keep to yourself or share with someone close to you. But how can a secret this large stay hidden between five people who disagreed on how to handle the situation in the first place? It can't.

And I'm scared of what that means for our futures.

Roman is the last to leave Squeak, taking his spot behind me and Seth. We only make it twenty feet from where we left her before I realize I'm still holding her cardigan.

"Wait," I say, holding it up. "I have to leave this with her."

Seth nods and he and Roman wait there while I rush back down to the stream and kneel beside Squeak's body. I shake out her cardigan and lay it down over her back like a blanket. A poor excuse for a meaningful gesture, but it's all I can do. Once we leave, it won't be long until woodland predators swoop in on her. And this—a light wool cardigan—won't protect her from them.

I shiver as I get up to leave, but I stop short as I catch a glimpse of something. My breath catches as I stare down at the back of Squeak's head. It's only now she's face down that I see it, wet and glistening. Her blond hair is stained dark at the base of her skull, and when I lean in closer, I catch the unmistakable metallic scent.

It's blood.

"Jade! Come on," I hear Seth's voice calling me.

I tuck the sweater tighter around her shoulders and slowly stand up, taking one last glance behind my shoulder before returning to the others, joining them in silence as we make the long walk back to the trailhead.

CHAPTER FORTY-SIX

NOW

I'm gasping in breaths as I pound the stairs trying to keep up with Seth, who takes them two at a time. Our heavy steps echo through the enclosed stairwell and I don't even care that my legs are already burning from the climb, there was no way I was going to stand around and wait for the elevator. I need to get to Penny.

"What was she thinking, taking Penny from her bed?" I hiss, clutching at the railing for support as we round another corner, two floors to go.

"It's Sacha, who the hell knows?" he pants, his face is tense, like he's already running through every worst-case scenario. "But if she thinks the way to win back our trust is to take Penny to play on the roof in the middle of the night, she's very much mistaken."

My mothering instincts are screaming at me. I *knew* I heard a noise coming from Penny's bedroom earlier, and I should have gone straight in to check on her but instead I told myself she was just stirring in her sleep, my instincts dampened as I lay embraced in a heated tangle with Seth.

Did Penny go willingly, or did Sacha have to carry her up

there? Did she even think to put a coat on her?

As I propel myself up the stairs, I vow to never again ignore it when my hackles go up unexpectedly. A mother's instincts are rarely wrong.

We hit the last bend and I can hear the roof door banging against the frame at the top of the stairwell. A moment later it's Seth who first pushes through it. I follow close behind, almost colliding with his back as we burst out onto the roof, the door slamming shut behind us.

The cold night air hits me like a slap across the face. I blink, looking out over the rooftop garden, the edges of the space barely visible in the moonlight. A line of makeshift flower boxes marks the farthest end, but it's too dark to see anything clearly as the wind makes my eyes water and sends my hair flying into my face. I squint into the darkness, my eyes darting everywhere, searching for Penny and Sacha.

"Sacha?" I shout into the wind, my voice raw and panicked.

"Penny!" Seth calls, cupping his hands around his mouth.

My eyes scan the roof, desperately looking for any sign of my daughter.

And then I hear it.

"Jade! Seth! Help!" Sacha's panicked voice comes from the other end of the roof.

I don't wait. I don't think. I just run, my feet slamming against the hard rooftop, Seth beside me, both of us dashing toward the sound of Sacha's terrified cries.

But my blood runs cold when I see her.

She's standing by the broken railing, pale as death, her hands shaking with panic like leaves in the wind as wet tears shimmer in her eyes. But I don't see Penny anywhere.

"I-I told her not to go so close to the edge," Sacha stammers. "But she wouldn't listen."

I feel my heart drop into my stomach as my eyes flick to the section of broken railing, rusted and loose, barely hanging on. The one I've been telling the building manager for months to fix, but he's never lifted a finger.

My legs try to give way where I stand, but Seth catches me and grabs my arms tight in his hands to stop me from collapsing.

"No!" I scream, my voice ragged. I feel dizzy. "Penny!"

I dart forward, the cold air rushing past me. Seth is right by my side, our breathing matched in fast, erratic gasps but as soon as we reach the railing, we both freeze. I reach out, grabbing the cold metal with both hands, my eyes scanning the street sixty feet below.

Seth and I stare down, trying to make sense of it. The streetlights below illuminate the pavement, but there's no small body, no figure lying crumpled on the concrete below. No Penny.

Just the usual hum of cars passing by in the distance.

My eyes move to Seth, who looks about as pale as I feel. He's trying to make sense of the same thing. He reaches for me, grabbing my arm, his grip like a vise.

"Where is she?" His voice cracks.

I shake my head. I don't understand. "She's not there. She's not down there."

I close my eyes for a moment, trying to steady my thoughts, my breath.

And then the realization hits me.

I turn sharply to see Sacha standing right behind us, smiling. A glint of metal reflects the moonlight, and I gasp when I see the large gardening shears in her hands. They're still shiny and sharp as razors, having sat unused in the small maintenance chest ever since Mr. Morris died.

This was a trap.

Seth turns, his eyes moving straight to the sharp metal in front of him. "What... what are you doing, Sacha?"

"The only thing I can do to be with Penny. You've left me no choice."

"What are you talking about?" I say, backing closer to the broken railing as the shears move toward us. "Where's Penny?"

"I'm talking about the same thing everyone else is. Jade and Seth, a couple on the brink of losing everything. Their finances in ruins, their marriage crumbling. Throw in an affair with a beautiful blond and you have yourself a recipe for murder–suicide."

Seth and I glance at each other, a terrified look of understanding passing between us.

Sacha grips the shears tightly. "It'll be impossible to tell which one of you pushed the other before jumping to your own tragic death."

I scan the roof again, my heart thudding. "Where is she? Where's Penny?"

"Don't worry about Penny. Despite what the two of you think, I would never do a thing to hurt that girl. I love her. And I promise, I'll raise her just like she's my own."

My mind suddenly flashes back to the conversation I had with Sacha about her desire to become a mother. All those questions she asked about what would happen to Penny if tragedy were to befall me and Seth. I swallow a hard lump in my throat. Sacha knows that if anything were to happen to either of us, she would—through a lack of any other family members fit for the job—be the one to gain guardianship of Penny.

"You're not touching her!" I shout, pushing my hair back as the wind thrusts it into my face. "She's our daughter and you have no right to her!"

Seth grips my arm. His other hand reaches out for the broken railing Sacha is inching us toward.

"Let's just talk about this, okay?" he says calmly. "It doesn't have to be this way. We can make a deal. You... you can come visit Penny once every week."

I doubt Sacha believes this any more than I do. This woman is certifiably insane and she's not going anywhere near our child if I have any say in it. But I keep my mouth shut, hoping that Sacha will agree and let us go.

"Do you think I'm stupid? No, wait, don't bother answering that. I already know. You've always seen me as the irresponsible, no good, idiot sister. You, Mom, Dad... all of you. We may be twins, but we were never equals in your mind, or in Mom and Dad's."

"That isn't true, Sacha." Seth's voice softens. "I never got any special treatment. I just kept my head down and kept out of trouble. That's why they never pushed back with me like they did with you. All they ever wanted was for you to succeed."

"We both know that isn't true!" Sacha scoffs, pointing the shears directly at her brother. "You got everything you ever asked for from the moment I can remember, and I got nothing. We turned eighteen on the same day, Seth. Who got a car?"

Seth rolls his eyes. "The car? You're *still* hung up on that? Sacha, they told you why they didn't get you one. You blew all the chances they gave you. Were they supposed to just do nothing as you failed school, too busy getting high and staying out all night with your friends? They tried to help you. But you pushed back at every turn. It's like you're determined to always be the victim!"

Sacha's eyes flash with anger and I'm starting to wish Seth would just shut up. He's not making this any better. I look around for an escape, but there's no getting past her. The shears are wide open and she looks set to strike.

"How about we discuss another *victim*, hey, Seth?" She gives her brother a piercing glare.

Seth stares back at his sister with some sort of saddened plea. "No, Sacha."

"Oh, come on! It'll be fun!" she taunts. "And really, what difference does it make now? It's been fifteen years since that night and we're the only three left alive who were there."

"Just stop!" Seth warns her.

Sacha snaps the shears close to Seth's face. "It's about time Jade knew the truth."

I look back and forth between them. "What? What truth?"

"You'll find out." Sacha's mouth twists into a dark grin. "But first, let's play a game. Truth, Truth, Lie. I think you guys already know it."

CHAPTER FORTY-SEVEN

Let's play a game.

Sacha's words are an echo from the past. Seth and I saw how she used this game to torture Squeak. And now she's going to use it to torture us. There's nothing I can do to stop her as she holds the shears out, never loosening her grip.

"Usual rules," she continues. "I'll tell you three facts, and you figure out which two are true, and which one is the lie. Jade, this round is just for you since Seth will already know the answer."

I swallow down a lump in my throat, but I nod in acceptance. After all, what other choice do I have but to play Sacha's sadistic game?

"Number one," Sacha begins without hesitation. "I slipped a generous amount of cocaine into Squeak's drinks that night. It wasn't my fault I forgot Roman's story about her weak heart."

My stomach drops as I remember Squeak knocking back drinks, her demeanor changing rapidly at one point. I'd attributed this to the effects of the alcohol, but this makes much more sense. Sacha is telling the truth. *She* did this. She spiked Squeak's drinks. That explains her collapsing out in the woods, her blue lips, the vomit on the ground. Squeak wasn't made like everyone else. Her small body and weakened heart just couldn't take that kind of concoction.

But that doesn't explain the other thing. The thing that has been nagging at the back of my mind for years. The thing that kept me up for nights on end, long after we left Squeak's body abandoned and alone that night. The blood on the back of her head.

I look to Seth, but he's staring up at the black sky, a pained look on his face, and I see it now. He knew about the drugs. He knew about Sacha spiking Squeak's drink. But how could he not tell me? Why would he protect his psychopathic sister like this? Unless she had something on him, too. A bargaining chip. Something that would keep them both quiet.

"Number two," Sacha says, her words flavored with glee. "Seth lied to everyone. He *did* find Squeak after she ran off. I know this, Jade, because when I left you there, slowing me down as you fumbled with your laces in the dark, I went looking for her by myself. I'd remembered what Roman had said about her heart, and I wanted to find her in case something bad happened. But what I came across instead was Seth and Squeak, alone. They didn't see me, but Squeak was crying hysterically while Seth tried to calm her down. He hugged the pathetic, wet-faced girl and she must have gotten the wrong signal or something because next thing I know, I see her grabbing his face and shoving her tongue so far down his throat she must have hit lungs."

I say nothing.

"And three," Sacha snips the shears at us in punctuation. "Seth didn't kiss Squeak back. He pushed her away. But... well, this is the thing, Jade. She was on him so tightly, he didn't just push her lightly. He pushed her hard. I saw it. And I saw her head hit that rock on the ground when she went down. He didn't stop to help her up. He didn't ask if she was okay. He just turned around and ran. He left her there."

Something deep inside me shifts. Something in my core. This can't be right. This one has to be the lie. *It has to be.*

Seth is squeezing his eyes shut, like he can just tune it out. Make it all disappear. But Sacha isn't done.

"So, Jade, you care to take a guess at which one is the lie?"

I gulp down a choked sob at the back of my throat, already knowing what's coming next.

"Oh gosh," she says, taking one hand from the shears and slapping the top of her head. "I always mess this game up, don't I? Silly me. All three of those facts were true."

There it is. The words I knew were coming but didn't want to hear. Because the ramifications of this are too big for me to wrap my head around right now.

I struggle to breathe as I blink back tears.

"Jade, I didn't kill her. I swear." Seth grabs my hands, desperately trying to lock eyes with me. "I was just trying to help her feel better after Sacha had torn her to shreds with that game, but she took it the wrong way and just attacked me! I tried to shake her off, but I guess I didn't think about how light she was. Yes, she hit her head, but I could see she was fine. I didn't know how to react, or what to say, so I left her. I've regretted it every day of my life. But how could I have known what would happen? I figured she'd follow me back to the circle. But she never did."

He shakes me, trying to get me to look at him, but I can't.

"I didn't kill Squeak, Jade, you have to believe me!" Seth shouts again.

"But you may as well have," Sacha says. "If you'd just brought her back to the clearing, if you hadn't pushed her away and then ran off, maybe she would have survived. Brady knew CPR, the cars weren't far away, we could have saved her."

"How could I have known she was going to die?" Seth spits at his sister. "And you, you're no better. You left her, too! You followed me instead. You knew I suspected you'd spiked Squeak's drink, I'd asked you earlier that night and you denied it. But you knew I didn't believe you and were worried I'd tell the others. So when you saw Squeak kiss me, you took the chance to keep me quiet."

I can't listen anymore. This is why he and Sacha were acting so strangely that night.

By the time our group made a pact to never tell anyone about Squeak's death, the two of them had already made a pact of their own. And despite being twins, sharing the same DNA, being born together, raised together, that pact may have been the only thing that ever bonded them. A dark and twisted kind of bond, not the kind created by love. And it's likely the reason they still hate each other to this day.

Seth looks Sacha directly in the eyes. "I knew if you told Jade that you saw me kissing her, she'd believe you. You'd already freaked her out with your lies about me staring at Squeak all night. Just like the lies you told her about me and my ex-girlfriend. Just like the lies you told her about me having an affair with Isabella."

I look to Sacha, seeking confirmation.

She nods. "Fine. You got me. None of that was true. Seth is the golden child, perfect as always."

My heart would soar with relief if I wasn't backed up against a broken railing with a sixty-foot drop behind me. Seth never cheated on me. Ever. It was all lies. Lies made up by a sister who couldn't bear the fact that her twin brother could never do wrong in their parents' eyes.

"And fine. I left Squeak, too. But what was I going to do, go over and give her a shoulder to cry on? It's not like I knew she was going to die. Nobody even invited her there that night,

Roman only brought her out of pity. Plus…" Sacha's face darkens, "…that was supposed to be the night Brady and I finally hooked up and she got in my way. Not that we ever got to, after all. The idiot was so traumatized by her death that he got into his car one night so wasted he couldn't see straight and drove headfirst into a truck before we ever got a chance."

I ignore Sacha's crude words about a person who was once a close friend of ours. And I doubt that's the reason Brady never wanted to hook up with her. Brady couldn't stand Sacha's brash in-your-face advances. He may have been popular with girls in high school, but I think the reason he was so attracted to Squeak was because she was the first girl who didn't make an idiot out of herself by throwing herself at him. She was quiet and refined and smart, but she was also beautiful in her own delicate way.

But what's the point in telling Sacha now that she didn't stand a chance with Brady? He's been dead for over a decade. Roman is gone, too. And Seth and I… Well, we did something that Sacha never even attempted to do. We grew up.

"But then, I've never had much luck with men," Sacha muses. "All of them either cheat, lie, or leave. The one time I thought I'd found someone special, I brought up having children and he ran for the hills. But now I have the chance to have a child of my own, no man needed."

Seth risks a step forward. "You're not having Penny. She's not some doll you get to play with and throw away when you get bored. She's our daughter. And she needs us."

For a moment I think Sacha is about to spit back some cruel retort, but then her eyes begin to glimmer with tears. "I love Penny. And she loves me. She looks up to me. Nobody in my life ever has loved me unconditionally like that."

This might be sweet if she weren't talking about killing me and Seth in order to keep Penny for herself. I've always known Sacha is deeply disturbed, and I'm not sure what's scarier, the thought of falling off this roof and dying on the sidewalk below or a woman with the emotional IQ of a scented candle being the one to raise my little girl.

Seth seems to be weighing this up in his mind too, and I watch him come to a conclusion in real time as he lunges forward and grabs one blade of the shears.

It looks like he's about to make sure that if we die tonight there'll be no mistaking this scene for some marital murder–suicide. And Sacha will never get her hands on our child.

The sharp metal digs into Seth's hand and blood begins to pour down his arm.

"Wha-what are you doing?" Sacha shrieks. "Let go!"

If Sacha were to push those handles together right now, Seth would risk losing his fingers. But she's so shocked by this bold move that she just tugs the shears back, ripping further through his skin. Despite the pain he must be feeling, Seth doesn't let go. He keeps his grip on the shears as blood pools on the ground below.

"Let go, Seth, or these are going right through your hand!" Sacha's panicking now, having expected us to just follow her orders and jump from the building so she can live happily ever after with our daughter.

But I know Seth. And I know there's nothing he wouldn't do to keep Penny safe from this woman.

Sacha keeps tugging and tugging the shears back, but Seth doesn't budge as he uses his free hand to grab her right arm.

"Let me go!" Sacha shouts.

"No, Sacha! I'm not going to let you do thi–"

The rest of Seth's sentence is cut short with the sickening sound of crunching bone as Sacha closes the shears. A throaty scream bursts from Seth's mouth and in the low light I see four of his fingers fall to the ground by his feet. My body doesn't wait a moment to respond as a cold sweat breaks out all over me. I sink to the ground, nearly fainting in horror as I stare at the shorn-off digits lying bloodied by his shoes.

Sacha's mouth hangs open in shock as Seth cries out in pain, but he doesn't loosen his grip on her arm as he tries to make her drop the shears. She pushes back at him, edging them both closer and closer to the broken rail. I want to help him, I want to grab her and pull her off him, but I can't move. I can't get up. And I can smell the blood seeping from Seth's discarded fingers beside me.

"What are you doing? Let go of me!" Sacha roars at him and tries to twist out of his grasp.

"Put the shears down, Sacha!" he shouts as he tries to push her back, but it's clear the blood loss and shock is beginning to weaken him.

Sacha has him right at the edge, ready to push him over the drop. I muster every ounce of strength I have to heave myself off the ground, nearly gagging as I step over Seth's bloodied fingers. I finally steady my footing but just as I reach for Sacha's other arm, it happens as if in slow motion. Seth loses his grip on Sacha and falls backward toward the broken railing. He lands just short of the edge, but Sacha comes crashing down fast toward the gap.

I lunge forward and try to grab her, to pull her backward to safety. But it's too late.

All I hear as she falls sixty feet to the street below is the desperate final scream of a broken woman.

Then silence.

EPILOGUE

"Okay, the trick is, you have to tap the bucket with the shovel three times, then say the magic word, *abracadabra*!" Seth grins. "Then lift the bucket and hey presto, we have our first sandcastle!"

An unceasing smile is glued to my face as I sit on the warm sand, watching Seth and Penny play. Seth's left hand moves with surprising precision as he shapes the sand, though it's clear from the deep concentration lines on his face that he's still struggling to adapt to using his non-dominant hand full-time.

His right hand—still wrapped up safely eight weeks out of surgery—rests at his side.

The doctors say the surgery was a success. The severed fingers were recovered in time and the surgeons managed to reattach them all, though it had taken them over nine hours.

Seth has a long road of recovery ahead of him. It could take months for the sensation and movement to come back, and there's a chance that neither will ever fully return. He tells me all he feels is numbness under the dressings, but he hasn't complained. Not even once. And luckily, being temporarily one hand down hasn't affected his ability to jump right into his new position at Sentinel Dynamics, who have been very supportive. And Seth wasn't kidding; the pay is great. Enough that our monthly bills are fully covered, our credit card debt is nearly wiped off, and we are on our first weekend away at the coast in a long time.

I don't know if Seth realizes it, but the fact that he's out here laughing and making sandcastles with Penny means more to me than anything else in the world. It's a sign of recovery, of healing. Both for him and for our family.

Penny turned five last week and seems to remain reasonably unaffected by the memory of having been bundled out of bed by Sacha that night and being dropped off at Mrs. Morris's apartment. As Mrs. Morris tells it, she was happy to let a sleepy Penny sit and watch cartoons on the couch after Sacha explained that her brother's marital issues were coming to a boil and she was afraid for Penny's safety.

Thankfully, Sacha's plan to frame it as us falling from the roof in a murder–suicide hadn't worked out for her. And though we've explained to Penny as best we can that her aunt is no longer with us, it's difficult to tell how much she understands death at this age. Sometimes it seems like she still expects to see Sacha show up at the door, ready to play with her again. It's sad, and though I wish things had ended differently, Penny is better off never getting to find out for herself who her aunt really was.

One person Penny seems to have forgotten about completely is her imaginary friend, Izzy-Bella. And I can't say I'm sad to see the back of both her *and* the real Isabella now that Seth has secured a job and no longer works with any of the team at Vanguard. Though I have to keep reminding myself that Isabella never did anything other than help secure my husband the job of his dreams. Despite what Sacha tried to make me believe.

One thing that Sacha did get right was her suspicion about

Roman. It turns out he did leave a note confessing about that night, just as she predicted.

It was enough to make local news: a man who couldn't live with the regret of covering up his cousin's accidental death fifteen years ago makes a parting confession to his family, leaving details of her final resting place.

Not that there would be anything left of her to find now.

One detail Roman didn't mention was the names of the friends who were with him that night. He could have taken us all down with him, but he didn't. And that's the Roman I always want to remember. The Roman who would do anything to protect his friends, his family. Even if that meant doing something awful. Even if it ultimately cost him his life.

The sun's heat presses down on my back as I bury my feet in the warm sand. I listen to the sound of the waves lapping at the shore and breathe in the mingling scents of saltwater and coconut sunscreen.

Seth and Penny are in their own little world as he lets her bury his feet in the sand, his toes disappearing under the dry grains, bit by bit, as she scoops and pours.

I can't help but think of the things I've buried, too. The memories, the nightmares, the secrets.

Because the thing I didn't tell Sacha or Seth that night on the roof is that I saw Squeak kissing Seth in those woods, too.

I was trying to find my way back to the clearing when I saw her hands around his neck, her lips on his. Reeling from the betrayal, I ran away.

It wasn't until Sacha had us backed up against that broken railing, the shears pointed our way, that I learned Seth had pushed Squeak away soon afterwards. If only I'd stopped long enough to see him reject Squeak... Well, things might have ended differently. But by that time, I had already fled. And when Seth had returned to the clearing without Squeak, claiming he hadn't seen her, I knew he was lying. But I was so scared of losing him—of losing my first love—that I said nothing.

Penny's laughter breaks through my thoughts as she sprints toward a line of seagulls near the water, waving her arms like she's trying to take off. The gulls scatter and Penny's face flushes with the kind of joy that only comes when you're five and everything feels like a game.

It's only as you get older you realize that unless you're careful, games can be deadly.

Fifteen years ago, Sacha's love of games set off a chain reaction that led to endless years of pain for more than just those of us there to play with her that night. And now I can't help but think that maybe if things had gone differently, Squeak, Brady, Roman and Sacha would still be alive today.

If Sacha hadn't spiked Squeak's drink. If we hadn't played that stupid game. If Squeak hadn't run off. If she hadn't hit her head when she fell. And if Seth hadn't fled from her misguided advances, leaving her out there alone in the dark.

Or maybe if when I found Squeak—the girl who I'd just seen trying to steal the love of my life—alone and dying that night, covered in vomit, her slow, blinking eyes pleading silently at me for help as her heart gave way...

Well, I suppose if I hadn't then waited for fifteen long minutes as I silently watched the life drain out of her before I finally screamed and cried out for the others' help—maybe Brady could have used his first aid skills to perform CPR, and Roman could have driven his cousin to get medical care, and maybe, just maybe, Squeak could have survived.

Seth sits next to me, his good hand finding mine in the sand below, wrapping our fingers together. We watch our daughter's carefree leaps as she chases the gulls, who squawk and flap their wings. It looks like she's having the time of her life.

It's the weirdest thing, though. As happy as Penny seems,

she doesn't really talk very much since Sacha's death. When we play games, she's always quiet. And when I take her to friends' parties, she runs around with the other kids, but I never see her talking back to them anymore. She just nods quietly, barely making a peep. I'm sure this is normal though, and just a phase she'll grow out of.

Seth's gaze lingers on her, then drifts over to me, a silent promise passing between us as we enjoy the sunshine. The simple times.

This, right here, is what we are protecting. What we will always protect.

There's an old adage that says the only way two people can keep a secret is if one of them is dead. But six of us went into those woods that night, and five of us left with a secret that shaped the rest of our lives. Brady got drunk and drove to his fiery death. Roman, filled with guilt and regret, eventually took his own life. And Sacha—clearly believing that old adage—had tried to kill me and Seth, ready to take what we had as her own, and bury the shared secrets we held along with us.

But the thing that Sacha didn't understand was this: like the tall, sprawling trees in the woods that night, Seth and I have roots. Roots that have spent many years growing and entwining together underground. And so linked are our roots, that we are no longer two, but one.

And there's no secret in the world that he and I can't keep.

AUTHOR'S NOTE

Thank you so much for picking up this book and joining Jade and Seth in their twisted love story. I had so much fun writing this, and I hope you enjoyed reading it, too.

If you liked *Let's Play a Game*, please consider taking a moment to leave a review on Amazon or Goodreads, as this is the best way to help new readers discover my books.

If you're interested in joining my advance reader team for future releases, or just want to drop me a message, you can contact me via the form on my website: www.nancysavagebooks.com

ALSO BY NANCY SAVAGE

The Couple in Cabin 14

Pretty Pictures

The Motel

ACKNOWLEDGMENTS

A huge thank you to the brilliant team at Bloodhound Books – Tara Lyons, Hannah Deuce, Lexi Curtis, Betsy Reavley, Fred Freeman, and the wider team. I'm endlessly grateful for everything you do to bring my books to life!

A big thank you to Abbie Rutherford, my amazing editor. Your kindness and encouragement over the past two years have meant more to me than I can say.

To Jared: I wouldn't have made it past my first paragraph, let alone to publishing my fourth book, without your constant support, help, and belief in me. Thank you!

Thank you to my mother, Kerri, for being so generous with your time and for helping me get my manuscripts into their best shape. It means the world to me.

To my incredible children – you inspire and motivate me every single day. I'm so grateful to be your mama.

And thank you, dear reader, for spending your time with this story. I'm so glad you're here.

A NOTE FROM THE PUBLISHER

Thank you for reading this book. If you enjoyed it, please do consider leaving a review on Amazon to help others find it too.

Follow Bloodhound Books on your socials.

www.ingramcontent.com/pod-product-compliance
Ingram Content Group UK Ltd.
Pitfield, Milton Keynes, MK11 3LW, UK
UKHW040251280426
12108UKWH00068B/405

9 781917 705790